GENTLE JULIA

BOOTH TARKINGTON

1st WORLD
LIBRARY
Literary Society

Gentle Julia

Booth Tarkington

© 1st World Library, 2006
PO Box 2211
Fairfield, IA 52556
www.1stworldlibrary.com
First Edition

LCCN: 2007920624

Softcover ISBN: 978-1-4218-3932-5
Hardcover ISBN: 978-1-4218-3832-8
eBook ISBN: 978-1-4218-4032-1

Purchase *"Gentle Julia"*
as a traditional bound book at:
www.1stWorldLibrary.com/purchase.asp?ISBN=978-1-4218-3932-5

1st World Library is a literary, educational organization
dedicated to:

- Creating a free internet library of downloadable ebooks

- Hosting writing competitions and offering book
  publishing scholarships.

Interested in more 1st World Library books?
contact: literacy@1stworldlibrary.com
Check us out at: www.1stworldlibrary.com

1st World Library Literary Society

Giving Back to the World

"If you want to work on the core problem, it's early school literacy."

- James Barksdale, former CEO of Netscape

"No skill is more crucial to the future of a child, or to a democratic and prosperous society, than literacy."

- Los Angeles Times

Literacy... means far more than learning how to read and write... The aim is to transmit... knowledge and promote social participation."

- UNESCO

"Literacy is not a luxury, it is a right and a responsibility. If our world is to meet the challenges of the twenty-first century we must harness the energy and creativity of all our citizens."

- President Bill Clinton

"Parents should be encouraged to read to their children, and teachers should be equipped with all available techniques for teaching literacy, so the varying needs and capacities of individual kids can be taken into account."

- Hugh Mackay

TO M. L. K.

"Rising to the point of order, this one said that since the morgue was not yet established as the central monument and inspiration of our settlement, and true philosophy was as well expounded in the convivial manner as in the miserable, he claimed for himself, not the license, but the right, to sing a ballad, if he chose, upon even so solemn a matter as the misuse of the town pump by witches."

CHAPTER ONE

Superciliousness is not safe after all, because a person who forms the habit of wearing it may some day find his lower lip grown permanently projected beyond the upper, so that he can't get it back, and must go through life looking like the King of Spain. This was once foretold as a probable culmination of Florence Atwater's still plastic profile, if Florence didn't change her way of thinking; and upon Florence's remarking dreamily that the King of Spain was an awf'ly han'some man, her mother retorted: "But not for a girl!" She meant, of course, that a girl who looked too much like the King of Spain would not be handsome, but her daughter decided to misunderstand her.

"Why, mamma, he's my Very Ideal! I'd marry him to-morrow!"

Mrs. Atwater paused in her darning, and let the stocking collapse flaccidly into the work-basket in her lap. "Not at barely thirteen, would you?" she said. "It seems to me you're just a shade too young to be marrying a man who's already got a wife and several children. Where did you pick up that 'I'd-marry-him-to-morrow,' Florence?"

"Oh, I hear that everywhere!" returned the damsel, lightly. "Everybody says things like that. I heard Aunt Julia say it. I heard Kitty Silver say it."

"About the King of Spain?" Mrs. Atwater inquired.

"I don't know who they were saying it about," said Florence, "but they were saying it. I don't mean they were saying it together; I heard one say it one time and the other say it some other time. I think Kitty Silver was saying it about some coloured man. She proba'ly wouldn't want to marry any white man; at least I don't expect she would. She's *been* married to a couple of coloured men, anyhow; and she was married twice to one of 'em, and the other one died in between. Anyhow, that's what she told me. She weighed over two hunderd pounds the first time she was married, and she weighed over two hunderd-and-seventy the last time she was married to the first one over again, but she says she don't know how much she weighed when she was married to the one in between. She says she never got weighed all the time she was married to that one. Did Kitty Silver ever tell you that, mamma?"

"Yes, often!" Mrs. Atwater replied. "I don't think it's very entertaining; and it's not what we were talking about. I was trying to tell you—"

"I know," Florence interrupted. "You said I'd get my face so's my underlip wouldn't go back where it ought to, if I didn't quit turning up my nose at people I think are beneath contemp'. I guess the best thing would be to just feel that way without letting on by my face, and then there wouldn't be any danger."

"No," said Mrs. Atwater. "That's not what I meant. You mustn't let your feelings get *their* nose turned up, or their underlip out, either, because feelings can grow warped just as well as—"

But her remarks had already caused her daughter to follow a trail of thought divergent from the main road along which the mother feebly struggled to progress. "Mamma," said Florence, "do you b'lieve it's true if a person swallows an apple-seed or a lemon-seed or a watermelon-seed, f'r instance, do you think they'd have a tree grow up inside of 'em? Henry Rooter said it would, yesterday."

Mrs. Atwater looked a little anxious. "Did you swallow some sort of seed?" she asked.

"It was only some grape-seeds, mamma; and you needn't think I got to take anything for it, because I've swallowed a million, I guess, in my time!"

"In your time?" her mother repeated, seemingly mystified.

"Yes, and so have you and papa," Florence went on. "I've seen you when you ate grapes. Henry said maybe not, about grapes, because I told him all what I've just been telling you, mamma, how I must have swallowed a million, in my time, and he said grape-seeds weren't big enough to get a good holt, but he said if I was to swallow an apple-seed a tree would start up, and in a year or two, maybe, it would grow up so't I couldn't get my mouth shut on account the branches."

"Nonsense!"

"Henry said another boy told *him*, but he said you could ask anybody and they'd tell you it was true. Henry said this boy that told him's uncle died of it when he was eleven years old, and this boy knew a grown woman that was pretty sick from it right now. I expect Henry wasn't telling such a falsehood about it, mamma, but proba'ly this boy did, because I didn't believe it for a minute! Henry Rooter says he never told a lie *yet*, in his whole life, mamma, and he wasn't going to begin now." She paused for a moment, then added: "I don't believe a word he says!"

She continued to meditate disapprovingly upon Henry Rooter. "Old thing!" she murmured gloomily, for she had indeed known moments of apprehension concerning the grape-seeds. "Nothing but an old thing—what he is!" she repeated inaudibly.

"Florence," said Mrs. Atwater, "don't you want to slip over to grandpa's and ask Aunt Julia if she has a very large darning needle? And don't forget not to look supercilious when you meet people on the way. Even your grandfather has been noticing it, and he was the one that spoke of it to me. Don't forget!"

"Yes'm."

Florence went out of the house somewhat moodily, but afternoon sunshine enlivened her; and, opening the picket gate, she stepped forth with a fair renewal of her chosen manner toward the public, though just at that moment no public was in sight. Miss Atwater's underlip resumed the position for which her mother had predicted that regal Spanish fixity, and her eyebrows and nose were all three perceptibly elevated. At the same time, her eyelids were half lowered, while the corners of her mouth somewhat deepened, as by a veiled mirth, so that this well-dressed child strolled down the shady sidewalk wearing an expression not merely of high-bred contempt but also of mysterious derision. It was an expression that should have put any pedestrian in his place, and it seems a pity that the long street before her appeared to be empty of human life. No one even so much as glanced from a window of any of the comfortable houses, set back at the end of their "front walks" and basking amid pleasant lawns; for, naturally, this was the "best residence street" in the town, since all the Atwaters and other relatives of Florence dwelt there. Happily, an old gentleman turned a corner before she had gone a hundred yards, and, as he turned in her direction, it became certain that they would meet. He was a stranger—that is to say, he was unknown to Florence—and he was well dressed; while his appearance of age (proba'ly at least forty or sixty or something) indicated that he might have sense enough to be interested in other interesting persons.

An extraordinary change took place upon the surface of Florence Atwater: all superciliousness and derision of the world vanished; her eyes opened wide, and into them came a look at once far-away and intently fixed. Also, a frown of concentration appeared upon her brow, and her lips moved silently, but with rapidity, as if she repeated to herself something of almost tragic import. Florence had recently read a newspaper account of the earlier struggles of a now successful actress: As a girl, this determined genius went about the streets repeating the lines of various roles to herself—constantly rehearsing, in fact, upon the public thoroughfares, so carried away was she by her intended profession and so set upon becoming famous. This was what Florence was doing now, except that she rehearsed no role in particular, and the words formed by her lips were neither sequential nor consequential, being, in fact, the following: "Oh, the darkness ... never, never, never! ... you couldn't ... he wouldn't ... Ah, mother! ... Where the river swings so slowly ... Ah, *no!*" Nevertheless, she was doing all she could for the elderly stranger, and as they came closer, encountered, and passed on, she had the definite impression that he did indeed take her to be a struggling young actress who would some day be famous—and then he might see her on a night of triumph and recognize her as the girl he had passed on the street, that day, so long ago! But by this time, the episode was concluded; the footsteps of him for whom she was performing had become inaudible behind her, and she began to forget him; which was as well, since he went out of her life then, and the two never met again. The struggling young actress disappeared, and the previous superiority was resumed. It became elaborately emphasized as a boy of her own age emerged from the "side yard" of a house at the next corner and came into her view.

The boy caught sight of Florence in plenty of time to observe this emphasis, which was all too obviously produced by her sensations at sight of himself; and, after staring at her for a moment, he allowed his own expression to become one of painful fatigue. Then he slowly swung about, as if to return into that side-yard obscurity whence he had come; making clear by this pantomime that he reciprocally found the sight of her insufferable. In truth, he did; for he was not only her neighbour but her first-cousin as well, and a short month older, though taller than she—tall beyond his years, taller than need be, in fact, and still in knickerbockers. However, his parents may not have been mistaken in the matter, for it was plain that he looked as well in knickerbockers as he could have looked in anything. He had no visible beauty, though it was possible to hope for him that by the time he reached manhood he would be more tightly put together than he seemed at present; and indeed he himself appeared to have some consciousness of insecurity in the fastenings of his members, for it was his habit (observable even now as he turned to avoid Miss Atwater) to haul at himself, to sag and hitch about inside his clothes, and to corkscrew his neck against the swathing of his collar. And yet there were times, as the most affectionate of his aunts had remarked, when, for a moment or so, he appeared to be almost knowing; and, seeing him walking before her, she had almost taken him for a young man; and sometimes he said something in a settled kind of way that was almost adult. This fondest aunt went on to add, however, that of course, the next minute after one of these fleeting spells, he was sure to be overtaken by his more accustomed moods, when his eye would again fix itself with fundamental aimlessness upon nothing. In brief, he was at the age when he spent most of his time changing his mind about things, or, rather, when his mind spent most of its time changing him about things; and this was what happened now.

After turning his back on the hateful sight well known to him as his cousin Florence at her freshest, he turned again, came forth from his place of residence, and joining her upon the pavement, walked beside her, accompanying her without greeting or inquiry. His expression of fatigue, indicating her insufferableness, had not abated; neither had her air of being a duchess looking at bugs.

"You *are* a pretty one!" he said; but his intention was perceived to be far indeed from his words.

"Oh, *am* I, Mister Herbert Atwater?" Florence responded. "I'm *awf'ly* glad *you* think so!"

"I mean about what Henry Rooter said," her cousin explained.

"Henry Rooter told me he made you believe you were goin' to have a grapevine climbin' up from inside of you because you ate some grapes with the seeds in 'em. He says you thought you'd haf to get a carpenter to build a little arbour so you could swallow it for the grapevine to grow on. He says—"

Florence had become an angry pink. "That little Henry Rooter is the worst falsehooder in this town; and I never believed a word he said in his life! Anyway, what affairs is it of yours, I'd like you to please be so kind and obliging for to tell me, Mister Herbert Illingsworth Atwater, Exquire!"

"What affairs?" Herbert echoed in plaintive satire. "What affairs is it of mine? That's just the trouble! It's *got* to be my affairs because you're my first-cousin. My goodness *I* didn't have anything to do with you being my cousin, did I?"

"Well, *I* didn't!"

"That's neither here nor there," said Herbert. "What *I* want to know is, how long you goin' to keep this up?"

"Keep what up?"

"I mean, how do you think I like havin' somebody like Henry Rooter comin' round me tellin' what they made a cousin of mine believe, and more than thirteen years old, goin' on fourteen ever since about a month ago!"

Florence shouted: "Oh, for goodness' *sakes!*" then moderated the volume but not the intensity of her tone. "Kindly reply to *this.* Whoever asked you to come and take a walk with me to-day?"

Herbert protested to heaven. "Why, I wouldn't take a walk with you if every policeman in this town tried to make me! I wouldn't take a walk with you if they brought a million horses and—"

"I wouldn't take a walk with *you*," Florence interrupted, "if they brought a million million horses and cows and camels and—"

"No, you wouldn't," Herbert said. "Not if *I* could help it!"

But by this time Florence had regained her derisive superciliousness. "There's a few things you *could* help," she said; and the incautious Herbert challenged her with the inquiry she desired.

"What could I help?"

"I should think you could help bumpin' into me every second when I'm takin' a walk on my own affairs, and walk along on your own side of the sidewalk, anyway, and not be so awkward a person has to keep trippin' over you about every time I try to take a step!"

Herbert withdrew temporarily to his own side of the pavement. "Who?" he demanded hotly. "*Who* says I'm awkward?"

"All the fam'ly," Miss Atwater returned, with a light but infuriating laugh. "You bump into 'em sideways and keep gettin' half in front of 'em whenever they try to take a step, and then when it looks as if they'd pretty near fall over you—"

"You look here!"

"And besides all that," Florence went on, undisturbed, "why, you generally keep kind of snorting, or somep'n, and then making all those noises in your neck. You were doin' it at grandpa's last Sunday dinner because every time there wasn't anybody talking, why, everybody could hear you plain as everything, and you ought to've seen grandpa look at you! He looked as if you'd set him crazy if you didn't quit that chuttering and cluckling!"

Herbert's expression partook of a furious astonishment. "I

don't any such thing!" he burst out. "I guess I wouldn't talk much about last Sunday dinner, if I was *you* neither. Who got caught eatin' off the ice cream freezer spoon out on the back porch, if you please? Yes, and I guess you better study a little grammar, while you're about it. There's no such words in the English language as 'cluckling' and 'chuttering.'"

"I don't care what language they're in," the stubborn Florence insisted. "It's what you do, just the same: cluckling and chuttering!"

Herbert's manners went to pieces. "Oh, dry up!" he bellowed.

"That's a *nice* way to talk! So gentlemanly—"

"Well, you try be a lady, then!"

"Try!" Florence echoed. "Well, after that, I'll just politely thank you to dry up, yourself, Mister Herbert Atwater!"

At this Herbert became moody. "Oh, pfuff!" he said; and for some moments walked in silence. Then he asked: "Where you goin', Florence?"

The damsel paused at a gate opening upon a broad lawn evenly divided by a brick walk that led to the white-painted wooden veranda of an ample and honest old brick house. "Righ' there to grandpa's, since you haf to know!" she said. "And thank you for your delightful comp'ny which I never asked for, if you care to hear the truth for once in your life!"

Herbert meditated. "Well, I got nothin' else to do, as I know of," he said. "Let's go around to the back door so's to see if Kitty Silver's got anything."

Then, not amiably, but at least inconsequently, they passed inside the gate together. Their brows were fairly unclouded; no special marks of conflict remained; for they had met and conversed in a manner customary rather than unusual.

They followed a branch of the brick walk and passed round the south side of the house, where a small orchard of apple-trees showed generous promise. Hundreds of gay little round apples among the leaves glanced the high lights to and fro on their polished green cheeks as a breeze hopped through the yard, while the shade beneath trembled with coquettishly moving disks of sunshine like golden plates. A pattern of orange light and blue shadow was laid like a fanciful plaid over the lattice and the wide, slightly sagging steps of the elderly "back porch"; and here, taking her ease upon these steps, sat a middle-aged coloured woman of continental proportions. Beyond all contest, she was the largest coloured woman in that town, though her height was not unusual, and she had a rather small face. That is to say, as Florence had once explained to her, her face was small but the other parts of her head were terribly wide. Beside her was a circular brown basket, of a type suggesting arts-and-crafts; it was made with a cover, and there was a bow of brown silk upon the handle.

"What you been up to to-day, Kitty Silver?" Herbert asked genially. "Any thing special?" For this was the sequel to his "so's we can see if Kitty Silver's got anything." But Mrs. Silver discouraged him.

"No, I ain't," she replied. "I ain't, an' I ain't goin' to."

"I thought you pretty near always made cookies on Tuesday," he said.

"Well, I ain't *this* Tuesday," said Kitty Silver. "I ain't, and I ain't goin' to. You might dess well g'on home ri' now. I ain't, an' I ain't goin' to."

Docility was no element of Mrs. Silver's present mood, and Herbert's hopeful eyes became blank, as his gaze wandered from her head to the brown basket beside her. The basket did not interest him; the ribbon gave it a quality almost at once excluding it from his consciousness. On the contrary, the ribbon had drawn Florence's attention, and she stared at the basket eagerly.

"What you got there, Kitty Silver?" she asked.

"What I got where?"

"In that basket."

"Nemmine what I got 'n 'at basket," said Mrs. Silver crossly, but added inconsistently: "I dess *wish* somebody ast me what I got 'n 'at basket! *I* ain't no cat-washwoman fer *no*body!"

"Cats!" Florence cried. "Are there cats in that basket, Kitty Silver? Let's look at 'em!"

The lid of the basket, lifted by the eager, slim hand of Miss Atwater, rose to disclose two cats of an age slightly beyond kittenhood. They were of a breed unfamiliar to Florence, and she did not obey the impulse that usually makes a girl seize upon any young cat at sight and caress it. Instead, she looked at them with some perplexity, and after a moment inquired: "Are they really cats, Kitty Silver, do you b'lieve?"

"Cats what she done tole *me*," the coloured woman replied. "You betta shet lid down, you don' wan' 'em run away, 'cause they ain't yoosta livin' 'n 'at basket yit; an' no matter whut kine o' cats they is or they isn't, *one* thing true: they *wile* cats!"

"But what makes their hair so long?" Florence asked. "I never saw cats with hair a couple inches long like that."

"Miss Julia say they Berjum cats."

"What?"

"I ain't tellin' no mo'n she tole me. You' aunt say they Berjum cats."

"Persian," said Herbert. "That's nothing. I've seen plenty

Persian cats. My goodness, I should think you'd seen a Persian cat at yow age. Thirteen goin' on fourteen!"

"Well, I *have* seen Persian cats plenty times, I guess," Florence said. "I thought Persian cats were white, and these are kind of gray."

At this Kitty Silver permitted herself to utter an embittered laugh. "You wrong!" she said. "These cats, they white; yes'm!"

"Why, they aren't either! They're gray as—"

"No'm," said Mrs. Silver. "They plum spang white, else you' Aunt Julia gone out her mind; me or her, one. I say: 'Miss Julia, them gray cats.' 'White,' she say. 'Them two cats is white cats,' she say. 'Them cats been crated,' she say. 'They been livin' in a crate on a dirty express train fer th'ee fo' days,' she say. 'Them cats gone got all smoke' up thataway,' she say. 'No'm, Miss Julia,' I say, 'No'm, Miss Julia, they ain't *no* train,' I say, 'they ain't *no* train kin take an' smoke two white cats up like these cats so's they hair is gray clean plum up to they hide.' You betta put the lid down, I tell you!"

Florence complied, just in time to prevent one of the young cats from leaping out of the basket, but she did not fasten the cover. Instead, she knelt, and, allowing a space of half an inch to intervene between the basket and the rim of the cover, peered within at the occupants. "I believe the one to this side's a he," she said. "It's got greenisher eyes than the other one; that's the way you can always tell. I b'lieve this one's a he and the other one's a she."

"I ain't stedyin' about no he an' she!"

"What did Aunt Julia say?" Florence asked.

"Whut you' Aunt Julia say when?"

"When you told her these were gray cats and not white cats?"

"She tole me take an' clean 'em," said Kitty Silver. "She say, she say she want 'em clean' up spick an' spang befo' Mista Sammerses git here to call an' see 'em." And she added morosely: "I ain't no cat-washwoman!"

"She wants you to bathe 'em?" Florence inquired, but Kitty Silver did not reply immediately. She breathed audibly, with a strange effect upon vasty outward portions of her, and then gave an incomparably dulcet imitation of her own voice, as she interpreted her use of it during the recent interview.

'Miss Julia, ma'am,' I say—'Miss Julia, ma'am, my bizniss cookin' vittles,' I say. 'Miss Julia, ma'am,' I tole her, 'Miss Julia, ma'am, I cook fer you' pa, an' cook fer you' fam'ly year in, year out, an' I hope an' pursue, whiles some might make complaint, I take whatever I find, an' I leave whatever I find. No'm, Miss Julia, ma'am,' I say—'no'm, Miss Julia, ma'am, I ain't no cat-washwoman!'"

"What did Aunt Julia say then?"

"She say, she say: 'Di'n I tell you take them cats downstairs an' clean 'em?' she say. I ain't *no*body's cat-washwoman!"

Florence was becoming more and more interested. "I should think that would be kind of fun," she said. "To be a cat-washwoman. *I* wouldn't mind that at all: I'd kind of like it. I expect if you was a cat-washwoman, Kitty Silver, you'd be pretty near the only one was in the world. I wonder if they do have 'em any place, cat-washwomen."

"I don' know if they got 'em some place," said Kitty Silver, "an' I don't know if they ain't got 'em no place; but I bet if they do got 'em any place, it's some place else from here!"

Florence looked thoughtful. "Who was it you said is going to call this evening and see 'em?"

"Mista Sammerses."

"She means Newland Sanders," Herbert explained. "Aunt Julia says all her callers that ever came to this house in their lives, Kitty Silver never got the name right of a single one of 'em!"

"Newland Sanders is the one with the little moustache," Florence said. "Is that the one you mean by 'Sammerses,' Kitty Silver?"

"Mista Sammerses who you' Aunt Julia tole *me*," Mrs. Silver responded stubbornly. "He ain't got no moustache whut you kin look at—dess some blackish whut don' reach out mo'n halfway todes the bofe ends of his mouf."

"Well," said Florence, "was Mr. Sanders the one gave her these Persian cats, Kitty Silver?"

"I reckon." Mrs. Silver breathed audibly again, and her expression was strongly resentful. "When she go fer a walk 'long with any them callers she stop an' make a big fuss over any li'l ole dog or cat an' I don't know whut all, an' after they done buy her all the candy from all the candy sto's in the livin' worl', an' all the flowers from all the greenhouses they is, it's a wonder some of 'em ain't sen' her a mule fer a present, 'cause seem like to me they done sen' her mos' every kine of animal they is! Firs' come Airydale dog you' grampaw tuck an' give away to the milkman; 'n'en come two mo' pups; I don't know whut they is, 'cause they bofe had dess sense enough to run away after you' grampaw try learn 'em how much he ain't like no pups; an' nex' come them two canaries hangin' in the dinin'-room now, an' nex'—di'n' I holler so's they could a-hear me all way down town? Di'n' I walk in my kitchen one mawnin' right slam in the face of ole warty allagatuh three foot long a-lookin' at me over the aidge o' my kitchen sink?"

"It was Mr. Clairdyce gave her that," said Florence. "He'd been to Florida; but she didn't care for it very much, and she didn't make any fuss at all when grandpa got the florist to take it. Grandpa hates animals."

"He don' hate 'em no wuss'n whut I do," said Kitty Silver. "An' he ain't got to ketch 'em lookin' at him outen of his kitchen sink—an' he ain't fixin' to be no cat-washwoman neither!"

"*Are* you fixing to?" Florence asked quickly. "You don't need to do it, Kitty Silver. I'd be willing to, and so'd Herbert. Wouldn't you, Herbert?"

Herbert deliberated within himself, then brightened. "I'd just as soon," he said. "I'd kind of like to see how a cat acts when it's getting bathed."

"I think it would be spesh'ly inter'sting to wash Persian cats," Florence added, with increasing enthusiasm. "I never washed a cat in my life."

"Neither have I," said Herbert. "I always thought they did it themselves."

Kitty Silver sniffed. "Ain't I says so to you' Aunt Julia? She done tole me, 'No,' she say. She say, she say Berjum cats ain't wash they self; they got to take an' git somebody else to wash 'em!"

"If we're goin' to bathe 'em," said Florence, "we ought to know their names, so's we can tell 'em to hold still and everything. You can't do much with an animal unless you know their name. Did Aunt Julia tell you these cats' names, Kitty Silver?"

"She say they name Feef an' Meemuh. Yes'm! Feef an' Meemuh! Whut kine o' name is Feef an' Meemuh fer cat name!"

"Oh, those are lovely names!" Florence assured her, and, turning to Herbert, explained: "She means Fifi and Mimi."

"Feef an' Meemuh," said Kitty Silver. "Them name don' suit

me, an' them long-hair cats don' suit me neither." Here she lifted the cover of the basket a little, and gazed nervously within. "Look at there!" she said. "Look at the way they lookin' at me! Don't you look at *me* thataway, you Feef an' Meemuh!" She clapped the lid down and fastened it. "Fixin' to jump out an' grab me, was you?"

"I guess, maybe," said Florence, "maybe I better go ask Aunt Julia if I and Herbert can't wash 'em. I guess I better go *ask* her anyhow." And she ran up the steps and skipped into the house by way of the kitchen. A moment later she appeared in the open doorway of a room upstairs.

CHAPTER TWO

It was a pretty room, lightly scented with the pink geraniums and blue lobelia and coral fuchsias that poised, urgent with colour, in the window-boxes at the open windows. Sunshine paused delicately just inside, where forms of pale-blue birds and lavender flowers curled up and down the cretonne curtains; and a tempered, respectful light fell upon a cushioned *chaise longue*; for there fluffily reclined, in garments of tender fabric and gentle colours, the prettiest twenty-year-old girl in that creditably supplied town.

It must be said that no stranger would have taken Florence at first glance to be her niece, though everybody admitted that Florence's hair was pretty. ("I'll say *that* for her," was the family way of putting it.). Florence did not care for her hair herself; it was dark and thick and long, like her Aunt Julia's; but Florence—even in the realistic presence of a mirror—preferred to think of herself as an ashen blonde, and also as about a foot taller than she was. Persistence kept this picture habitually in her mind, which, of course, helps to explain her feeling that she was justified in wearing that manner of superciliousness deplored by her mother. More middle-aged gentlemen than are suspected believe that they look like the waspen youths in the magazine advertisements of clothes; and this impression of theirs accounts (as with Florence) for much that is seemingly inexplicable in their behaviour.

Florence's Aunt Julia was reading an exquisitely made little book, which bore her initials stamped in gold upon the cover;

and it had evidently reached her by a recent delivery of the mail, for wrappings bearing cancelled stamps lay upon the floor beside the *chaise longue*. It was a special sort of book, since its interior was not printed, but all laboriously written with pen and ink—poems, in truth, containing more references to a lady named Julia than have appeared in any other poems since Herrick's. So warmly interested in the reading as to be rather pink, though not always with entire approval, this Julia nevertheless, at the sound of footsteps, closed the book and placed it beneath one of the cushions assisting the *chaise longue* to make her position a comfortable one. Her greeting was not enthusiastic.

"What do you want, Florence?"

"I was going to ask you if Herbert and me—I mean: Was it Noble Dill gave you Fifi and Mimi, Aunt Julia?"

"Noble Dill? No."

"I wish it was," Florence said. "I'd like these cats better if they were from Noble Dill."

"Why?" Julia inquired. "Why are you so partial to Mr. Noble Dill?"

"I think he's *so* much the most inter'sting looking of all that come to see you. Are you *sure* it wasn't Noble Dill gave you these cats, Aunt Julia?"

A look of weariness became plainly visible upon Miss Julia Atwater's charming face. "I do wish you'd hurry and grow up, Florence," she said.

"I do, too! What for, Aunt Julia?"

"So there'd be somebody else in the family of an eligible age. I really think it's an outrageous position to be in," Julia continued, with languid vehemence—"to be the only girl between thirteen and forty-one in a large connection of near relatives, including children, who all seem to think they haven't anything to think of but Who comes to see her, and Who came to see her yesterday, and Who was here the day before, and Who's coming to-morrow, and Who's she going to marry! You really ought to grow up and help me out, because I'm getting tired of it. No. It wasn't Noble Dill but Mr. Newland Sanders that sent me Fifi and Mimi—and I want you to keep away from 'em."

"Why?" asked Florence.

"Because they're very rare cats, and you aren't ordinarily a very careful sort of person, Florence, if you don't mind my saying so. Besides, if I let you go near them, the next thing Herbert would be over here mussing around, and he can't go near *anything* without ruining it! It's just in him; he can't help it."

Florence looked thoughtful for a brief moment; then she asked: "Did Newland Sanders send 'em with the names already to them?"

"No," said Julia, emphasizing the patience of her tone somewhat. "I named them after they got here. Mr. Sanders hasn't seen them yet. He had them shipped to me. He's coming this evening. Anything more to-day, Florence?"

"Well, I was thinking," said Florence. "What do you think grandpa'll think about these cats?"

"I don't believe there'll be any more outrages," Julia returned, and her dark eyes showed a moment's animation. "I told him at breakfast that the Reign of Terror was ended, and he and everybody else had to keep away from Fifi and Mimi. Is that about all, Florence?"

"You let Kitty Silver go near 'em, though. She says she's fixing to wash 'em."

Julia smiled faintly. "I thought she would! I had to go so far as to tell her that as long as I'm housekeeper in my father's house she'd do what I say or find some other place. She behaved outrageously and pretended to believe the natural colour of Fifi and Mimi is gray!"

"I expect," said Florence, after pondering seriously for a little while—"I expect it would take quite some time to dry them."

"No doubt. But I'd rather you didn't assist. I'd rather you weren't even around looking on, Florence."

A shade fell upon her niece's face at this. "Why, Aunt Julia, I couldn't do any harm to Fifi and Mimi just *lookin'* at 'em, could I?"

Julia laughed. "That's the trouble; you never do 'just look' at anything you're interested in, and, if you don't mind my saying so, you've got rather a record, dear! Now, don't you care: you can find lots of other pleasant things to do at home—or over at Herbert's, or Aunt Fanny's. You run along now and—"

"Well—" Florence said, moving as if to depart.

"You might as well go out by the front door, child," Julia suggested, with a little watchful urgency. "You come over some day when Fifi and Mimi have got used to the place, and you can look at them all you want to."

"Well, I just—"

But as Florence seemed disposed still to linger, her aunt's manner became more severe, and she half rose from her reclining position.

"No, I really mean it! Fifi and Mimi are royal-bred Persian cats with a wonderful pedigree, and I don't know how much trouble and expense it cost Mr. Sanders to get them for me.

They're entirely different from ordinary cats; they're very fine and queer, and if anything happens to them, after all the trouble papa's made over other presents I've had, I'll go straight to a sanitarium! No, Florence, you keep away from the kitchen to-day, and I'd like to hear the front door as you go out."

"Well," said Florence; "I do wish if these cats are as fine as all that, it was Noble Dill that gave 'em to you. I'd like these cats lots better if *he* gave 'em to you, wouldn't you?"

"No, I wouldn't."

"Well—" Florence said again, and departed.

Twenty is an unsuspicious age, except when it fears that its dignity or grace may be threatened from without; and it might have been a "bad sign" in revelation of Julia Atwater's character if she had failed to accept the muffled metallic clash of the front door's closing as a token that her niece had taken a complete departure for home. A supplemental confirmation came a moment later, fainter but no less conclusive: the distant slamming of the front gate; and it made a clear picture of an obedient Florence on her homeward way. Peace came upon Julia: she read in her book, while at times she dropped a languid, graceful arm, and, with the pretty hand at the slimmer end of it, groped in a dark shelter beneath her couch to make a selection, merely by her well-experienced sense of touch, from a frilled white box that lay in concealment there. Then, bringing forth a crystalline violet become scented sugar, or a bit of fruit translucent in hardened sirup, she would delicately set it on the way to that attractive dissolution hoped for it by the wistful donor—and all without removing her shadowy eyes from the little volume and its patient struggle for dignified rhymes with "Julia." Florence was no longer in her beautiful relative's thoughts.

Florence was idly in the thoughts, however, of Mrs. Balche, the next-door neighbour to the south. Happening to glance from a bay-window, she negligently marked how the child walked to the front gate, opened it, paused for a moment's meditation, then hurled the gate to a vigorous closure, herself remaining within its protection. "Odd!" Mrs. Balche murmured.

Having thus eloquently closed the gate, Florence slowly turned and moved toward the rear of the house, quickening her steps as she went, until at a run she disappeared from the scope of Mrs. Balche's gaze, cut off by the intervening foliage of Mr. Atwater's small orchard. Mrs. Balche felt no great interest; nevertheless, she paused at the sound of a boy's voice, half husky, half shrill, in an early stage of change. "What she say, Flor'nce? D'she say we could?" But there came a warning "*Hush up!*" from Florence, and then, in a lowered tone, the boy's voice said: "Look here; these are mighty funny-actin' cats. I think they're kind of crazy or somep'n. Kitty Silver's fixed a washtub full o' suds for us."

Mrs. Balche was reminded of her own cat, and went to give it a little cream. Mrs. Balche was a retired widow, without children, and too timid to like dogs; but after a suitable interval, following the loss of her husband, she accepted from a friend the gift of a white kitten, and named it Violet. It may be said that Mrs. Balche, having few interests in life, and being of a sequestering nature, lived for Violet, and that so much devotion was not good for the latter's health. In his youth, after having shown sufficient spirit to lose an eye during a sporting absence of three nights and days, Violet was not again permitted enough freedom of action to repeat this disloyalty; though, now, in his advanced middle-age, he had been fed to such a state that he seldom cared to move, other than by a slow, sneering wavement of the tail when friendly words were addressed to him; and consequently, as he seemed beyond all capacity or desire to run away, or to run at all, Mrs. Balche allowed him complete liberty of action.

She found him asleep upon her "back porch," and placed beside him a saucer of cream, the second since his luncheon. Then she watched him affectionately as he opened his eye, turned toward the saucer his noble Henry-the-Eighth head with its great furred jowls, and began the process of rising for more food, which was all that ever seemed even feebly to rouse his mind. When he had risen, there was little space between him anywhere and the floor.

Violet took his cream without enthusiasm, pausing at times and turning his head away. In fact, he persisted only out of an incorrigible sensuality, and finally withdrew a pace or two, leaving creamy traces still upon the saucer. With a multitude of fond words his kind mistress drew his attention to these, whereupon, making a visible effort, he returned and disposed of them.

"Dat's de 'itty darlin'," she said, stooping to stroke him. "Eat um all up nice clean. Dood for ole sweet sin!" She continued to stroke him, and Violet half closed his eye, but not with love or serenity, for he simultaneously gestured with his tail, meaning to say: "Oh, do take your hands off o' me!" Then he opened the eye and paid a little attention to sounds from the neighbouring yard. A high fence, shrubberies, and foliage concealed that yard from the view of Violet, but the sounds were eloquent to him, since they were those made by members of his own general species when threatening atrocities. The accent may have been foreign, but Violet caught perfectly the sense of what was being said, and instinctively he muttered reciprocal curses within himself.

"What a matta, honey?" his companion inquired sympathetically. "Ess, bad people f ighten poor Violet!"

From beyond the fence came the murmurings of a boy and a girl in hushed but urgent conversation; and with these sounds there mingled watery agitations, splashings and the like, as well as those low vocalizings that Violet had recognized; but suddenly there were muffled explosions, like fireworks choked in feather beds; and the human voices grew uncontrollably somewhat louder, so that their import was distinguishable. "*Ow!*" "Hush up, can't you? You want to bring the whole town to—*ow!*" "Hush up yourself!" "Oh, *goodness!*" "Look out! Don't let her—" "Well, look what she's *doin'* to me, can't you?" "For Heavenses' sakes, catch holt and—*Ow!*"

Then came a husky voice, inevitably that of a horrified coloured person hastening from a distance: "Oh, my soul!" There was a scurrying, and the girl was heard in furious yet hoarsely guarded vehemence: "Bring the clo'es prop! Bring the clo'es prop! We can poke that one down from the garage, anyway. *Oh, my goodness, look at 'er go!*"

Mrs. Balche shook her head. "Naughty children!" she said, as she picked up the saucer and went to the kitchen door, which she held open for Violet to enter. "Want to come with mamma?"

But Violet had lost even the faint interest in life he had shown a few moments earlier. He settled himself to another stupor in the sun.

"Well, well," Mrs. Balche said indulgently. "Afterwhile shall have some more nice keem."

*   *   *   *   *

Sunset was beginning to be hinted, two hours later, when, in another quarter of the town, a little girl of seven or eight, at play on the domestic side of an alley gate, became aware of an older girl regarding her fixedly over the top of the gate. The little girl felt embarrassed and paused in her gayeties, enfolding in her arms her pet and playmate. "Howdy' do," said the stranger, in a serious tone. "What'll you take for that cat?"

The little girl made no reply, and the stranger, opening the gate, came into the yard. She looked weary, rather bedraggled, yet hurried: her air was predominantly one of anxiety. "I'll give you a quarter for that cat," she said. "I want an all-white cat, but this one's only got that one gray spot over its eye, and I don't believe there's an all-white cat left in town, leastways that anybody's willing to part with. I'll give you twenty-five cents for it. I haven't got it with me, but I'll promise to give it to you day after to-morrow."

The little girl still made no reply, but continued to stare, her eyes widening, and the caller spoke with desperation.

"See here," she said, "I *got* to have a whitish cat! That'n isn't worth more'n a quarter, but I'll give you thirty-five cents for her, money down, day after to-morrow."

At this, the frightened child set the cat upon the ground and fled into the house. Florence Atwater was left alone; that is to say, she was the only human being in the yard, or in sight. Nevertheless, a human voice spoke, not far behind her. It came through a knot-hole in the fence, and it was a voice almost of passion.

"*You grab it!*"

Florence stood in silence, motionless; there was a solemnity about her. The voice exhorted. "My goodness!" it said. "She didn't say she *wouldn't* sell it, did she? You can bring her the money like you said you would, can't you? I got *mine*, didn't I, almost without any trouble at all! My Heavens! Ain't Kitty Silver pretty near crazy? Just think of the position we've put her into! I tell you, you *got* to!"

But now Florence moved. She moved slowly at first: then with more decision and rapidity.

*　　*　　*　　*　　*

That evening's dusk had deepened into blue night when the two cousins, each with a scant, uneasy dinner eaten, met by appointment in the alley behind their mutual grandfather's place of residence, and, having climbed the back fence, approached the kitchen. Suddenly Florence lifted her right hand, and took between thumb and forefinger a lock of hair upon the back of Herbert's head.

"Well, for Heavenses' sakes!" he burst out, justifiably protesting.

"Hush!" Florence warned him. "Kitty Silver's talkin' to somebody in there. It might be Aunt Julia! C'm'ere!"

She led him to a position beneath an open window of the kitchen. Here they sat upon the ground, with their backs against the stone foundation of the house, and listened to voices and the clink of dishes being washed.

"She's got another ole coloured darky woman in there with her," said Florence. "It's a woman belongs to her church and comes to see her 'most every evening. Listen; she's telling her about it. I bet we could get the real truth of it maybe better this way than if we went in and asked her right out. Anyway, it isn't eavesdropping if you listen when people are talkin' about you, yourself. It's only wrong when it isn't any of your own bus—"

"For Heavenses' sakes hush *up*!" her cousin remonstrated. "Listen!"

"'No'm, Miss Julia, ma'am,' I say"—thus came the voice of Mrs. Silver—"'no'm, Miss Julia, ma'am. Them the same two cats you han' me, Miss Julia, ma'am,' I say. 'Leas'wise,' I say, 'them the two same cats whut was in nat closed-up brown basket when I open it up an' take an' fix to wash 'em. Somebody might 'a' took an' change 'em 'fo' they got to *me*,' I say, 'Miss Julia, ma'am, but all the change happen to 'em sence they been in charge of *me*, that's the gray whut come off 'em whiles I washin' 'em an' dryin' 'em in corn meal and flannel. I dunno how much *washin'* 'em change 'em, Miss Julia, ma'am,' I say, "'cause how much they change or ain't change, that's fer you to say and me not to jedge,' I say."

"Lan' o' misery!" cried the visitor, chuckling delightedly. "I wonder how you done kep' you face, Miss Kitty. What Miss Julia say?"

A loud, irresponsible outburst of mirth on the part of Mrs. Silver followed. When she could again control herself, she replied more definitely. "Miss Julia say, she say she ain't never hear no sech outragelous sto'y in her life! She *tuck* on! Hallelujah! An' all time, Miz Johnson, I give you my word, I stannin' there holdin' nat basket, carryin' on up hill an' down dale how them the same two Berjum cats Mista Sammerses sen' her: an' trouble enough dess ten'in' to that basket, lemme say to you, Miz Johnson, as anybody kin tell you whutever tried to take care o' two cats whut ain't yoosta each other in the same basket. An' every blessed minute I stannin' there, can't I hear that ole Miz Blatch nex' do', out in her back yod an' her front yod, an' plum out in the street, hollerin': 'Kitty? Kitty? Kitty?' '*Yes!* Miss Julia say, she say, 'Fine sto'y!' she say. 'Them two cats you claim my Berjum cats, they got short hair, an' they ain't the same age an' they ain't even nowheres near the same *size*,' she say. 'One of 'em's as fat as *bofe* them Berjum cats,' she say: 'an' it's on'y got one eye,' she say. 'Well, Miss Julia, ma'am,' I say—'*one* thing; they come out white, all 'cept dess around that there skinnier one's eye,' I say: 'dess the same you tell me they goin' to,' I say. 'You right about *that* much, ma'am!' I say."

"Oh, me!" Mrs. Johnson moaned, worn with applausive laughter. "What she respon' then?"

"I set that basket down," said Kitty Silver, "an' I start fer the do', whiles she unfasten the lid fer to take one mo' look at 'em, I reckon: but open window mighty close by, an' nat skinny white cat make one jump, an' after li'l while I lookin' out thishere window an' see that ole fat Miz Blatch's tom, waddlin' crost the yod todes home."

"What she doin' now?" Mrs. Johnson inquired.

"Who? Miss Julia? She settin' out on the front po'che talkin' to

Mista Sammerses."

"My name! How she goin' fix it with *him*, after all thishere dishcumaraddle?"

"Who? Miss Julia? Leave her alone, honey! She take an' begin talk so fas' an' talk so sweet, no young man ain't goin' to ricklect he ever give her no cats, not till he's gone an' halfway home! But I ain't tole you the en' of it, Miz Johnson, an' the en' of it's the bes' part whut happen."

"What's that, Miss Kitty?"

"Look!" said Mrs. Silver. "Mista Atwater gone in yonder, after I come out, an' ast whut all them goin's-on about. Well suh, an' di'n' he come walkin' out in my kitchen an' slip me two bright spang new silbuh dolluhs right in my han'?"

"My name!"

"Yessuh!" said Mrs. Silver triumphantly. And in the darkness outside the window Florence drew a deep breath. "I'd of felt just awful about this," she said, "if Noble Dill had given Aunt Julia those Persian cats."

"Why?" Herbert inquired, puzzled by her way of looking at things. "I don't see why it would make it any worse *who* gave 'em to her."

"Well, it would," Florence said. "But anyway, I think we did rather wrong. Did you notice what Kitty Silver said about what grandpa did?"

"Well?"

"I think we ought to tell him our share of it," Florence returned thoughtfully. "I don't want to go to bed to-night with all this on my mind, and I'm going to find grandpa right now and confess every bit of it to him."

Herbert hopefully decided to go with her.

CHAPTER THREE

Julia, like Herbert, had been a little puzzled by Florence's expression of a partiality for the young man, Noble Dill; it was not customary for anybody to confess a weakness for him. However, the aunt dismissed the subject from her mind, as other matters pressed sharply upon her attention; she had more worries than most people guessed.

The responsibilities of a lady who is almost officially the prettiest person in a town persistently claiming sixty-five thousand inhabitants are often heavier than the world suspects, and there were moments when Julia found the position so trying that she would have preferred to resign. She was a warm-hearted, appreciative girl, naturally unable to close her eyes to sterling merit wherever it appeared: and it was not without warrant that she complained of her relatives. The whole family, including the children, she said, regaled themselves with her private affairs as a substitute for theatre-going. But one day, a week after the irretrievable disappearance of Fifi and Mimi, she went so far as to admit a note of unconscious confession into her protest that she was getting pretty tired of being mistaken for a three-ring circus! Such was her despairing expression, and the confession lies in her use of the word "three."

The misleading moderation of "three" was pointed out to her by her niece, whose mind at once violently seized upon the word and divested it of context—a process both feminine and instinctive, for this child was already beginning to be feminine.

Booth Tarkington

"Three!" she said. "Why, Aunt Julia, you must be crazy! There's Newland Sanders and Noble Dill and that old widower, Ridgley, that grandpa hates so, and Mister Clairdyce and George Plum and the two new ones from out of town that Aunt Fanny Patterson said you had at church Sunday morning—Herbert said he didn't like one of 'em's looks much, Aunt Julia. And there's Parker Kent Usher and that funny-lookin' one with the little piece of whiskers under his underlip that Noble Dill got so mad at when they were calling, and Uncle Joe laughed about, and I don't know who all! Anyhow, there's an awful lot more than three, Aunt Julia."

Julia looked down with little favour upon the talkative caller. Florence was seated upon the shady steps of the veranda, and Julia, dressed for a walk, occupied a wicker chair above her. "Julia, dressed for a walk"—how scant the words! It was a summer walk that Julia had dressed for: and she was all too dashingly a picture of coolness on a hot day: a brunette in murmurous white, though her little hat was a film of blackest blue, and thus also in belt and parasol she had almost matched the colour of her eyes. Probably no human-made fabric could have come nearer to matching them, though she had once met a great traveller—at least he went far enough in his search for comparisons—who told her that the Czarina of Russia had owned a deep sapphire of precisely the colour, but the Czarina's was the only sapphire yet discovered that had it. One of Newland Sanders's longest Poems-to-Julia was entitled "Black Sapphires."

Julia's harmonies in black sapphire were uncalled for. If she really had been as kind as she was too often capable of looking, she would have fastened patches over both eyes—one patch would have been useless—and she would have worn flat shoes and patronized a dressmaker with genius enough to misrepresent her. But Julia was not great enough for such generosities: she should have been locked up till she passed sixty; her sufferings deserve no pity.

And yet an attack of the mumps during the winter had

brought Julia more sympathy than the epidemic of typhoid fever in the Old Ladies' Infirmary brought all of the nine old ladies who were under treatment there. Julia was confined to her room for almost a month, during which a florist's wagon seemed permanent before the house: and a confectioner's frequently stood beside the florist's. Young Florence, an immune who had known the mumps in infancy, became an almost constant attendant upon the patient, with the result that the niece contracted an illness briefer than the aunt's, but more than equalling it in poignancy, caused by the poor child's economic struggle against waste. Florence's convalescence took place in her own home without any inquiries whatever from the outer world, but Julia's was spent in great part at the telephone. Even a poem was repeated to her by the instrument:

How the world blooms anew
To think that you
Can speak again,
Can hear
The words of men
And the dear
Own voice of you.

This was Newland Sanders. He was just out of college, a reviewer, a poet, and once, momentarily, an atheist. It was Newland who was present and said such a remarkable thing when Julia had the accident to her thumb-nail in closing the double doors between the living-room and the library, where her peculiar old father sat reading. "To see you suffer," Newland said passionately as she nursed her injury:—"to see you in pain, that is the one thing in the universe which I feel beyond all my capacities. Do you know, when you are made to suffer pain, then I feel that there is no God!"

This strong declaration struck Herbert as one of the most impressive things he had ever heard, though he could not account for its being said to any aunt of his. Herbert had just dropped in without the formality of ringing the bell, and had paused in the hall, outside the open door of the living-room.

He considered the matter, after Newland had spoken, and concluded to return to his own place of residence without disturbing anybody at his grandfather's. At home he found his mother and father entertaining one of his uncles, one of his aunts, two of his great-uncles, one of his great-aunts, and one of his grown-up cousins, at cards: and he proved to be warranted in believing that they would all like to know what he had heard. Newland's statement became quite celebrated throughout the family: and Julia, who had perceived almost a sacred something in his original fervour, changed her mind after hearing the words musingly repeated, over and over, by her fat old Uncle Joe.

Florence thought proper to remind her of this to-day, after Julia's protest containing the too moderately confessional word "three."

"If you don't want to be such a circus," the niece continued, reasoning perfectly, "I don't see what you always keep leadin' all of 'em on all the time just the same for."

"Who've you heard saying that, Florence?" her aunt demanded.

"Aunt Fanny Patterson," Florence replied absently. "F'r instance, Aunt Julia, I don't see what you want to go walking with Newland Sanders for, when you said yourself you wished he was dead, or somep'n, after there got to be so muck talk in the family and everywhere about his sayin' all that about the Bible when you hurt your thumb. All the family—"

Julia sighed profoundly. "I wish 'all the family' would try to think about themselves for just a little while! There's entirely too little self-centredness among my relatives to suit me!"

"Why, it's only because you're related to me that *I* pay the very *slightest* attention to what goes on here," Florence protested. "It's my own grandfather's house, isn't it? Well, if you didn't live here, and if you wasn't my own grandfather's daughter,

Aunt Julia, I wouldn't ever pay the *very* slightest attention to you! Anyway, I don't *much* criticize all these people that keep calling on you—anyway not half as much as Herbert does. Herbert thinks he always hass to act so critical, now his voice is changing."

"At your age," said Julia, "my mind was on my schoolbooks."

"Why, Aunt Julia!" Florence exclaimed in frank surprise. "Grandpa says just the opposite from that. I've heard him say, time and time and time again, you always *were* this way, ever since you were four years old."

"What way?" asked her aunt.

"Like you are now, Aunt Julia. Grandpa says by the time you were fourteen it got so bad he had to get a new front gate, the way they leaned on it. He says he hoped when you grew up he'd get a little peace in his own house, but he says it's worse, and never for one minute the livelong day can he—"

"I know," Julia interrupted. "He talks like a Christian Martyr and behaves like Nero. I might warn you to keep away from him, by the way, Florence. He says that either you or Herbert was over here yesterday and used his spectacles to cut a magazine with, and broke them. I wouldn't be around here much if I were you until he's got over it."

"It must have been Herbert broke 'em," said Florence promptly.

"Papa thinks it was you. Kitty Silver told him it was."

"Mean ole reptile!" said Florence, alluding to Mrs. Silver; then she added serenely, "Well, grandpa don't get home till five o'clock, and it's only about a quarter of two now. Aunt Julia, what are you waitin' around here for?"

"I told you; I'm going walking."

"I mean: Who with?"

Miss Atwater permitted herself a light moan. "With Mr. Sanders and Mr. Ridgely, Florence."

Florence's eyes grew large and eager. "Why, Aunt Julia, I thought those two didn't speak to each other any more!"

"They don't," Julia assented in a lifeless voice. "It just happened that Mr. Sanders and Mr. Ridgley and Mr. Dill, all three, asked me to take a walk this afternoon at two o'clock."

"But Noble Dill isn't going?"

"No," said Julia. "I was fortunate enough to remember that I'd already promised someone else when he asked me. That's what I didn't remember when Mr. Ridgely asked me."

"I'd have gone with Noble Dill," Florence said firmly. "Noble Dill is my Very Ideal! I'd marry him to-morrow."

"It seems to me," her aunt remarked, "I heard your mother telling somebody the other day that you had said the same thing about the King of Spain."

Florence laughed. "Oh, that was only a passing fancy," she said lightly. "Aunt Julia, what's Newland Sanders supposed to do?"

"I think he hasn't entered any business or profession yet."

"I bet he couldn't," her niece declared. "What's that old Ridgely supposed to be? Just a widower?"

"Never mind!"

"And that George Plum's supposed to do something or other around Uncle Joe's ole bank, isn't he?" Florence continued.

"'Supposed'!" Julia protested. "What is all this 'supposed to be'? Where did you catch that horrible habit? You know the whole family worries over your superciliousness, Florence; but until now I've always thought it was just the way your face felt easiest. If it's going to break out in your talk, too, it's time you began to cure yourself of it."

"Oh, it doesn't hurt anything!" Florence made careless response, and, as she saw the thin figure of young Mr. Sanders approaching in the distance, "Look!" she cried, pointing. "Why, he doesn't even *compare* to Noble Dill!"

"Don't point at people!"

"Well, he's nothing much to point at!" She lowered her finger. "It's no depredation to me, Aunt Julia, to give up pointing at Newland Sanders. Atch'ly, I wouldn't give Noble Dill's little finger for a hunderd and fifty Newland Sanderses!"

Julia smiled faintly as she watched Mr. Sanders, who seemed not yet to be aware of her, because he thought it would be better to reach the gate and lift his hat just there. "What *has* brought on all this tenderness in favour of Mr. Dill, Florence?"

Her niece's eyes, concentrated in thought, then became dreamy. "I like him because he's so uncouth," she said. "I think he's the uncouthest of any person I ever saw."

"'Uncouth'?"

"Yes," said Florence. "Herbert said I was uncouth, and I looked it up in the ditchanary. It said, 'Rare, exquisite, elegant, unknown, obs, unfamiliar, strange,' and a whole lot else. I never did know a word that means so much, I guess. What's 'obs' mean, Aunt Julia?"

"Hush!" said Julia, rising, for Mr. Sanders had made a little startled movement as he reached the gate and caught sight of her; and now, straw hat in hand, he was coming up the brick walk that led to the veranda. His eyes were fixed upon Julia with an intensity that seemed to affect his breathing; there was a hushedness about him. And Florence, in fascination, watched Julia's expression and posture take on those little changes that always seemed demanded of her by the approach of a young or youngish man, or a nicely dressed old one. By almost imperceptible processes the commonplace moment became dramatic at once.

"You!" said Newland in a low voice.

And Julia, with an implication as flattering as the gesture was graceful, did not wait till he was within reach, but suddenly extended her welcoming hand at arm's length. He sprang forward convulsively and grasped it, as if forever.

"You see my little niece?" Julia said. "I think you know her."

"Know her?" Mr. Sanders repeated; then roused his faculties and gave Florence a few fingers dangling coldly after their recent emotion. "Florence. Oh, yes, Florence."

Florence had not risen, but remained seated upon the steps, her look and air committed to that mood of which so much complaint had been made. "How do you do," she said. "There's Mr. Ridgely."

"Where?" Newland asked loudly.

"Comin' in at the gate," said Florence. "He's goin' walkin' with you, too."

In this crisis, Mr. Sanders's feeling was obviously one of startled anguish. He turned to Julia.

"Why, this is terrible!" he said. "You told me—"

"Sh!" she warned him; and whispered hastily, all in a breath: "*Couldn't-be-helped-explain-next-time-I-see-you.*" Then she advanced a gracious step to meet the newcomer.

But the superciliousness of Florence visibly increased with this advent: Mr. Ridgely was easily old enough to be her grandfather, yet she seemed to wish it evident that she would not have cared for him even in that capacity. He was, in truth, one of those widowers who feel younger than ever, and behave as they feel. Since his loss he had shown the greatest willingness to forego whatever advantages age and experience had given him over the descendants of his old friends and colleagues, and his cheerfulness as well as his susceptibility to all that was charming had begun to make him so famous in the town that some of his contemporaries seemed to know scarce another topic. And Julia had a kinder heart, as her father bitterly complained, than most girls.

The widower came, holding out to her a votive cluster of violets, a pink rose among them, their stems wrapped in purple; and upon the lapel of his jovial flannel coat were other violets about a pink rosebud.

"How pretty of you!" said Julia, taking the offering; and as she pinned it at her waist, she added rather nervously, "I believe you know Mr. Sanders; he is going with us."

She was warranted in believing the gentlemen to be acquainted, because no longer ago than the previous week they both had stated, in her presence and simultaneously, that any further communication between them would be omitted for life. Julia realized, of course, that Mr. Ridgely must find the present meeting as trying as Newland did, and, to help him bear it, she contrived to make him hear the hurried whisper: "*Couldn't-be-helped-explain-some-day.*"

Then with a laugh not altogether assured, she took up her parasol. "Shall we be starting?" she inquired.

"Here's Noble Dill," said Florence, "I guess he's goin' to try to go walkin' with you, too, Aunt Julia."

Julia turned, for in fact the gate at that moment clicked behind the nervously advancing form of Noble Dill. He came with, a bravado that was merely pitiable and he tried to snap his Orduma cigarette away with thumb and forefinger in a careless fashion, only to see it publicly disappear through an open cellar window of the house.

"I hope there's no excelsior down there," said Newland Sanders. "A good many houses have burned to the ground just that way."

"It fell on the cement floor," Florence reported, peering into the window. "It'll go out pretty soon."

"Then I suppose we might as well do the same thing," said Newland, addressing Julia first and Mr. Dill second. "Miss Atwater and I are just starting for a walk."

Mr. Ridgely also addressed the new arrival. "Miss Atwater and I are just starting for a walk."

"You see, Noble," said the kind-hearted Julia, "I did tell you I had another engagement."

"I came by here," Mr. Dill began in a tone commingling timidity, love, and a fatal stubbornness; "I came by here—I mean I just happened to be passing—and I thought if it was a walking-*party*, well, why not go along? That's the way it struck me." He paused, coughing for courage and trying to look easily genial, but not succeeding; then he added, "Well, as I say, that's the way it struck me—as it were. I suppose we might as well be starting."

"Yes, we might," Newland Sanders said quickly; and he placed himself at Julia's left, seizing upon her parasol and opening it with determination.

Mr. Ridgely had kept himself closely at the lady's right. "You were mistaken, my boy," he said, falsely benevolent. "It isn't a party—though there's Miss Florence, Noble. Nobody's asked her to go walking to-day!"

Now, Florence took this satire literally. She jumped up and said brightly: "I just as soon! Let's *do* have a walking-party. I just as soon walk with Mr. Dill as anybody, and we can all keep together, kind of." With that, she stepped confidently to the side of her selected escort, who appeared to be at a loss how to avert her kindness.

There was a moment of hesitation, during which a malevolent pleasure slightly disfigured the countenances of the two gentlemen with Julia; but when Florence pointed to a house across the street and remarked, "There's Great-Uncle Milford and Aunt C'nelia; they been lookin' out of their second guestroom window about half an hour," Julia uttered an exclamation.

"Murder!" she said, and moved with decision toward the gate. "Let's go!"

Thus the little procession started, Mr. Sanders and the sprightly widower at Beauty's side, with Florence and Mr. Dill so close behind that, before they had gone a block, Newland found it necessary to warn this rear rank that the heels of his new shoes were not part of the pavement. After that the rear rank, a little abashed, consented to fall back some paces. Julia's heightened colour, meanwhile, was little abated by some slight episodes attending the progress of the walking-party. Her Aunt Fanny Patterson, rocking upon a veranda, rose and evidently called to someone within the house, whereupon she was joined by her invalid sister, Aunt Harriet, with a trained nurse and two elderly domestics, a solemnly whispering audience. And in the front yard of "the Henry Atwater house," at the next corner, Herbert underwent a genuine bedazzlement, but he affected more. His violent gaze dwelt upon Florence, and he permitted his legs slowly to crumple under him, until, just as the party came nearest him, he lay prostrate upon his back in a swoon. Afterward he rose and for a time followed in a burlesque manner; then decided to return home.

"Old heathen!" said Florence, glancing back over her shoulder as he disappeared from view.

Mr. Dill was startled from a reverie inspired by the back of Julia's head. "'Heathen'?" he said, in plaintive inquiry.

"I meant Herbert," Florence informed him. "Cousin Herbert Atwater. He was following us, walking Dutch."

"'Cousin Herbert Atwater'?" said Noble dreamily. "'Dutch'?"

"He won't any more," said Florence. "He always hass to show off, now his voice is changing." She spoke, and she also walked, with dignity—a rather dashing kind of dignity, which was what Herbert's eccentricity of gait intended to point out injuriously. In fact, never before had Florence been so impressed with herself; never before, indeed, had she been a member of a grown-up non-family party; never before had she gone walking with an actual adult young man for her escort; and she felt that she owed it to her position to appear in as brilliant an aspect as possible. She managed to give herself a rhythmical, switching motion, causing her kneelength skirt to swing from side to side—a pomp that brought her a great deal of satisfaction as she now and then caught the effect by twisting her neck enough to see down behind, over her shoulder.

But her poise was temporarily threatened when the walking-party passed her own house. Her mother happened to be sitting near an open window upstairs, and, after gazing forth with warm interest at Julia and her two outwalkers, Mrs. Atwater's astonished eyes fell upon Florence taking care of the overflow. Florence bowed graciously.

"Florence!" her mother called down from the window: whereupon both Florence and her Aunt Julia were instantly apprehensive, for Mrs. George Atwater's lack of tact was a legend in the family. "Florence! Where on earth are you going?"

"Never mind!" Florence thought best to respond. "Never mind!"

"You'd better come *in*," Mrs. Atwater called, her voice necessarily louder as the party moved onward.

"Never mind!" Florence called back.

Mrs. Atwater leaned out of the window. "Where are you going? Come back and get your *hat*. You'll get a *sunstroke*!"

Florence was able to conceal her indignation, and merely waved a hand in airy dismissal as they passed from Mrs. Atwater's sight, leaving her still shouting.

The daughter smiled negligently and shrugged her shoulders. "She'll get over it!" she said.

"Who?"

"My mother. She was the one makin' all that noise," said Florence. "Sometimes I do what she says: sometimes I don't. It's all accordings to the way I feel." She looked up in her companion's face, and her expression became politely fond as she thought how uncouth he was, for in Florence's eye Noble Dill was truly rare, exquisite, and unfamiliar; and she believed that he was obs, too, whatever that meant. She often thought about him, and no longer ago than yesterday she had told Kitty Silver that she couldn't see "how Aunt Julia could *look* at anybody else!"

Florence's selection of Noble Dill for the bright favourite of her dreams was one of her own mysteries. Noble was not beautiful, neither did he present to the ordinary eye of man anything especially rare, exquisite, unfamiliar, or even so distinguished as to be obsolete. He was about twenty-two, but not one of those book-read sportsmen of that age, confident in clothes and manner, easy travellers and debonair; that is to say, Noble was not of the worldly type twenty-two. True, he had graduated from the High-school before entering his father's Real Estate and Insurance office, but his geographical experiences (in particular) had been limited to three or four railway excursions, at special rates, to such points of interest as Mammoth Cave and Petoskey, Michigan. His other experiences were not more sparkling, and except for the emotions within him, he was in all the qualities of his mind as well as in his bodily contours and the apparel sheltering the latter, the most commonplace person in Florence's visible world. The inner areas of the first and second fingers of his left hand bore cigarette stains, seemingly indelible: the first and second fingers of his right hand were strongly ornamented in a like manner; tokens proving him ambidextrous to but a limited extent, however. Moreover, his garments and garnitures were not comparable to those of either Newland Sanders or that dapper antique, Mr. Ridgely. Noble's straw hat might have brightened under the treatment of lemon juice or other restorative; his scarf was folded to hide a spot that worked steadily toward a complete visibility, and some recent efforts upon his trousers with a tepid iron, in his bedchamber at home, counteracted but feebly that tendency of cloth to sculpture itself in hummocks upon repeated pressure of the human knee.

All in all, nothing except the expression of Noble's face and the somewhat ill-chosen pansy in his buttonhole hinted of the remarkable. Yet even here was a thing for which he was not responsible himself; it was altogether the work of Julia. What her work was, in the case of Noble Dill, may be expressed in a word—a word used not only by the whole Atwater family connection, in completely expressing Noble's condition, but by Noble's own family connection as well. This complete word was "awful."

Florence was the one exception on the Atwater side: she was far, far from thinking or speaking of Noble Dill in that way, although, until she looked up "uncouth" in Webster's Collegiate Dictionary, she had not found suitable means to describe him. And now, as she walked at his side, she found her sensations to be nothing short of thrilling. For it must be borne in mind that this was her first and wholly unexpected outburst into society; the experience was that of an obscure aerolite suddenly become a noble meteor. She longed to say or do something magnificent—something strange and exhilarating, in keeping with her new station in life.

It was this longing, and by no means a confirmed unveracity, that prompted her to amplify her comments upon her own filial independence. "Oh, I guess I pretty near never do anything I don't want to," she said. "I kind of run the house to suit myself. I guess if the truth had to be told, I just about run the whole Atwater family, when it comes to that!"

The statement was so noticeable that it succeeded in turning Noble's attention from the back of Julia's head. "You do?" he said. "Well, that seems queer," he added absently.

"Oh, I don't know!" she laughed. In her increasing exaltation things appeared actually to be as she wished them to be; an atmosphere both queenly and adventurous seemed to invest her, and any remnants of human caution in her were assuaged by the circumstance that her Aunt Julia's attention was subject to the strong demands necessarily imposed upon anybody taking a walk between two gentlemen who do not "speak" to each other. "Oh, I don't know," said Florence. "The family's used to it by this time, I guess. The way I do things, they haf to be, I guess. When they don't like it I don't say much for a while, then I just—" She paused, waiting for her imagination to supply a sequel to the drama just sketched. "Well, I guess they kind of find out they better step around pretty lively," she concluded darkly. "They don't bother around *too* much!"

"I suppose not," said Noble, his vacancy and credulity continuing to dovetail perfectly.

"You bet not!" the exuberant Florence thought proper to suggest as a preferable expression. And then she had an inspiration to enliven his dreamy interest in her conversation. "Grandpa, he's the one I kind of run most of all of 'em. He's about fifty or sixty, and so he hasn't got too much sense. What I mean, he hasn't got too much sense *left*, you know. So I haf to sort of take holt every now and then." She lowered her voice a little, some faint whisper of discretion reaching her inward ear. "Aunt Julia can't do a thing with him. I guess that's maybe the reason she kind of depen's on me so much; or anyway somep'n like that. You know, f'r instance, I had to help talk grandpa into lettin' her send to New York for her things. Aunt Julia gets all her things in New York."

Undeniably, Mr. Dill's interest flickered up. "*Things?*" he repeated inquiringly. "Her things?"

"Yes. Everything she wears, you know."

"Oh, yes."

"What I was goin' to tell you," Florence continued, "you know grandpa just about hates everybody. Anyhow, he'd like to have some peace and quiet once in a while in his own house, he says, instead of all this moil and turmoil, and because the doctor said all the matter with her was she eats too much candy, and they keep sendin' more all the time—and there's somep'n the trouble with grandpa: it makes him sick to smell violets: he had it ever since he was a little boy, and he can't help it; and he hates animals, and they keep sendin' her Airedales and Persian kittens, and then there was that alligator came from Florida and upset Kitty Silver terribly—and so, you see, grandpa just hates the whole everlasting business."

Mr. Dill nodded and spoke with conviction: "He's absolutely right; absolutely!"

"Well, some ways he is," said Florence; and she added confidentially: "The trouble is, he seems to think you're about as bad as any of 'em."

"What?"

"*Well!*" Florence exclaimed, with upward gestures both of eye and of hand, to signify what she left untold of Mr. Atwater's orations upon his favourite subject: Noble Dill. "It's torrable!" she added.

Noble breathed heavily, but a thought struggled in him and a brightening appeared upon him. "You mean——" he began. "Do you mean it's terrible for your Aunt Julia? Do you mean his injustice about me makes her feel terribly?"

"No," said Florence. "No: I mean the way he goes on about everybody. But Aunt Julia's kind of used to it. And anyhow you needn't worry about him 'long as I'm on your side. He won't do anything much to you if I say not to. Hardly anything at all." And then, with almost a tenderness, as she marked the visibly insufficient reassurance of her companion, she said handsomely: "He won't say a word. I'll tell him not to."

Noble was dazed; no novelty, for he had been dazed almost continually during the past seven months, since a night when dancing with Julia, whom he had known all his life, he "noticed for the first time what she looked like." (This was his mother's description.) Somewhere, he vaguely recalled, he had read of the extraordinary influence possessed by certain angelic kinds of children; he knew, too, what favourite grandchildren can do with grandfathers. The effect upon him was altogether base; he immediately sought by flattery to increase and retain Florence's kindness. "I always *thought* you seemed to know more than most girls of your age," he began.

It was a great afternoon for Florence. From time to time she glanced over her shoulder at the switching skirt, and increased its radius of action, though this probably required more exercise, compared to the extent of ground covered, than any lady member of a walking-party had ever before taken, merely as a pedestrian. Meanwhile, she chattered on, but found time to listen to the pleasant things said to her by her companion; and though most of these were, in truth, rather vague, she was won to him more than he knew. Henceforth she was to be his champion indeed, sometimes with greater energy than he would need.

... The two were left alone together by Julia's gate when the walk (as short as Julia dared to make it) was over.

"Well," Florence said, "I've had quite a nice time. I hope you enjoyed yourself nicely, too, Mr. Dill." Then her eye rose to the overhanging branch of a shade-tree near them. "Would you like to see me chin myself?" she asked, stepping beneath the branch. "I bet I could skin-the-cat on that limb! Would you like to see me do it?"

"I would *so*!" the flatterer enthused.

She became thoughtful, remembering that she was now a lady who took walks with grown gentlemen. "I can, but I won't," she said. "I used to do lots of things like that. I used to whenever I felt like it. I could chin myself four times and Herbert only three. I was lots better than Herbert when I used to do all kinds of things like that."

"Were you?"

She laughed as in a musing retrospect of times gone by. "I guess I used to be a pretty queer kind of a girl in those days," she said. "Well—I s'pose we ought to say good-bye for the present, so to speak, Mr. Dill."

"I'm afraid so."

"Well—" She stood looking at him expectantly, but he said nothing more. "Well, good-bye for the present, Mr. Dill," she said again, and, turning, walked away with dignity. But a moment later she forgot all about her skirt and scampered.

CHAPTER FOUR

Mrs. Dill, Noble's mother, talked of organizing a Young Men's Mothers' Club against Julia, nevertheless she acknowledged that in one solitary way Noble was being improved by the experience. His two previous attacks of love (one at twelve, and the other at eighteen) had been incomparably lighter, and the changes in him, noted at home, merely a slight general irritability and a lack of domestic punctuality due to too much punctuality elsewhere. But, when his Julia Atwater trouble came, the very first symptom he manifested was a strange new effort to become beautiful; his mother even discovered that he sometimes worked with pumice stone upon the cigarette stains on his fingers.

The most curious thing about his condition was that for a long time he took it for granted that his family did not know what was the matter with him; and this shows as nothing else could the meekness and tact of the Dills; for, excluding bad cooks and the dangerously insane, the persons most disturbing to the serenity of households are young lovers. But the world has had to accommodate itself to them because young lovers cannot possibly accommodate themselves to the world. For the young lover there is no general life of the species; for him the universe is a delicate blush under a single bonnet. He has but an irritated perception of every vital thing in nature except the vital thing under this bonnet; all else is trivial intrusion. But whatever does concern the centrifugal bonnet, whatever concerns it in the remotest—ah, *then* he springs to life! So Noble Dill sat through a Sunday dinner at home, seemingly drugged to a torpor, while the family talk went on about him; but when his father, in the course of some remarks upon politics, happened to mention the name of the county-treasurer, Charles J. Patterson, Noble's startled attention to the conversation was so conspicuous as to be disconcerting. Mrs. Dill signalled with her head that comment should be omitted, and Mr. Dill became, for the moment, one factor in a fairly clear example of telepathic communication, for it is impossible to believe that his wife's almost imperceptible gesture was what caused him to remember that Charles J. Patterson was Julia Atwater's uncle.

That name, Charles J. Patterson, coming thus upon Noble's ear, was like an unexpected shrine on the wayside where plods the fanatic pilgrim; and yet Mr. Patterson was the most casual of Julia's uncles-by-marriage: he neither had nor desired any effect upon her destiny. To Noble he seemed a being ineffably privileged and fateful, and something of the same quality invested the wooden gateposts in front of Julia's house; invested everything that had to do with her. What he felt about her father, that august old danger, himself, was not only the uncalled-for affection inevitable toward Julia's next of kin, but also a kind of horror due to the irresponsible and awful power possessed by a sacred girl's parent. Florence's offer of protection had not entirely reassured the young lover, and, in sum, Noble loved Mr. Atwater, but often, in his reveries, when he had rescued him from drowning or being burned to death, he preferred to picture the peculiar old man's injuries as ultimately fatal.

For the other Atwaters his feeling held less of apprehension, more of tenderness; and whenever he saw one of them he became deferential and a little short of breath. Thus, on a sunny afternoon, having been home to lunch after his morning labour downtown, he paused in passing young Herbert's place of residence and timidly began a conversation with this glamoured nephew. It happened that during the course of the morning Herbert had chosen a life career for himself; he had decided to become a scientific specialist, an entomologist; and he was now on his knees studying the manners and customs of the bug inhabitants of the lawn before the house, employing for his purpose a large magnifying lens, or "reading glass." (His discovery of this implement in the attic, coincidentally with his reading a recent "Sunday Supplement" article on bugs, had led to his sudden choice of a vocation.)

"Did somebody—ah, have any of the family lost anything, Herbert?" Noble asked in a gentle voice, speaking across the fence.

Herbert did not look up, nor did he relax the scientific frown upon his brow. "No," he said. "They always *are* losin' things, espesh'ly Aunt Julia, when she comes over here, or anywheres else; but I wouldn't waste *my* time lookin' for any old earrings or such. I got more important things to do on my hands."

"*Has* your Aunt Julia lost an earring, Herbert?"

"Her? Well, she nearly always *has* lost somep'n or other, but that isn't bother'n' *me* any. I got better things to do with my time." Herbert spoke without interrupting his occupation or relaxing his forehead. "Nacher'l history is a *little* more important to the inhabitants of our universe than a lot o' worthless jew'lry, I guess," he continued; and his pride in discovering that he could say things like this was so great that his frown gave way temporarily to a look of pleased surprise, then came back again to express an importance much increased. He rose, approached the fence, and condescended to lean upon it. "I don't guess there's one person in a thousand," he said, "that knows what they *ought* to know about our inseck friends."

"No," Mr. Dill agreed readily. "I guess that's so. I guess you're right about that, Herbert. When did your Aunt Julia lose the earring, Herbert?"

"I d' know," said Herbert. "Now, you take my own father and mother: What do they know? Well, mighty little. They may have had to learn a little teeny bit about insecks when they were in school, but whatever little it was they went and forgot it proba'ly long before they were married. Well, that's no way. F'r instance, you take a pinchin' bug: What do you suppose my father and mother know about its position in the inseck world?"

"Well—" said Noble uneasily. "Well—" He coughed, and hastened to add: "But as I was saying, if she lost her earring somewhere in your yard, or—"

The scientific boy evidently did not follow this line of thought, for he interrupted: "Why, they wouldn't know a thing about it, and a pinchin' bug isn't one of the highest insecks at all. Ants are way up compared to most pinchin' bugs. Ants are way up anyway. Now, you take an ant—" He paused. "Well, everybody ought to know a lot more'n they do about ants. It takes time, and you got to study 'em the right way, and of course there's lots of people wouldn't know how to do it. I'm goin' to get a book I been readin' about. It's called 'The Ant.'"

For a moment Noble was confused; he followed his young friend's discourse but hazily, and Herbert pronounced the word "ant" precisely as he pronounced the word "aunt." The result was that Noble began to say something rather dreamy concerning the book just mentioned, but, realizing that he was being misunderstood, he changed his murmur into a cough, and inquired:

"When was she over here, Herbert?"

"Who?"

"Your Aunt Julia."

"Yesterday evening," said Herbert. "Now, f'r instance, you take a common lightning-bug—"

"Did she lose it, then?"

"Lose what?"

"Her earring."

"I d' know," said Herbert. "You take the common lightning-bug or, as it's called in some countries, the firefly—"

He continued, quoting and misquoting the entomological authority of the recent "Sunday Supplement"; but his friend on the other side of the fence was inattentive to the lecture. Noble's mind was occupied with a wonder; he had realized, though dimly, that here was he, trying to make starry Julia the subject of a conversation with a person who had the dear privilege of being closely related to her—and preferred to talk about bugs.

Herbert talked at considerable length about lightning-bugs, but as his voice happened rather precociously to be already in a state of adolescent change, the sound was not soothing; yet Noble lingered. Nephews were queer, but this one was Julia's, and he finally mentioned her again, as incidental to lightning-bugs; whereupon the mere hearer of sounds became instantly a listener to words.

"Well, and then I says," Herbert continued;—"I says: 'It's phosphorus, Aunt Julia.' I guess there's hardly anybody in the world doesn't know more than Aunt Julia, except about dresses and parasols and every other useless thing under the sun. She says: 'My! I always thought it was sulphur!' Said nobody ever *told* her it wasn't sulphur! I asked her: I said: 'You mean to sit there and tell me you don't know the difference?' And she says: 'I don't care one way or the other,' she says. She said she just as soon a lightning-bug made his light with sulphur as with phosphorus; it didn't make any difference to her, she says, and they could go ahead and make their light any way they wanted, *she* wouldn't interfere! I had a whole hatful of 'em, and she told me not to take 'em into their house, because grandpa hates insecks as much as he does animals and violets, and she said they never owned a microscope or a magnifying-glass in their lives, and wouldn't let me hunt for one. All in the world she knows is how to sit on the front porch and say: 'Oh you don't mean *that!*' to somebody like Newland Sanders or that ole widower!"

"When?" Noble asked impulsively. "When did she say that?"

"Oh, I d' know," said Herbert. "I expect she proba'ly says it to somebody or other about every evening there is."

"She does?"

"Florence says so," Herbert informed him carelessly. "Florence goes over to grandpa's after dark and sits on the ground up against the porch and listens."

Noble first looked startled then uneasily reminiscent. "I don't believe Florence ought to do that," he said gravely.

"*I* wouldn't do it!" Herbert was emphatic.

"That's right, Herbert. I'm glad you wouldn't."

"No, sir," the manly boy declared. "You wouldn't never catch *me* takin' my death o' cold sittin' on the damp grass in the night air just to listen to a lot o' tooty-tooty about 'I've named a star for you,' and all such. You wouldn't catch me—"

Noble partly concealed a sudden anguish. "Who?" he interrupted. "Who did she say *that* to?"

"She didn't. They say it to her, and she says? 'Oh, you don't mean that!' and of course then they haf to go on and say some more. Florence says—" He checked himself. "Oh, I forgot! I promised Florence I wouldn't tell anything about all this."

"It's safe," Noble assured him quickly. "I'm quite a friend of Florence's and it's absolutely safe with me. I won't speak of it to anybody, Herbert. Who was it told her he'd named a star for her?"

"It was the way some ole poem began. Newland Sanders wrote it. Florence found it under Aunt Julia's sofa-cushions and read it all through, but *I* wouldn't wade through all that tooty-tooty for a million dollars, and I told her to put it back before Aunt Julia noticed. Well, about every day he writes her a fresh one, and then in the evening he stays later than the rest, and reads 'em to her—and you ought to hear grandpa when *he* gets to talkin' about it!"

"He's perfectly right," said Noble. "Perfectly! What does he say when he talks about it, Herbert?"

"Oh, he says all this and that; and then he kind of mutters around, and you can't tell just what all the words are exactly, so't he can deny it if any o' the family accuses him of swearing or anything." And Herbert added casually: "He was kind of goin' on like that about you, night before last."

"About *me*! Why, what could he say about *me*?"

"Oh, all this and that."

"But what did he find to say?"

"Well, he heard her tellin' you how you oughtn't to smoke so many cigarettes and all about how it was killin' you, and you sayin' you guessed it wouldn't matter if you *did* die, and Aunt Julia sayin' 'Oh, you don't mean that,' and all this and such and so on, you know. He can hear anything on the porch pretty good from the lib'ary; and Florence told me about that, besides, because she was sittin' in the grass and all. She told Great-Uncle Joe and Aunt Hattie about it, too."

"My heavens!" Noble gasped, as for the first time he realized to what trumpeting publicity that seemingly hushed and moonlit bower, sacred to Julia, had been given over. He gulped, flushed, repeated "My heavens!" and then was able to add, with a feeble suggestion of lightness: "I suppose your grandfather understood it was just a sort of joke, didn't he?"

"No," said Herbert, and continued in a friendly way, for he was flattered by Noble's interest in his remarks, and began to feel a liking for him. "No. He said Aunt Julia only talked like that because she couldn't think of anything else to say, and it was wearin' him out. He said all the good it did was to make you smoke more to make her think how reckless you were; but the worst part of it was, he'd be the only one to suffer, because it blows all through the house and he's got to sit in it. He said he just could stand the smell of *some* cigarettes, but if you burned any more o' yours on his porch he was goin' to ask your father to raise your salary for collectin' real-estate rents, so't you'd feel able to buy some real tobacco. He—"

But the flushed listener felt that he had heard as much as he was called upon to bear; and he interrupted, in a voice almost out of control, to say that he must be "getting on downtown." His young friend, diverted from bugs, showed the greatest willingness to continue the narrative indefinitely, evidently being in possession of copious material; but Noble turned to depart. An afterthought detained him. "Where was it she lost her earring?"

"Who?"

"Your Aunt Julia."

"Why, *I* didn't say she lost any earring," Herbert returned. "I said she always *was* losin' 'em: I didn't say she did."

"Then you didn't mean—"

"No," said Herbert, "*I* haven't heard of her losin' anything at all, lately." Here he added: "Well, grandpa kept goin' on about you, and he told her—Well, so long!" And gazed after the departing Mr. Dill in some surprise at the abruptness of the latter's leave-taking. Then, wondering how the back of Noble's neck could have got itself so fiery sunburnt, Herbert returned to his researches in the grass.

*   *   *   *   *

The peaceful street, shady and fragrant with summer, was so quiet that the footfalls of the striding Noble were like an interruption of coughing in a silent church. As he seethed adown the warm sidewalk the soles of his shoes smote the pavement, for mentally he was walking not upon cement but upon Mr. Atwater.

Unconsciously his pace presently became slower for a more concentrated brooding upon this slanderous old man who took advantage of his position to poison his daughter's mind against the only one of her suitors who cared in the highest way. And upon this there came an infinitesimal consolation in the midst of anguish, for he thought of what Herbert had told him about Mr. Newland Sanders's poems to Julia, and he had a strong conviction that one time or another Mr. Atwater must have spoken even more disparagingly of these poems and their author than he had of Orduma cigarettes and their smoker. Perhaps the old man was not altogether vile.

This charitable moment passed. He recalled the little moonlit drama on the embowered veranda, when Julia, in her voice of plucked harp strings, told him that he smoked too much, and he had said it didn't matter; nobody would care much if he died—and Julia said gently that his mother would, and other people, too; he mustn't talk so recklessly. Out of this the old eavesdropper had viciously represented him to be a poser, not really reckless at all; had insulted his cigarettes and his salary. Well, Noble would show him! He had doubts about being able to show Mr. Atwater anything important connected with the cigarettes or the salary, but he *could* prove how reckless he was. With that, a vision formed before him: he saw Julia and her father standing spellbound at a crossing while a smiling youth stood directly between the rails in the middle of the street and let a charging trolley-car destroy him—not instantly, for he would live long enough to whisper, as the stricken pair bent over him: "Now, Julia, which do you believe: your father, or me?" And then with a slight, dying sneer: "Well, Mr. Atwater, is *this* reckless enough to suit you?"

*   *   *   *   *

Town squirrels flitted along their high paths in the shade-tree branches above the embittered young lover, and he noticed them not at all, which was but little less than he noticed the elderly human couple who observed him from a side-yard as he passed by. Mr. and Mrs. Burgess had been happily married for fifty-three years and four months. Mr. Burgess lay in a hammock between two maple trees, and was soothingly swung by means of a string connecting the hammock and the rocking-chair in which sat Mrs Burgess, acting as a mild motor for both the chair and the hammock. "That's Noble Dill walking along the sidewalk," Mrs. Burgess said, interpreting for her husband's failing eyes. "I bowed to him, but he hardly seemed to see us and just barely lifted his hat. He needn't be cross with *us* because some other young man's probably taking Julia Atwater out driving!"

"Yes, he need!" Mr. Burgess declared. "A boy in his condition needs to be cross with everything. Sometimes they get so cross they go and drink liquor. Don't you remember?"

She laughed. "I remember once!" she assented, and laughed again.

"Why, it's a terrible time of life," her husband went on. "Poets and suchlike always take on about young love as if it were a charming and romantic experience, but really it's just a series of mortifications. The young lover is always wanting to do something dashing and romantic and Sir Walter Raleigh-like, but in ordinary times about the wildest thing he can do, if he can afford it, is to learn to run a Ford. And he can't stand a word of criticism; he can't stand being made the least little bit of fun of; and yet all the while his state of mind lays him particularly open to all the things he can't stand. He can't stand anything, and he has to stand everything. Why, it's a *horrible* time of life, mamma!"

"Yes, it is," she assented placidly. "I'm glad we don't have to go through it again, Freddie; though you're only eighty-two, and with a girl like Julia Atwater around nobody ought to be sure."

CHAPTER FIVE

Although Noble had saluted the old couple so crossly, thus unconsciously making them, as he made the sidewalk, proxy for Mr. Atwater, so to speak, yet the sight of them penetrated his outer layers of preoccupation and had an effect upon him. In the midst of his suffering his imagination paused for a shudder: What miserable old gray shadows those two were! Thank Heaven he and Julia could never be like that! And in the haze that rose before his mind's eye he saw himself leading Julia through years of adventure in far parts of the world: there were glimpses of himself fighting grotesque figures on the edge of Himalayan precipices at dawn, while Julia knelt by the tent on the glacier and prayed for him. He saw head-waiters bowing him and Julia to tables in "strange, foreign cafes," and when they were seated, and he had ordered dishes that amazed her, he would say in a low voice: "Don't look now, but do you see that heavy-shouldered man with the insignia, sitting with that adventuress and those eight officers who are really his guards? Don't be alarmed, Julia, but I am here to *get* that man! Perhaps you remember what your father once said of me? Now, when what I have to do here is done, perhaps you may wish to write home and mention a few things to that old man!" And then a boy's changing voice seemed to sound again close by: "He said he just could stand the smell of *some* cigarettes, but if you burned any more o' yours on his porch—" And Noble came back miserably to town again.

From an upper window of a new stucco house two maidens of nineteen peered down at him. The shade of a striped awning protected the window from the strong sun and the maidens from the sight of man—the latter protection being especially fortunate, since they were preparing to take a conversational afternoon nap, were robed with little substance, and their heads appeared to be antlered; for they caught sight of Noble just as they were preparing to put silk-and-lace things they called "caps" on their heads.

"Who's that?" the visiting one asked.

"It's Noble Dill; he's kind of one of the crowd."

"Is he nice?"

"Oh, sort of. Kind of shambles around."

"Looks like last year's straw hat to me," the visiting one giggled.

"Oh, he tries to dress—lately, that is—but he never did know how."

"Looks mad about something."

"Yes. He's one of the ones in love with that Julia Atwater I told you about."

"Has he got any chance with her?"

"Noble Dill? Mercy!"

"Is he much in love with her?"

"'Much'? *Murder!*"

The visiting one turned from the window and yawned. "Come on: let's lie down and talk about some of the nice ones!"

The second house beyond this was—it was the house of Julia!

And what a glamour of summer light lay upon it because it was the house of Julia! The texture of the sunshine came under a spell here; glowing flakes of amber were afloat; a powder of opals and rubies fell silently adrizzle through the trees. The very air changed, beating faintly with a fairy music, for breathing it was breathing sorcery: elfin symphonies went tinkling through it. The grass in the next yard to Julia's was just grass, but every blade of grass in her yard was cut of jewels.

Julia's house was also the house of that person who through some ungovernable horseplay of destiny happened to be her father: and this gave the enchanted spot a background of lurking cyclone—no one could tell at what instant there might rise above the roseate pleasance a funnel-shaped cloud. With young Herbert's injurious narrative fresh in his mind, Noble quickened his steps; but as he reached the farther fence post, marking the southward limit of Mr. Atwater's property, he halted short, startled beautifully. Through the open front door, just passed, a voice had called his name; a voice of such arresting sweetness that his breath stopped, like his feet.

"Oh, Noble!" it called again.

He turned back, and any one who might have seen his face then would have known what was the matter with him, and must have been only the more sure of it because his mouth was open. The next instant the adequate reason for his disorder came lightly through the open door and down to the gate.

Julia was kind, much too kind! She had heard that her Aunt Harriet and her Uncle Joe were frequently describing Mr. Atwater's most recent explosion to other members of the extensive Atwater family league; and though she had not discovered how Aunt Harriet and Uncle Joe had obtained their material, yet, in Julia's way of wording her thoughts, an account of the episode was "all over town," and she was almost certain that by this time Noble Dill had heard it. And so, lest he should suffer, the too-gentle creature seized the first opportunity to cheer him up. That was the most harmful thing about Julia; when anybody liked her—even Noble Dill—she couldn't bear to have him worried. She was the sympathetic princess who wouldn't have her puppy's tail chopped off all at once, but only a little at a time.

"I just happened to see you going by," she said, and then, with an astounding perfection of seriousness, she added the question: "Did you *mind* my calling to you and stopping you, Noble?"

He leaned, drooping, upon the gatepost, seeming to yearn toward it; his expression was such that this gatepost need not have been surprised if Noble had knelt to it.

"Why, no," he said hoarsely. "No, I don't have to be back at the office any particular time. No."

"I just wanted to ask you—" She hesitated. "Well, it really doesn't amount to anything—it's nothing so important I couldn't have spoken to you about it some other time."

"Well," said Noble, and then on the spur of the moment he continued darkly: "There might not be any other time."

"How do you mean, Noble?"

He smiled faintly. "I'm thinking of going away." This was true; nevertheless, it was the first time he had thought of it. "Going away," he repeated in a murmur. "From this old town."

A shadowy, sweet reproach came upon Julia's eyes. "You mean—for good, Noble?" she asked in a low voice, although no one knew better than she what trouble such performances often cost her, later. "Noble, you don't mean—"

He made a vocal sound conveying recklessness, something resembling a reckless laugh. "I might go—any day! Just as it happens to strike me."

"But where to, Noble?"

"I don't—Well, maybe to China."

"China!" she cried in amazement. "Why, Noble Dill!"

"There's lots of openings in China," he said. "A white man can get a commission in the Chinese army any day."

"And so," she said, "you mean you'd rather be an officer in the Chinese army than stay—here?" With that, she bit her lip and averted her face for an instant, then turned to him again, quite calm. Julia could not help doing these things; she was born that way, and no punishment changed her.

"Julia—" the dazzled Noble began, but he stopped with this beginning, his voice seeming to have exhausted itself upon the name.

"When do you think you'll start?" she asked.

His voice returned. "I don't know *just* when," he said; and he began to feel a little too much committed to this sudden plan of departure, and to wonder how it had come about. "I—I haven't set any day—exactly."

"Have you talked it over with your mother yet, Noble?"

"Not yet—exactly," he said, and was conscious of a distaste for China as something unpleasant and imminent. "I thought I'd wait till—till it was certain I *would* go."

"When will that be, Noble?" And in spite of herself, Julia spoke in the tone of one who controls herself to ask in calmness: "Is my name on the list for the guillotine?"

"Well," he said, "it'll be as soon as I've made up my mind to go. I probably won't go before then; not till I've made up my mind to."

"But you might do that any day, mightn't you?"

Noble began to feel relieved; he seemed to have hit upon a way out. "Yes; and then I'd be gone," he said firmly. "But probably I wouldn't go at all unless I decided to." This seemed to save him from China, and he added recklessly: "I guess I wouldn't be missed much around this old town if I did go."

"Yes, you would," Julia said quickly. "Your family'd miss you—and so would everybody."

"Julia, *you* wouldn't—"

She laughed lightly. "Of course I should, and so would papa."

Noble released the gatepost and appeared to slant backward. "What?"

"Papa was talking about you this very morning at breakfast," she said; and she spoke the truth. "He said he *dreamed* about you last night."

"He did?"

Julia nodded sunnily. "He dreamed that you and he were the very greatest friends!" This also was true, so far as it went; she only omitted to state that Mr. Atwater had gone on to classify his dream as a nightmare. "There!" she cried. "Why, of course he'd miss you—he'd miss you as much as he'd miss any friend of mine that comes here."

Noble felt a sudden rush of tenderness toward Mr. Atwater; it is always possible to misjudge a man for a few hasty words. And Julia went on quickly:

"I never saw anybody like you, Noble Dill!" she exclaimed. "I don't suppose there's anybody in the United States except you that would be capable of doing things like going off to be an officer in the Chinese army—all just any minute like this. I've always declared you were about the most reckless man I know!"

Noble shook his head. "No," he said judicially. "I'm not reckless; it's just that I don't care what happens."

Julia became grave. "Don't you?"

"To me," he said hurriedly. "I mean I don't care what happens to myself. I mean that's more the way I am than just reckless."

She was content to let his analysis stand, though she shook her head, as if knowing herself to be wiser than he about his recklessness. A cheerfulness came upon them; and the Chinese question seemed to have been settled by these indirect processes;—in fact, neither of them ever mentioned it again. "I mustn't keep you," she said, "especially when you ought to be getting on downtown to business, but—Oh!" She gave the little cry of a forgetful person reminded. "I almost forgot what I ran out to ask you!"

"What was it, Julia?" Noble spoke huskily, in a low voice. "What is it you want me to do, Julia?"

She gave a little fluttering laugh, half timid, half confiding. "You know how funny papa is about tobacco smoke?" (But she hurried on without waiting for an answer.) "Well, he is. He's the funniest old thing; he doesn't like *any* kind very much except his own special cheroot things. He growls about every other kind, but the cigars Mr. *Ridgely* smokes when he comes here, papa really *does* make a fuss over! And, you see, I don't like to say 'No' when Mr. Ridgely asks if he can smoke, because it always makes men so uncomfortable if they can't when they're sitting on a veranda, so I wondered if I could just tactfully get him to buy something different from his cigars?—and I thought the best thing would be to suggest those cigarettes you always have, Noble. They're the ones papa makes the *least* fuss about and seems to stand the best—next to his own, he seems to like them the most, I mean—but I'd forgotten the name of them. That's what I ran out to ask you."

"Orduma," said Noble. "Orduma Egyptian Cigarettes."

"Would you mind giving me one—just to show Mr. Ridgely?"

Noble gave her an Orduma cigarette.

"Oh, thank you!" she said gratefully. "I mustn't keep you another minute, because I know your father wouldn't know *what* to do at the office without you! Thank you so much for this!" She turned and walked quickly halfway up the path, then paused, looking back over her shoulder. "I'll only show it to him, Noble," she said. "I won't give it to him!"

She bit her lip as if she had said more than she should have; shook her head as in self-chiding; then laughed, and in a flash touched the tiny white cylinder to her lips, waved it to him;— then ran to the veranda and up the steps and into the house. She felt satisfied that she had set matters right, this kind Julia!

CHAPTER SIX

Before she thus set matters right with Noble he had been unhappy and his condition had been bad; now he was happy, but his condition was worse. In truth, he was much, much too happy; nothing rational remained in his mind. No elfin orchestra seemed to buzz in his ears as he went down the street, but a loud, triumphing brass band. His unathletic chest was inflated; he heaved up with joy; and a little child, playing on the next corner, turned and followed him for some distance, trying to imitate his proud, singular walk. Restored to too much pride, Noble became also much too humane; he thought of Mr. Atwater's dream, and felt almost a motherly need to cherish and protect him, to be indeed his friend. There was a warm spot in Noble's chest, produced in part by a yearning toward that splendid old man. Noble had a good home, sixty-six dollars in the bank and a dollar and forty cents in his pockets; he would have given all for a chance to show Mr. Atwater how well he understood him now, at last, and how deeply he appreciated his favour.

Students of alcoholic intoxication have observed that in their cups commonplace people, and not geniuses, do the most unusual things. So with all other intoxications. Noble Dill was indeed no genius, and some friend should have kept an eye upon him to-day; he was not himself. All afternoon in a mood of tropic sunrise he collected rents, or with glad vagueness consented instantly to their postponement. "I've come about the rent again," he said beamingly to one delinquent tenant of his father's best client; and turned and walked away, humming a waltz-song, while the man was still coughing as a preliminary to argument.

Late in the afternoon, as the entranced collector sat musing alone near a window in his father's office, his exalted mood was not affected by the falling of a preternatural darkness over the town, nor was he roused to action by any perception of the fact that the other clerks and the members of the firm had gone home an hour ago; that the clock showed him his own duty to lock up the office and not keep his mother "waiting dinner"; and that he would be caught in a most outrageous thunderstorm if he didn't hurry. No; he sat, smiling fondly, by the open window, and at times made a fragmentary gesture as of some heroic or benevolent impulse in rehearsal.

Meanwhile, paunchy with wind and wetness, unmannerly clouds came smoking out of the blackened west. Rumbling, they drew on. Then from cloud to cloud dizzy amazements of white fire staggered, crackled and boomed on to the assault; the doors of the winds were opened; the tanks of deluge were unbottomed; and the storm took the town. So, presently, Noble noticed that it was raining and decided to go home.

With an idea that he was fulfilling his customary duties, he locked the doors of the two inner rooms, dropped the keys gently into a wastebasket, and passing by an umbrella which stood in a corner, went out to the corridor, and thence stepped into the street of whooping rain.

Here he became so practical as to turn up his collar; and, substantially aided by the wind at his back, he was not long in leaving the purlieus of commerce behind him for Julia's Street. Other people lived on this street—he did, himself, for that matter; and, in fact, it was the longest street in the town; moreover, it had an official name with which the word "Julia" was entirely unconnected; but for Noble Dill (and probably for Newland Sanders and for some others in age from nineteen to sixty) it was "Julia's Street" and no other.

It was a tumultuous street as Noble splashed along the sidewalk. Incredibly elastic, the shade-trees were practising calisthenics, though now and then one outdid itself and lost a branch; thunder and lightning romped like loosed scandal; rain hissed upon the pavement and capered ankle-high. It was a storm that asked to be left to itself for a time, after giving fair warning that the request would be made; and Noble and the only other pedestrian in sight had themselves to blame for getting caught.

This other pedestrian was some forty or fifty yards in advance of Noble and moved in the same direction at about the same gait. He wore an old overcoat, running with water; the brim of his straw hat sagged about his head, so that he appeared to be wearing a bucket; he was a sodden and pathetic figure. Noble himself was as sodden; his hands were wet in his very pockets; his elbows seemed to spout; yet he spared a generous pity for the desolate figure struggling on before him.

All at once Noble's heart did something queer within his wet bosom. He recognized that figure, and he was not mistaken. Except the One figure, and those of his own father and mother and three sisters, this was the shape that Noble would most infallibly recognize anywhere in the world and under any conditions. In spite of the dusk and the riot of the storm, Noble knew that none other than Mr. Atwater splashed before him.

He dismissed a project for seizing upon a fallen branch and running forward to walk beside Mr. Atwater and hold the branch over his venerated head. All the branches were too wet; and Noble feared that Mr. Atwater might think the picture odd and decline to be thus protected. Yet he felt that something ought to be done to shelter Julia's father and perhaps save him from pneumonia; surely there was some simple, helpful, dashing thing that ordinary people couldn't think of, but that Noble could. He would do it and not stay to be thanked. And then, to-morrow evening, not sooner, he would go to Julia and smile and say; "Your father didn't get too wet, I hope, after all?" And Julia: "Oh, Noble, he's talked of you all day long as his 'new Sir Walter Raleigh'!"

Suddenly will-o'-the-wisp opportunity flickered before him, and in his high mood he paused not at all to consider it, but insanely chased it. He had just reached a crossing, and down the cross street, walking away from Noble, was the dim figure of a man carrying an umbrella. It was just perceptible that he was a fat man, struggling with seeming feebleness in the wind and making poor progress. Mr. Atwater, moving up Julia's Street, was out of sight from the cross street where struggled the fat man.

Noble ran swiftly down the cross street, jerked the umbrella from the fat man's grasp; ran back, with hoarse sounds dying out behind him in the riotous dusk; turned the corner, sped after Mr. Atwater, overtook him, and thrust the umbrella upon him. Then, not pausing the shortest instant for thanks or even recognition, the impulsive boy sped onward, proud and joyous in the storm, leaving his beneficiary far behind him.

In his young enthusiasm he had indeed done something for Mr. Atwater. In fact, Noble's kindness had done as much for Mr. Atwater as Julia's gentleness had done for Noble, but how much both Julia and Noble had done was not revealed in full until the next evening.

That was a warm and moonshiny night of air unusually dry, and yet Florence sneezed frequently as she sat upon the "side porch" at the house of her Great-Aunt Carrie and her Great-Uncle Joseph. Florence had a cold in the head, though how it got to her head was a process involved in the mysterious ways of colds, since Florence's was easily to be connected with Herbert's remark that he wouldn't ever be caught takin' his death o' cold sittin' on the damp grass in the night air just to listen to a lot o' tooty-tooty. It appeared from Florence's narrative to those interested listeners, Aunt Carrie and Uncle Joseph, that she had been sitting on the grass in the night air when both air and grass were extraordinarily damp. In brief, she had been at her post soon after the storm cleared on the preceding evening, but she had heard no tooty-tooty; her overhearings were of sterner stuff.

"Well, what did Julia say *then*?" Aunt Carrie asked eagerly.

"She said she'd go up and lock herself in her room and stuff cushions over her ears if grandpa didn't quit makin' such a fuss."

"And what did he say?"

"He made more rumpus than ever," said Florence. "He went on and on, and told the whole thing over and over again; he seemed like he couldn't tell it enough, and every time he told it his voice got higher and higher till it was kind of squealy. He said he'd had his raincoat on and he didn't want an umberella anyhow, and hadn't ever carried one a single time in fourteen years! And he took on about Noble Dill and all this and that about how you *bet* he knew who it was! He said he could tell Noble Dill in the dark any time by his cigarette smell, and, anyway, it wasn't too dark so's he couldn't see his skimpy little shoulders, and anyway he saw his face. And he said Noble didn't *hand* him the umberella; he stuck it all down over him like he was somep'n on fire he wanted to put out; and before he could get out of it and throw it away this ole fat man that it belonged to and was chasin' Noble, he ran up to grandpa from behind and took hold of him, or somep'n, and they slipped, and got to fussin' against each other; and then after a while they got up and grandpa saw it was somebody he knew and told him for Heaven's sake why didn't he take his ole umberella and go on home; and so he did, because it was raining, and I guess he proba'ly had to give up; he couldn't out-talk grandpa."

"No," said Uncle Joe. "He couldn't, whoever he was. But what happened about Noble Dill?"

Florence paused to accumulate and explode a sneeze, then

responded pleasantly: "He said he was goin' to kill him. He said he often and often wanted to, and now he *was*. That's the reason I guess Aunt Julia wrote that note this morning."

"What note?" Aunt Carrie inquired. "You haven't told us of that."

"I was over there before noon," said Florence, "and Aunt Julia gave me a quarter and said she'd write a note for me to take to Noble Dill's house when he came home for lunch, and give it to him. She kind of slipped it to me, because grandpa came in there, pokin' around, while she was just finishin' writin' it. She didn't put any envelope on it even, and she never said a single thing to *me* about its bein' private or my not readin' it if I wanted to, or anything."

"Of course you didn't," said Aunt Carrie. "You didn't, did you, Florence?"

"Why, she didn't *say* not to," Florence protested, surprised. "It wasn't even in an envelope."

Mr. Joseph Atwater coughed. "I hardly think we ought to ask what the note said, even if Florence was—well, indiscreet enough to read it."

"No," said his wife. "I hardly think so either. It didn't say anything important anyhow, probably."

"It began, 'Dear Noble,'" said Florence promptly. "Dear Noble'; that's the way it began. It said how grandpa was just all upset to think he'd accepted an umberella from him when Noble didn't have another one for himself like that, and grandpa was so embarrassed to think he'd let Noble do so much for him, and everything, he just didn't know *what* to do, and proba'ly it would be tactful if he wouldn't come to the house till grandpa got over being embarrassed and everything. She said not to come till she let him know."

"Did you notice Noble when he read it?" asked Aunt Carrie.

"Yessir! And would you believe it; he just looked *too* happy!" Florence made answer, not wholly comprehending with what truth.

"I'll bet," said Uncle Joseph;—"I'll bet a thousand dollars that if Julia told Noble Dill he was six feet tall, Noble would go and order his next suit of clothes to fit a six-foot man."

And his wife complemented this with a generalization, simple, yet of a significance too little recognized. "They don't see a thing!" she said. "The young men that buzz around a girl's house don't see a *thing* of what goes on there! Inside, I mean."

Yet at that very moment a young man was seeing something inside a girl's house a little way down that same street. That same street was Julia's Street and the house was Julia's. Inside the house, in the library, sat Mr. Atwater, trying to read a work by Thomas Carlyle, while a rhythmic murmur came annoyingly from the veranda. The young man, watching him attentively, saw him lift his head and sniff the air with suspicion, but the watcher took this pantomime to be an expression of distaste for certain versifyings, and sharing that distaste, approved. Mr. Atwater sniffed again, threw down his book and strode out to the veranda. There sat dark-haired Julia in a silver dress, and near by, Newland Sanders read a long young poem from the manuscript.

"Who is smoking out here?" Mr. Atwater inquired in a dead voice.

"Nobody, sir," said Newland with eagerness. "*I* don't smoke. I have never touched tobacco in any form in my life."

Mr. Atwater sniffed once more, found purity; and returned to the library. But here the air seemed faintly impregnated with Orduma cigarettes. "Curious!" he said as he composed himself once more to read—and presently the odour seemed to wear away and vanish. Mr. Atwater was relieved; the last thing he could have wished was to be haunted by Noble Dill.

Yet for that while he was. Too honourable to follow such an example as Florence's, Noble, of course, would not spy or eavesdrop near the veranda where Julia sat, but he thought there could be no harm in watching Mr. Atwater read. Looking at Mr. Atwater was at least the next thing to looking at Julia. And so, out in the night, Noble was seated upon the top of the side fence, looking through the library window at Mr. Atwater.

After a while Noble lit another Orduma cigarette and puffed strongly to start it. The smoke was almost invisible in the moonlight, but the night breeze, stirring gently, wafted it toward the house, where the open window made an inward draft and carried it heartily about the library.

Noble was surprised to see Mr. Atwater rise suddenly to his feet. He smote his brow, put out the light, and stamped upstairs to his own room.

His purpose to retire was understood when the watcher saw a light in the bedroom window overhead. Noble thought of the good, peculiar old man now disrobing there, and he smiled to himself at a whimsical thought: What form would Mr. Atwater's embarrassment take, what would be his feeling, and what would he do, if he knew that Noble was there now, beneath his window and thinking of him?

In the moonlight Noble sat upon the fence, and smoked Orduma cigarettes, and looked up with affection at the bright window of Mr. Atwater's bedchamber. Abruptly the light in that window went out.

"Saying his prayers now," said Noble. "I wonder if—" But, not to be vain, he laughed at himself and left the thought unfinished.

CHAPTER SEVEN

A week later, on a hot July afternoon, Miss Florence Atwater, recovered from her cold, stood in the shady back yard of her place of residence and yawned more extensively than any one would have believed possible, judging by her face in repose. Three of her friends, congenial in age and sex, were out of town for the summer; two had been ascertained, by telephonic inquiries, to be taking commanded siestas; and neither the other one nor Florence had yet forgotten that yesterday, although they were too religious to commit themselves to a refusal to meet as sisters in the Great Beyond, they had taken the expurgated oath that by Everything they would never speak to each other again so long as they both should live.

Florence was at the end of her resources. She had sought distraction in experimental cookery; but, having scorched a finger, and having been told by the cook that a person's own kitchen wasn't worth the price at eleven dollars a week if it had to git all smelled up with broiled rubber when the femometer stood at ninety-sevvum degrees in the shade, the experimenter abusedly turned her back on the morose woman and went out to the back yard for a little peace.

After an interval of torpor, she decided to go and see what Herbert was doing—a move not short of desperation, on account of Herbert's new manner toward her. For a week Herbert had steadily pursued his scientific career, and he seemed to feel that in it he had attained a distinction beyond the reach of Florence. What made it ridiculous for her to hope was, of course, the fact that she was a girl, and Herbert had explained this to her in a cold, unpleasant way; for it is true that what is called "feminism" must be acquired by men, and is not a condition, or taste, natural to them. At thirteen it has not been acquired.

She found him at home. He was importantly engaged in a room in the cellar, where were loosely stored all manner of incapacitated household devices; two broken clothes-wringers, a crippled and rusted sewing-machine, an ice-cream freezer in like condition, a cracked and discarded marble mantelpiece, chipped porcelain and chinaware of all sorts, rusted stove lids and flatirons, half a dozen dead mops and brooms. This was the laboratory, and here, in congenial solitude, Herbert conducted his investigations. That is to say, until Florence arrived he was undisturbed by human intrusion, but he was not alone—far from it! There was, in fact, almost too much life in the place.

Where the light fell clearest from the cobwebby windows at the ground level overhead, he had placed a long deal table, once a helpmate in the kitchen, but now a colourless antique on three legs and two starch boxes. Upon the table were seven or eight glass jars, formerly used for preserves and pickles, and a dozen jelly glasses (with only streaks and bits of jelly in them now) and five or six small round pasteboard pill-boxes. The jars were covered, some with their own patent tops, others with shingles or bits of board, and one with a brick. The jelly glasses stood inverted, and were inhabited; so were the preserve jars and pickle jars; and so were the pill-boxes, which evidently contained star boarders, for they were pierced with "breathing holes," and one of them, standing upon its side like a little wheel, now and then moved in a faint, ghostly manner as if about to start rolling on its own account—whereupon Herbert glanced up and addressed it sternly, though somewhat inconsistently: "You shut up!"

In the display of so much experimental paraphernalia, there may have been a hint that Herbert's was a scientific nature craving rather quantity than quality; his collection certainly possessed the virtue of multitudinousness, if that be a virtue; and the birds in the neighbourhood must have been undergoing a great deal of disappointment. In brief, as many bugs as Herbert now owned have seldom been seen in the custody of any private individual. And nearly all of them were alive, energetic and swearing, though several of the preserve jars had been imperfectly drained of their heavy syrups, and in one of them a great many spiders seemed to be having, of the whole collection, the poorest time; being pretty well mired down and yet still subject to disagreements among themselves. The habits of this group, under such unusual surroundings, formed the subject of Herbert's special study at the moment of Florence's arrival. He was seated at the table and frowning with science as he observed the unfortunates through that magnifying-glass, his discovery of which was responsible for their present condition and his own choice of a career.

Florence paused in the doorway, but he gave no sign of recognition, unless his intensified preoccupation was a sign, and Florence, perceiving what line of conduct he meant to adopt, instinctively selected a reciprocal one for herself. "Herbert Atwater, you ought to be punished! I'm goin' to tell your father and mother."

"You g'way," Herbert returned, unmoved; and, without condescending to give her a glance, he set down the magnifying-glass, and with a pencil wrote something profoundly entomological in a soiled memorandum book upon the table. "Run away, Flor'nce. Run away somewheres and play."

Florence approached. "'Play'!" she echoed tartly. "I should think *you* wouldn't talk much about 'playin',' the way you're teasing those poor, poor little bugs!"

"'Teasing'!" Herbert exclaimed: "That shows! That shows!"

"Shows what?"

"How much you know!" He became despondent about her. "See here, Florence; it does look to me as though at your age a person ought to know anyway enough not to disturb me when I'm expairamenting, and everything. I should think—"

But she did not prove so meek as to await the conclusion of his remonstrance. "I never saw anything as wicked in my whole born days! What did any of those poor, poor little bugs ever do to *you*, I'd like to know, you got to go and confine 'em like this! And look how dirty your hands are!"

This final charge, wandering so far from her previous specifications of his guilt, was purely automatic and conventional; Florence often interjected it during the course of any cousinly discussion, whatever the subject in dispute, and she had not even glanced at Herbert's hands to assure herself that the accusation was warranted. But, as usual, the facts supported her; and they also supported Herbert in his immediate mechanical retort: "So're yours!"

"Not either!" But here Florence, after instinctively placing her hands behind her, brought forth the right one to point, and simultaneously uttered a loud cry: "Oh, *look* at your hands!" For now she did look at Herbert's hands, and was amazed.

"Well, what of it?"

"They're all lumpy!" she cried, and, as her gaze rose to his cheek, her finger followed her eyes and pointed to strange appearances there. "Look at your *face*!"

"Well, what of it?" he demanded, his tone not entirely free from braggadocio. "A girl can't make expairaments the way I do, because if one of these good ole bumblebees or hornets of mine was to give 'em a little sting, once in a while, while they was catchin' 'em and puttin' 'em in a jar, all they'd know how to do'd be to holler and run home to their mamma. Nobody with any gumption minds a few little stings after you put mud on 'em."

"I guess it serves you right," Florence said, "for persecutin' these poor, poor little bugs."

Herbert became plaintive. "Look here, Florence; I do wish you'd go on back home where you belong."

But Florence did not reply; instead she picked up the magnifying-glass, and, gazing through it at a pickle jar of mixed beetles, caterpillars, angleworms, and potato bugs, permitted herself to shudder. "Vile things!" she said.

"They are not, either!" Herbert retorted hotly. "They're about the finest insecks that you or anybody else ever saw, and you ought to be ashamed—"

"I ought?" his cousin cried. "Well, I should think you're the one ought to be ashamed, if anybody ought! Down here in the cellar playin' with all these vile bugs that ought to be given their liberty, or thrown down the sewer, or somep'n!" Again, as she peered through the lens, she shuddered. "Vile—"

"Florence," he said sternly, "you lay down that magnifying-glass."

"Why?"

"Because you don't know how to handle it. A magnifying-glass has got to be handled in just the right way, and you couldn't learn if you tried a thousand years. That's a mighty fine magnifying-glass, and I don't intend to have it ruined."

"Why, just lookin' through it can't spoil it, can it?" she inquired, surprised.

"You lay it down," said Herbert darkly. "Lookin' through it the wrong way isn't going to do it any *good*."

"Why, how could just *lookin'* through it—"

"Lookin' through it the wrong way isn't goin' to *help* it any, I tell you!" he insisted. "You're old enough to know that, and I'm not goin' to have my magnifying-glass spoiled and all my insecks wasted just because of a mere whin of yours!"

"A what?"

"A mere whin, I said!"

"What's a whin?"

"Never you mind," said Herbert ominously. "You'll proba'ly find out some day when you aren't expectin' to!"

Undeniably, Florence was somewhat impressed: she replaced the magnifying-glass upon the table and picked up the notebook.

"You lay that down, too," said Herbert instantly.

"Oh, maybe it's somep'n you're *'shamed* to—"

"Go on and read it, then," he said, suddenly changing his mind, for he was confident that she would find matter here that might cause her to appreciate at least a little of her own inferiority.

"'Nots'," Florence began. "'Nots'—"

"Notes!" he corrected her fiercely.

"'Notes'," she read. "'Notes on our inseck friends. The spidder—'"

"*Spider!*"

"'The spider spends his time mostly in cobwebs which he digilently spins between posts and catches flies to eat them. They are different coloured and sizes and have legs in pairs.

Booth Tarkington

Spiders also spin their webs in corners or in weeds or on a fence and sometimes in the grass. They are more able to get about quicker than catapillars or fishing worms, but cannot fly such as pinching bugs, lightning bugs, and birds because having no wings, nor jump as far as the grass hoper—'"

"Grasshopper!" Herbert shouted.

"I'm readin' it the way it's spelled," Florence explained. "Anyway, it don't make much sense."

Herbert was at least enough of an author to be furious. "Lay it down!" he said bitterly. "And go on back home to your dolls."

"Dolls certainly would be *cleaner* than vile bugs," Florence retorted, tossing the book upon the table. "But in regards to that, I haven't had any," she went on, airily—"not for years and years and years and—"

He interrupted her, his voice again plaintive. "See here, Florence, how do you expect me to get my *work* done, with you everlastin'ly talkin' and goin' on around here like this? Can't you see I've got somep'n pretty important on my hands?"

Florence became thoughtful. "I never did see as many bugs before, all together this way," she said. "What you goin' to do with 'em, Herbert?"

"I'm makin' my expairaments."

But her thoughtfulness increased. "It seems to me," she said slowly:—"Herbert, it seems to me there must be some awful inter'sting thing we could do with so many bugs all together like this."

"'We'!" he cried. "My goodness, whose insecks do you think these insecks are?"

"I just know there's somep'n," she went on, following her own line of thought, and indifferent to his outburst. "There's somep'n we could do with 'em that we'd never forget, if we could only think of it."

In spite of himself, Herbert was interested. "Well, what?" he asked. "What could we do with 'em we'd never forget?"

In her eyes there was a far-away light as of a seeress groping. "I don't just know exackly, but I know there's *somep'n*—if we could only think of it—if we could just—" And her voice became inaudible, as in dreamy concentration she seated herself upon the discarded ice-cream freezer, and rested her elbows upon her knees and her chin upon the palms of her hands.

In silence then, she thought and thought. Herbert also was silent, for he, too, was trying to think, not knowing that already he had proved himself to be wax in her hands, and that he was destined further to show himself thus malleable. Like many and many another of his sex, he never for an instant suspected that he spent the greater part of his time carrying out ideas implanted within him by a lady-friend. Florence was ever the imaginative one of those two, a maiden of unexpected fancies and inexplicable conceptions, a mind of quicksilver and mist. There was within her the seedling of a creative artist, and as she sat there, on the ice-cream freezer in Herbert's cellar, with the slowly growing roseate glow of deep preoccupation upon her, she looked strangely sweet and good, and even almost pretty.

CHAPTER EIGHT

"Do you s'pose," she said, at last, in a musing voice: "Herbert, do you s'pose maybe there's some poor family's children somewheres that haven't got any playthings or anything and we could take all these—"

But here Herbert proved unsympathetic. "I'm not goin' to give my insecks to any poor people's children," he said emphatically. "I don't care how poor they are!"

"Well, I thought maybe just as a surprise—"

"I won't do it. I had mighty hard work to catch this c'lection, and I'm not goin' to give it away to anybody, I don't care how surprised they'd be! Anyway, I'd never get any thanks for it; they wouldn't know how to handle 'em, and they'd get all stung up: and what'd be the use, anyhow? I don't see how *that's* goin' to be somep'n so interesting we'd never forget it."

"No," she said. "I guess it wouldn't. I just thought it would be kind of a bellnevolent thing to do."

This word disturbed Herbert, but he did not feel altogether secure in his own impression that "benovvalent" was the proper rendition of what she meant, and so refrained from criticism. Their musing was resumed.

"There's one thing I do wish," Florence said suddenly, after a time. "I wish we could find some way to use the c'lection that would be useful for Noble Dill."

Now, at this, her cousin's face showed simple amazement. "What on earth you talkin' about?"

"Noble Dill," she said dreamily. "He's the only one I like that comes to see Aunt Julia. Anyway, I like him the most."

"I bet Aunt Julia don't!"

"I don't care: he's the one *I* wish she'd get married to."

Herbert was astounded. "Noble Dill? Why, I heard mamma and Aunt Hattie and Uncle Joe talkin' about him yesterday."

"What'd they say?"

"Most of the time," said Herbert, "they just laughed. They said Noble Dill was the very last person in this town Aunt Julia'd ever dream o' marryin'. They said he wasn't anything: they said he wasn't handsome and he wasn't distingrished-looking—"

"I think he is," Florence interposed. "I think he's *very* distingrished-looking."

"Well, they said he wasn't, and they know more'n you do. Why, Noble Dill isn't hardly any taller'n I am myself, and he hasn't got any muscle partickyourly. Aunt Julia wouldn't look at him!"

"She does, too! My goodness, how could he sit on the porch, right in front of her, for two or three hours at a time, without her lookin' at him?"

"I don't care," Herbert insisted stubbornly. "*They* said Aunt Julia wouldn't. They said she was the worst flirt had ever been in the whole family and Noble Dill had the worst case they ever saw, but she wouldn't ever look at him, and if she did she'd be crazy."

"Well, anyway," said Florence, "I think he's the nicest of all that goes to see her, and I wish we could use this c'lection some way that would be nice for him."

Herbert renewed his protest. "How many times I got to tell you I had a hard enough time catchin' this c'lection, day in and day out, from before daylight till after dark, and then fixin' 'em all up like this and everything! I don't prapose to waste 'em just to suit Noble Dill, and I'm not goin' to give 'em away either. If anybody wanted to buy 'em and offered a good fair price, money down, why, I—"

"*That's* it, Herbert!" his lady-cousin exclaimed with sudden excitement. "Let's sell 'em!" She jumped up, her eyes bright. "I bet we could get maybe five dollars for 'em. We can pour the ones that are in the jars that haven't got tops and the ones in the jelly glasses and pill-boxes—we can pour all those into the jars that have got tops, and put the tops on again, and that'd just about fill those jars—and then we could put 'em in a basket and take 'em out and sell 'em!"

"Where could we sell 'em?" Herbert inquired, not convinced.

"At the fish store!" she cried. "Everybody uses bugs and worms for bait when they go fishing, don't they? I bet the fish man'll buy all the worms we got, even if he wouldn't buy anything else. I bet he'll buy all the others, too! I bet he never saw as much good bait as this all at one time in his whole life! I bet he'll give us five dollars—maybe more!"

Herbert was dazzled; the thought of this market was a revelation—nothing could have been more plausible. Considered as bait, the c'lection at once seemed to acquire a practical and financial value which it lacked, purely as a c'lection. And with that the amateur and scientist disappeared, giving way to the person of affairs. "'Give *us* five dollars'?" he said, in this capacity, and for deeper effect he used a rhetorical expression:

"Who do you think is the owner of all this fish bait, may I ask you, pray?"

"Yes, you *may*, pray!" was his cousin's instant and supercilious retort. "Pray where would you ever of got any five dollars from any fish man, if it hadn't been for me, pray? Pray, didn't I first sajest our doing somep'n with the bugs we'd never forget, and if the fish man gives us five dollars for 'em won't we remember it all our lives, pray? And, pray, what part did you think up of all this, pray? Not one single thing, and if you don't divide even with me, I'll run ahead and tell the fish man the whole c'lection has been in bottles that had old medicine and poison in 'em—and then where'll *you* be, pray?"

It is to be doubted that Florence possessed the cold-blooded capacities with which this impromptu in diplomacy seemed to invest her: probably she would never have gone so far. But the words sufficed; and Herbert was so perfectly intimidated that he was even unresentful. "Well, you can have your ole two dollars and a half, whether you got a right to it or not," he said. "But you got to carry the basket."

"No," said Florence. "This has got to be done right, Herbert. We're partners now and everything's got to be divided just exackly even. I'll carry the basket half the way and you carry it the other half."

"Well—" he grumbled, consenting.

"That's the only right way," she said sunnily. "You carry it till we get to the fish man's, and I'll carry it all the way back."

But even Herbert could perceive the inequality here. "It'll be empty then," he protested.

"Fair's fair and wrong's wrong," she returned firmly. "I spoke first to carry it on the way home, and the one that speaks first gets it!"

"Look here!"

"Herbert, we got to get all these bugs fixed up and ready," she urged. "We don't want to waste the whole afternoon just talkin' about it, do we? Besides, Herbert, on the way home you'll have two dollars and a half in your pocket, or anyway as much as you have left, if you buy some soda and candy and things, and you'll feel so fine then you won't mind whether you're carrying the basket or not."

The picture she now suggested to Herbert's mind was of himself carrying the basket both to the fish man and from the fish man: and he found himself anxious to protest, yet helpless in a maze of perplexity. "But wait a minute," he began. "You said—"

"Let's don't waste another minute," she interrupted briskly. "I shouldn't wonder it was after four o'clock by this time, and we both need money. Hurry, Herbert!"

"But didn't you say—" He paused to rub his head. "You said I'd feel so good I wouldn't mind if I—if—"

"No. I said, 'Hurry'!"

"Well—" And though he felt that a subtle injustice lurked somewhere, he was unable to think the matter out clearly into its composing elements, and gave up trying. Nevertheless, as he obeyed her, and began to "hurry," there remained with him an impression that by some foggy and underhand process he had been committed to acquiescence in an unfair division of labour.

In this he was not mistaken. An hour later he and Florence were on their way home from the fish man's place of business, and Herbert, having carried the basket thither, was now carrying it thence. Moreover, his burden was precisely as heavy on this homeward leg of the course as it had been on that terminating at the fish store, for, covered by a discreet newspaper, the preserve and pickle jars still remained within the basket, their crowding and indignant contents intact. The fish man had explained in terms derisive, but plain, the difference between a fish man and a fisherman. He had maintained his definitions of the two economic functions in spite of persistent arguments on the part of the bait-dealers, and in the face of reductions that finally removed ninety per cent. of their asking price. He wouldn't give fifty cents, or ten cents, or one cent, he said: and he couldn't furnish the address of anybody else that would. His fish came by express, he declared, again and again: and the only people he knew that did any fishing were mainly coloured, and dug their own bait; and though these might possibly be willing to accept the angle worms as a gift, they would probably incline to resent a generosity including so many spiders, not to speak of the dangerous winged members of the c'lection. On account of these latter, he jocosely professed himself to be anxious lest the tops of some of the jars might work loose—and altogether he was the most disheartening man they had ever met.

Anticlimax was never the stimulant of amiability, and, after an altercation on the pavement just outside of the store, during which the derisive fish man continually called to them to go on and take that there basket out of the neighbourhood, the cousins moved morbidly away, and walked for a time in silence.

They brooded. Herbert was even more embittered with Florence than he was with the fish man, and Florence found life full of unexpectedness; it had been so clear to her that the fish man would say: "Why, certainly. Here's five dollars; two dollars and a half for each of you. Would you care to have the jars back?" The facts, so contrary, seemed to wear the aspect of deliberate malice, and she felt ill-used, especially as she had several physical grievances, due to her assistance in pouring part of the c'lection into the jars with tops. In spite of every precaution three or four of the liveliest items had made their escape, during this pouring, and had behaved resentfully. Florence bore one result on the back of her left hand, two others on the thumb and second finger of her right hand, and another, naturally the most conspicuous, on the point of her chin. These had all been painful, in spite of mud poultices, but, excited by the anticipation of a kindly smiling fish man, and occupied with plans for getting Herbert to spend part of his two dollars and a half for mutual refreshment, she had borne up cheerfully. Now, comprehending that she had suffered in vain, she suffered anew, and hated bugs, all fish men, and the world.

It was Herbert who broke the silence and renewed the altercation. "How far you expeck me to go on luggin' this ole basket?" he demanded bitterly. "All the way home?"

"I don't care how far," she informed him. "You can throw it away if you want to. It's certainly no propaty of mine, thank you!"

"Look here, didn't you promise you'd carry it home?"

"I said I *spoke* to. I didn't say I *would* carry it."

"Well, I'd like to know the dif—"

But Florence cut him off. "I'll tell you the difference, since you're so anxious to know the truth, Mister Herbert Atwater! The difference is just this: you had no biznuss to meddle with those vile ole bugs in the first place, and get me all stung up so't I shouldn't wonder I'd haf to have the doctor, time I get home, and if I do I'm goin' to tell mamma all about it and make her send the bill to your father. I want you to know I *hurt*!"

"My goodness!" Herbert burst out. "Don't you s'pose *I* hurt any? I guess you don't hurt any worse than—"

She stopped him: "Listen!"

From down the street there came a brazen clamouring for the

right of way; it grew imperiously louder, and there were clatterings and whizzings of metallic bodies at speed, while little blurs and glistenings in the distance grew swiftly larger, taking shape as a fire engine and a hose-cart. Then, round the near-by corner, came perilously steering the long "hook-and-ladder wagon"; it made the turn and went by, with its firemen imperturbable on the running boards.

"Fire!" Florence cried joyfully. "Let's go!" And, pausing no instant, she made off up the street, shouting at the top of her voice: "*Fire! Fire! Fire! Fire!*"

Herbert followed. He was not so swift a runner as she, though this he never submitted to a test admitted to be fair and conclusive; and he found her demonstration of superiority particularly offensive now, as she called back over her shoulder: "Why don't you keep up with me? Can't you keep up?"

"I'd *show* you!" he panted. "If I didn't haf to lug this ole basket, I'd leave you a mile behind mighty quick."

"Well, why'n't you drop it, then?"

"You s'pose I'm goin' to throw my c'lection away after all the trouble I been *through* with it?"

She slackened her gait, dropping back beside him. "Well, then, if you think you could keep up with me if you didn't have it, why'n't you leave it somewhere, and come back and get it after the fire's over?"

"No place to leave it."

She laughed, and pointed. "Why'n't you leave it at grandpa's?"

"Will you wait for me and start fair?"

"Come on!" They obliqued across the street, still running forward, and at their grandfather's gate Herbert turned in and

Booth Tarkington

sped toward the house.

"Take it around to the kitchen and give it to Kitty Silver," Florence called. "Tell Kitty Silver to take care of it for you."

But Herbert was in no mind to follow her advice; a glance over his shoulder showed that Florence was taking another unfair advantage of him. "You wait!" he shouted. "You stand still till I get back there! You got half a mile start a'ready! You wait till we can start even!"

But Florence was skipping lightly away and she caroled over her shoulder, waving her hand in mocking farewell as she began to run:

"Ole Mister Slowpoke can't catch me!
Ole Mister Slowpoke couldn't catch a flea!"

"I'll show you!" he bellowed, and, not to lose more time, he dashed up the steps of the deserted veranda, thrust his basket deep underneath a wicker settee, and ran violently after his elusive cousin.

She kept a tantalizing distance between them, but when they reached the fire it was such a grand one they forgot all their differences—and also all about the basket.

CHAPTER NINE

Noble Dill came from his father's house, after dinner that evening, a youth in blossom, like the shrubberies and garden beds in the dim yards up and down Julia's Street. All cooled and bathed and in new clothes of white, he took his thrilled walk through the deep summer twilight, on his way to that ineffable Front Porch where sat Julia, misty in the dusk. The girlish little new moon had perished naively out of the sky; the final pinkness of the west was gone; blue evening held the quiet world; and overhead, between the branches of the maple trees, were powdered all those bright pin points of light that were to twinkle on generations of young lovers after Noble Dill, each one, like Noble, walking the same fragrant path in summer twilights to see the Prettiest Girl of All.

Now and then there came to the faintly throbbing ears of the pedestrian a murmur of voices from lawns where citizens sat cooling after the day's labour, or a tinkle of laughter from where maidens dull (not being Julia) sat on verandas vacant of beauty and glamour. For these poor things, Noble felt a wondering and disdainful pity; he pitied everything in the world that was not on the way to starry Julia.

Eight nights had passed since he, himself, had seen her, but to-day she had replied (over the telephone) that Mr. Atwater seemed to have settled down again, and she believed it might be no breach of tact for Noble to call that evening—especially as she would be on the veranda, and he needn't ring the bell. Would she be alone—for once? It was improbable, yet it could

Booth Tarkington

be hoped.

But as he came hoping up the street, another already sat beside Julia, sharing with her the wicker settee on the dim porch, and this was the horn-rimmed young poet. Newland had, as usual, a new poem with him; and as others had proved of late that they could sit on Julia's veranda as long as he could, he had seized the first opportunity to familiarize her with this latest work.

The veranda was dark, and to go indoors to the light might have involved too close a juxtaposition to peculiar old Mr. Atwater who was in the library; but the resourceful Newland, foreseeing everything, had brought with him a small pocket flashlight to illumine his manuscript. "It's *vers libre*, of course," he said as he moved the flashlight over the sheets of scribbled paper. "I think I told you I was beginning to give all the old forms up. It's the one new movement, and I felt I ought to master it."

"Of course," she said sympathetically, though with a little nervousness. "Be just a wee bit careful with the flashlight— about turning it toward the window, I mean—and read in your nice low voice. I always like poetry best when it's almost whispered. I think it sounds more musical that way, I mean."

Newland obeyed. His voice was hushed and profoundly appreciative of the music in itself and in his poem, as he read:

"I—And Love!
Lush white lilies line the pool
Like laces limned on looking-glasses!
I tread the lilies underfoot,
Careless how they love me!
Still white maidens woo me,
Win me not!
But thou!
Thou art a cornflower
Sapphire-eyed!

I bend!
Cornflower, I ask a question.
O flower, speak—"

Julia spoke. "I'm afraid," she said, while Newland's spirit filled with a bitterness extraordinary even in an interrupted poet;— "I'm afraid it's Mr. Dill coming up the walk. We'll have to postpone—" She rose and went to the steps to greet the approaching guest. "How nice of you to come!"

Noble, remaining on the lowest step, clung to her hand in a fever. "Nice to come!" he said hoarsely. "It's eight days—eight days—eight days since—"

"Mr. Sanders is here," she said. "It's so dark on this big veranda people can hardly see each other. Come up and sit with us. I don't have to introduce you two men to each other."

She did not, indeed. They said "H'lo, Dill" and "H'lo Sanders" in a manner of such slighting superiority that only the utmost familiarity could have bred a contempt so magnificent. Then, when the three were seated, Mr. Sanders thought well to add: "How's rent collecting these days, Dill? Still hustling around among those darky shanties over in Bucktown?"

In the dark Noble moved convulsively, but contrived to affect a light laugh, or a sound meant for one, as he replied, in a voice not entirely under control: "How's the ole poetry, Sanders?"

"What?" Newland demanded sharply. "What did you say?"

"I said: 'How's the ole poetry?' Do you read it to all your relations the way you used to?"

"See here, Dill!"

"Well, what you want, Sanders?"

"You try to talk about things you understand," said Newland. "You better keep your mind on collecting four dollars a week from some poor coloured widow, and don't—"

"I'd *rather* keep my mind on that!" Noble was inspired to retort. "Your Aunt Georgina told my mother that ever since you began thinkin' you could write poetry the life your family led was just—"

Newland interrupted. He knew the improper thing his Aunt Georgina had said, and he was again, and doubly, infuriated by the prospect of its repetition here. He began fiercely:

"Dill, you see here—"

"Your Aunt Georgina said—"

Both voices had risen. Plainly it was time for someone to say: "Gentlemen! Gentlemen!" Julia glanced anxiously through the darkness of the room beyond the open window beside her, to where the light of the library lamp shone upon a door ajar; and she was the more nervous because Noble, to give the effect of coolness, had lit an Orduma cigarette.

She laughed amiably, as if the two young gentlemen were as amiable as she. "I've thought of something," she said. "Let's take the settee and some chairs down on the lawn where we can sit and see the moon."

"There isn't any," Noble remarked vacantly.

"Let's go, anyhow," she said cheerily. "Come on."

Her purpose was effected; the belligerents were diverted, and Noble lifted the light wicker settee. "I'll carry this," he said. "It's no trouble. Sanders can carry a chair—I guess he'd be equal to that much." He stumbled, dropped the settee, and lifted a basket, its contents covered with a newspaper. "Somebody must have—"

"What is it?"

"It's a basket," said Noble.

"How curious!"

Julia peered through the darkness. "I wonder who could have left that market basket out *here*. I suppose—" She paused. "Our cook does do more idiotic things than—I'll go ask her if it's ours."

She stepped quickly into the house, leaving two concentrations of inimical silence behind her, but she returned almost immediately, followed by Kitty Silver.

"It's no use to argue," Julia was saying as they came. "You did your marketing and simply and plainly left it out there because you were too shiftless to—"

"No'm," Mrs. Silver protested in a high voice of defensive complaint. "No'm, Miss Julia, I ain' lef no baskit on *no* front po'che! I got jus' th'ee markit baskits in the livin' worl' an' they ev'y las' one an' all sittin' right where I kin lay my han's on 'em behime my back do'. No'm, Miss Julia, I take my solemn oaf I ain' lef no—" But here she debouched upon the porch, and in spite of the darkness perceived herself to be in the presence of distinguished callers. "Pahdon me," she said loftily, her tone altering at once, "I beg leaf to insis' I better take thishere baskit back to my kitchen an' see whut-all's insiden of it."

With an elegant gesture she received the basket from Noble Dill and took the handle over her ample forearm. "Hum!" she said. "Thishere ole basket kine o' heavy, too. I wunner whut-all she *is* got in her!" And she groped within the basket, beneath the newspaper.

Now, it was the breath of Kitty Silver's life to linger, when she could, in a high atmosphere; and she was a powerful gossip, exorbitantly interested in her young mistress's affairs and all callers. Therefore it was beyond her not to seize upon any excuse that might detain her for any time whatever in her present surroundings.

"Pusserve jugs," she said. "Pusserve or pickle. Cain't tell which."

"You can in the kitchen," Julia said, with pointed suggestion. "Of course you can't in the dark."

But still Mrs. Silver snatched at the fleeting moment and did not go. "Tell by smellin' 'em," she murmured, seemingly to herself.

With ease she unscrewed the top of one of the jars; then held the open jar to her nose. "Don't smell to me exackly like no pusserves," she said. "Nor yit like no pickles. Don't smell to me—" She hesitated, sniffed the jar again, and then inquired in a voice quickly grown anxious: "Whut *is* all thishere in thishere jug? Seem like to *me*—"

But here she interrupted herself to utter a muffled exclamation, not coherent. Instantly she added some words suitable to religious observances, but in a voice of passion. At the same time, with a fine gesture, she hurled the jar and the basket from her, and both came in contact with the wall, not far away, with a sound of breakage.

"Why, what—" Julia began. "Kitty Silver, are you crazy?"

But Kitty Silver was moving hurriedly toward the open front door, where appeared, at that moment, Mr. Atwater in his most irascible state of peculiarity.

He began: "What was that heathenish—"

Shouting, Mrs. Silver jostled by him, and, though she disappeared into the house, a trail of calamitous uproar marked her passage to the kitchen.

"What thing has happened?" Mr. Atwater demanded. "Is she—?"

His daughter interrupted him.

"*Oh*!" was all she said, and sped by him like a bit of blown thistledown, into the house. He grasped at her as she passed him; then suddenly he made other gestures, and, like Kitty Silver, used Jacobean phrases. But now there were no auditors, for Noble Dill and Newland Sanders, after thoughtlessly following a mutual and natural impulse to step over and examine the fallen basket, had both gone out to the street, where they lingered a while, then decided to go home.

... Later, that evening, Florence and Herbert remembered the c'lection; so they came for it, a mistake. Discovering the fragments upon the veranda, they made the much more important mistake of entering the house to demand an explanation, which they received immediately. It was delivered with so much vigour, indeed, that Florence was surprised and hurt. And yet, the most important of her dreamy wishes of the afternoon had been fulfilled: the c'lection had been useful to Noble Dill, for Mr. Atwater had smelled the smell of an Orduma cigarette and was just on the point of coming out to say some harsh things, when the c'lection interfered. And as Florence was really responsible for its having been in a position to interfere, so to say, she had actually in a manner protected her protege and also shown some of that power of which she had boasted when she told him that sometimes she made members of her family "step around pretty lively."

Another of her wishes appeared to be on the way to fulfilment, too. She had hoped that something memorable might be done with the c'lection, and the interview with her grandfather, her Aunt Julia, and Kitty Silver seemed to leave this beyond doubt.

CHAPTER TEN

Now August came, that florid lazy month when mid-summer dawdles along in trailing greeneries, and the day is like some jocund pagan, all flushed and asleep, with dripping beard rosy in a wine bowl of fat vine leaves. Yet, in this languorous time there may befall a brisker night, cool and lively as an intrusive boy—a night made for dancing. On such a night a hasty thought might put it as desirable that all the world should be twenty-two years old and in love, like Noble Dill.

Upon the white bed in his room, as he dressed, lay the flat black silhouettes of his short evening coat and trousers, side by side, trim from new pressing; and whenever he looked at them Noble felt rich, tall, distinguished, and dramatic. It is a mistake, as most literary legends are mistakes, to assume that girls are the only people subject to before-the-party exhilaration. At such times a girl is often in the anxious yet determined mood of a runner before a foot race, or she may be merely hopeful; some are merry and some are grim, but arithmetical calculation of some sort, whether glorious or uneasy, is busy in their eyes as they pin and pat before their mirrors. To behold romance gone light-headed, turn to the humbler sort of man-creature under twenty-three. Alone in his room, he may enact for you scenes of flowery grace and most capricious gallantry, rehearsals as unconscious as the curtsies of field daisies in a breeze. He has neither doubt nor certainty of his charm; he has no arithmetic at all, and is often so free of calculation that he does not even pull down the shades at his windows.

Unfortunately for the neighbours, and even for passers-by, since Noble's room had a window visible from the street, his prophetic mother had closed his shutters before he began to dress. Thus she deprived honest folk of what surely must have been to them the innocent pleasure of seeing a very young man in light but complete underwear, lifting from his head a Panama hat, new that day, in a series of courteous salutations. At times, during this same stage of his toilet, they might have had even more entertainment:—before putting on his socks Noble "one-stepped" for several minutes, still retaining upon his head the new hat. This was a hat of double value to him; not only was it pleasant to behold in his mirror, but it was engaged in solidifying for the evening the arrangement of his hair.

It may be admitted that he was a little giddy, for the dance was Julia's. Mr. Atwater had been summoned to New York on a blessed business that would keep him a fortnight, and his daughter, alert to the first flash of opportunity, had almost instantly summoned musicians, florists, a caterer, and set plans before them. Coincidentally, Noble had chanced to see Mr. Atwater driving down Julia's Street that morning, a travelling bag beside him, and, immediately putting aside for the day all business cares, hurried to the traveller's house. Thus he forestalled, for the time being, that competition which helped to make caring for Julia so continuous a strain upon whatever organ is the seat of the anxieties. Kind Julia, busy as she was, agreed to dance the first dance with him, and the last—those being considered of such significance that he would be entitled to the perquisites of a special cavalier; for instance, a seat beside her during the serving of the customary light repast. In such high fortune, no wonder he was a little giddy as he dressed!

The process of clothing himself was disconnected, being broken by various enacted fancies and interludes. Having approached the length of one sock toward the completion of his toilet, he absently dropped the other upon the floor, and danced again; his expression and attitude signifying that he clasped a revered partner. Releasing her from this respectful confinement, he offered the invisible lady a gracious arm and walked up and down the room with a stateliness tempered to rhythm, a cakewalk of strange refinement. Phrases seemed to be running in his head, impromptus symbolic of the touching and romantic, for he spoke them half aloud hi a wistful yet uplifted manner. "Oh, years!" he said. "Oh, years so fair; oh, night so rare!" Then he added, in a deeper voice:

"For life is but a golden dream so sweetly."

Other whimsies came forth from him as the dressing slowly continued, though one might easily be at fault in attempting to fathom what was his thought when, during the passage of his right foot through the corresponding leg of his trousers, he exclaimed commandingly:

"Now, Jocko, for the stirrup cup!"

Jack boots and a faithful squire, probably.

During the long and dreamy session with his neck gear he went back to the softer *motif*:

"Oh, years so fair; oh, night so rare!
For life is but a golden dream so sweetly."

Then, pausing abruptly to look at his coat, so smoothly folded upon the bed, he addressed it: "O noblest sample of the tailor's dext'rous art!"

This was too much courtesy, for the coat was "ready-made," and looked nobler upon the bed than upon its owner. In fact, it was by no means a dext'rous sample; but evidently Noble believed in it with a high and satisfying faith; and he repeated his compliment to it as he put it on:

"Come, noblest sample of the tailor's art; I'll don thee!"

During these processes he had been repeatedly summoned to

descend to the family dinner, and finally his mother came lamenting and called up from the front hall that "everything" was "all getting cold!"

But by this time he was on his way, and though he went back to leave his hat in his room, unwilling to confide it to the hat-rack below, he presently made his appearance in the dining-room and took his seat at the table. This mere sitting, however, appeared to be his whole conception of dining; he seemed as unaware of his mother's urging food upon him as if he had been a Noble Dill of waxwork. Several tunes he lifted a fork and set it down without guiding it to its accustomed destination. Food was far from his thoughts or desires, and if he really perceived its presence at all, it appeared to him as something vaguely ignoble upon the horizon.

But he was able to partake of coffee; drank two cups feverishly, his hand visibly unsteady; and when his mother pointed out this confirmation of many prophecies that cigarettes would ruin him, he asked if anybody had noticed whether or not it was cloudy outdoors. At that his father looked despondent, for the open windows of the dining-room revealed an evening of fragrant clarity.

"I see, I see," Noble returned pettishly when the fine state of this closely adjacent weather was pointed out to him by his old-maid sister. "It wouldn't be raining, of course. Not on a night like this." He jumped up. "It's time for me to go."

Mrs. Dill laughed. "It's only a little after seven. Julia won't be through her own dinner yet. You mustn't—"

But with a tremulous smile, Noble shook his head and hurriedly left the room. He went upstairs for his hat, and while there pinned a geranium blossom upon his lapel, for it may be admitted that in boutonnieres his taste was as yet unformed.

Coming down again, he took a stick under his arm and was about to set forth when he noticed a little drift of talcum powder upon one of his patent leather shoes. After carefully removing this accretion and adding a brighter lustre to the shoe by means of friction against the back of his ankle, he decided to return to his room and brush the affected portion of his trousers. Here a new reverie arrested him; he stood with the brush in his hand for some time; then, not having used it, he dropped it gently upon the bed, lit an Orduma cigarette, descended, and went forth to the quiet street.

As he walked along Julia's Street toward Julia's Party, there was something in his mien and look more dramatic than mere sprightliness; and when he came within sight of the ineffable house and saw its many lights shining before him, he breathed with profundity, half halting. Again he murmured:

"Oh, years so fair; oh, night so rare!
For life is but a golden dream so sweetly."

At the gate he hesitated. Perhaps—perhaps he was a little early. It might be better to walk round the block.

He executed this parade, and again hesitated at the gate. He could see into the brightly lighted hall, beyond the open double doors; and it contained nothing except its usual furniture. Once more he walked round the block. The hall was again in the same condition. Again he went on.

When he had been thrice round the block after that, he discovered human beings in the hall; they were Florence, in a gala costume, and Florence's mother, evidently arrived to be assistants at the party, for, with the helpful advice of a coloured manservant, they were arranging some bunches of flowers on two hall tables. Their leisurely manner somewhat emphasized the air of earliness that hung about the place, and Noble thought it better to continue to walk round the block. The third time after that, when he completed his circuit, the musicians were just arriving, and their silhouettes, headed by that of the burdened bass fiddler, staggered against the light of the glowing doorway like a fantasia of giant beetles. Noble felt that it would be better to let them get settled, and therefore walked round the block again.

Not far from the corner above Julia's, as he passed, a hoarse and unctuous voice, issuing out of an undistinguishable lawn, called his name: "Noble! Noble Dill!" And when Noble paused, Julia's Uncle Joseph came waddling forth from the dimness and rested his monstrous arms upon the top of the fence, where a street light revealed them as shirt-sleeved and equipped with a palm-leaf fan.

"What *is* the matter, Noble?" Mr. Atwater inquired earnestly.

"Matter?" Noble repeated. "Matter?"

"We're kind of upset," said Mr. Atwater. "My wife and I been just sittin' out here in our front yard, not doing any harm to anybody, and here it's nine times we've counted you passing the place—always going the same way!" He spoke as with complaint, a man with a grievance. "It's kind of ghostlike," he added. "We'd give a good deal to know what *you* make of it."

Noble was nonplussed. "Why—" he said. "Why—"

"How do you get *back*? That's the mystery!" said Mr. Atwater. "You're always walkin' down street and never up. You know my wife's never been too strong a woman, Noble, and all this isn't doing her any good. Besides, we sort of figured out that you ought really to be at Julia's dance this evening."

"I am," said Noble nervously. "I mean that's where I'm going. I'm going there. I'm going there."

"That's what's upsetting us so!" the fat man exclaimed. "You keep on going there! Just when we've decided you must *be* there, at last, here you come, going there again. Well, don't let me detain you. But if you do decide to go in, some time, Noble, I'm afraid you aren't going to be able to do much dancing."

Noble, who had begun to walk on, halted in sudden panic. Did this sinister fear of Mr. Atwater's mean that, as an uncle, he had heard Julia was suddenly ill?

"Why won't I?" he asked quickly. "Is anything—"

"Your poor feet!" said Mr. Atwater, withdrawing. "Good-night, Noble."

The youth went on, somewhat disturbed; it seemed to him that this uncle, though Julia's, was either going queer in the head or had chosen a poor occasion to be facetious. Next time, probably, it would be better to walk round the block below this. But it was no longer advisable to walk round any block. When he came to the happy gateway, the tuning of instruments and a fanfare of voices sounded from within the house; girls in light wraps were fluttering through the hall with young men; it was "time for the party!" And Noble went in.

Throughout the accomplishment of the entrance he made, his outside and his inside were directly contradictory. His inside was almost fluttering: there might have been a nest of nervous young birds in his chest; but as he went upstairs to the "gentlemen's dressing-room," to leave his hat and stick, this flopping and scrambling within him was never to be guessed from his outside. His outside was unsympathetic, even stately; he greeted his fellow guests with negligent hauteur, while his glance seemed to say: "Only peasantry here!"

CHAPTER ELEVEN

The stairway was crowded as he descended; and as he looked down upon the heads and shoulders of the throng below, in Julia's hall, the thought came to him that since he had the first and last dances and supper engaged with Julia, the hostess, this was almost the next thing to being the host. It was a pleasing thought, and a slight graciousness now flavoured his salutations.

At the foot of the stairs he became part of the file of young people who were moving into one of the large rooms where Julia stood to "receive." And then, between two heads before him, he caught a first glimpse of her;—and all the young birds fluttering in his chest burst into song; his heart fainted, his head ballooned, his feet seemed to dangle from him at the ends of two strings.

There glowed sapphire-eyed Julia; never had she been prettier.

The group closed, shutting out the vision, and he found himself able to dry his brow and get back his breath before moving forward in a cold and aristocratic attitude. Then he became incapable of any attitude—he was before her, and she greeted him. A buzzing of the universe confused him: he would have stood forever, but pressure from behind pushed him on; and so, enveloped in a scented cloud, he passed into a corner. He tried to remember what he had said to her, but could not; perhaps it would have discouraged him to know that all he had said was, "Well!"

Now there rattled out a challenge of drums; loud music struck upon the air. Starting instantly to go to Julia, Noble's left leg first received the electric impulse and crossed his laggard right; but he was no pacer, and thus stumbled upon himself and plunged. Still convulsive, he came headlong before her, and was the only person near who remained unaware that his dispersal of an intervening group had the appearance of extreme unconventionality. Noble knew nothing except that this was his dance with Her.

Then heaven played with him. She came close and touched him exquisitely. She placed a lovely hand upon his shoulder, her other lovely cool hand in one of his. The air filled with bursting stars.

They danced.

Noble was conscious of her within his clasping arm, but conscious of her as nothing human. The fluffy white bodice pressed by his hand seemed to be that of some angel doll; the charming shoulder that sometimes touched his was made of a divine mist. Only the pretty head, close to his, was actual; the black-sapphire eyes gave him a little blue-black glance, now and then, and seemed to laugh.

In truth, they did, though Julia's lips remained demure. So far as Noble was able to comprehend what he was doing, he was floating rhythmically to a faint, far music; but he was almost unconscious, especially from the knees down. But to the eye of observers incapable of perceiving that Noble was floating, it appeared that he was out of step most of the time, and danced rather hoppingly. However, these mannerisms were no novelty with him, and it cannot be denied that girls at dances usually hurried impulsively away to speak to somebody when they saw him coming. One such creature even went so far as to whisper to Julia now, during a collision: "How'd you get caught?"

Julia was loyal; she gave no sign of comprehension, but valiantly swung onward with Noble, bumped and bumping everywhere, in spite of the most extraordinary and graceful dexterity on her part.

"That's one reason she's such a terrible belle," a damsel whispered to another.

"What is?"

"The way she'll be just as nice to anybody like Noble Dill as she is to anybody," said the first. "Look at her now: she won't laugh at him a bit, though everybody else is."

"Well, I wouldn't laugh either," said the other. "Not in Julia's position. I'd be too busy being afraid."

"What of?"

"Of getting a sprained ankle!"

It is well that telepathy remains, as a science, lethargic. Speculation sets before us the prospect of a Life Beyond in which every thought is communicated without the intervention of speech: a state wherein all neighbours and neighbourhoods would promptly be dispersed and few friendships long endure, one fears. If to Noble Dill's active consciousness had penetrated merely the things thought about him and his dancing, in this one short period of time before the music for that dance stopped, he might easily have been understood if he had hurried forth, obtained explosives, and blown up the place, himself indeed included. As matters providentially were in reality, when the music stopped he stood confounded: he thought the dance had just begun.

His mouth remained open until the necessary gestures of articulation intermittently closed it as he said: "*Oh!* That was *divine!*"

Too-gentle Julia agreed.

"You said I could have part of some in between the first and last," he reminded her. "Can I have the first part of the next?"

She laughed. "I'm afraid not. The next is Mr. Clairdyce's and I really *promised* him I wouldn't give *any* of his away or let anybody cut in."

"Well, then," said Noble, frowning a little, "would you be willing for me to cut in on the third?"

"I'm afraid not. That's Newland Sanders', and I promised him the same thing."

"Well, the one after that?"

"No, that one's Mr. Clairdyce's, too."

"It *is*?" Noble was greatly disturbed.

"Yes."

"Two that quick with old Baldy Clairdyce!" he exclaimed, raising his voice, but unaware of the fervour with which he spoke. "Two with that old—"

"*Sh*, Noble," she said, though she laughed. "He isn't really old; he's just middle-aged, and only the least bit bald, just enough to be distinguished-looking."

"Well, you know what *I* think of him!" he returned with a vehemence not moderated. "*I* don't think he's distinguished-looking; I think he's simply and plainly a regular old—"

"*Sh!*" Julia warned him again. "He's standing with some people just behind us," she added.

"Well, then," said Noble, "can I cut in on the next one after that?"

She consulted a surreptitious little card. "I'm afraid you'll have to wait till quite a little later on, Noble. That one is poor Mr. Ridgely's. I promised him I wouldn't—"

"Then can I cut in on the next one after that?"

"It's Mr. Clairdyce's," said Julia—and she blushed.

"My goodness!" said Noble. "Oh, my goodness!"

"*Sh!* I'm afraid people—"

"Let's go out on the porch," said Noble, whose manner had suddenly become desperate. "Let's go out and get some air where we can talk this thing over."

"I'm afraid I'd better not just now," she returned, glancing over her shoulder. "You see, all the people aren't here yet."

"You've got an aunt here," said Noble, "and a sister-in-law and a little niece: I saw 'em. They can—"

"I'm afraid I'd better stay indoors just now," she said persuasively. "We can talk here just as well."

"We can't!" he insisted feverishly. "We can't, Julia! I've got something to say, Julia. Julia, you gave me the first dance and the last dance, and of course sitting together at supper, or whatever there is, and you know as well as I do that means it's just the same as if you weren't giving this party but it was somewhere else and I took you to it, and it's always understood you *never* dance more with anybody else than the one you went with, when you go with that person to a place, because that's the rights of it; and other towns it's just the same way; they do that way there, just the same as here; they do that way everywhere, because nobody else has got a right to cut in and dance more with you than the one you go with, when you goes to a place with that one. Julia, don't you see that's the regular way it is, and the only fair way it ought to be?"

"What?"

"Weren't you even *listening*?" he cried.

"Yes, indeed, but—"

"Julia," he said desperately, "let's go out on the porch. I want to explain just the way I feel. Let's go out on the porch, Julia. If we stay here, somebody's just bound to interrupt us any minute before I can explain the way I—"

But the prophecy was fulfilled even before it was concluded. A group of loudly chattering girls and their escorts of the moment bore down upon Julia, and shattered the tete-a-tete. Dislodged from Julia's side by a large and eager girl, whom he had hated ever since she was six years old and he five, Noble found himself staggering in a kind of suburb; for the large girl's disregard of him, as she shouldered in, was actually physical, and too powerful for him to resist. She wished to put her coarse arm round Julia's waist, it appeared, and the whole group burbled and clamoured: the party was *perfictly* glorious; so was the waxed floor; so was Julia, my *dear*, so was the music, the weather, and the din they made!

Noble felt that his rights were being outraged. Until the next dance began, every moment of her time was legally his—yet all he could even see of her was the top of her head. And the minutes were flying.

He stood on tiptoe, thrust his head forward over the large girl's odious shoulder, and shouted: "Julia! Let's go out on the porch!"

No one seemed to hear him.

"Julia—"

Boom! Rackety-*Boom*! The drummer walloped his drums; a saxophone squawked, and fiddles squealed. Hereupon appeared a tall authoritative man, at least thirty-two years old, and all swelled up with himself, as interpreted by Noble and several other friends of Julia's—though this, according to quite a number of people (all feminine) was only another way of saying that he was a person of commanding presence. He wore a fully developed moustache, an easy smile, clothes offensively knowing; and his hair began to show that scarcity which Julia felt gave him distinction—a curious theory, but natural to her age. What really did give this Clairdyce some air of distinction, however, was the calmness with which he walked through the group that had dislodged Noble Dill, and the assurance with which he put his arm about Julia and swept her away in the dance.

Noble was left alone in the middle of the floor, but not for long. Couples charged him, and he betook himself to the wall. The party, for him, was already ruined.

Sometimes, as he stood against the wall, there would be swirled to him, out of all the comminglements of other scents, a faint, faint hint of heliotrope and then Julia would be borne masterfully by, her flying skirts just touching him. And sometimes, out of the medley of all other sounds, there would reach his ear a little laugh like a run of lightly plucked harp strings, and he would see her shining dark hair above her partner's shoulder as they swept again near him for an instant. And always, though she herself might be concealed from him, he could only too painfully mark where she danced: the overtopping head of the tall Clairdyce was never lost to view. The face on the front part of that disliked head wore continuously a confident smile, which had a bad effect on Noble. It seemed to him desecration that a man with so gross a smile should be allowed to dance with Julia. And that she should smile back at her partner, and with such terrible kindness—as Noble twice saw her smile—this was like a calamity happening to her white soul without her knowing it. If she should ever marry that man—well, it would be the old story: May and December! Noble shuddered, and the drums, the fiddles, the bass fiddle, and the saxophone seemed to have an evil sound.

When the music stopped he caromed hastily through the room toward Julia, but she was in a thicket of her guests when he arrived, and for several moments Mr. Clairdyce's broad back kept intervening—almost intentionally, it seemed. When Noble tried to place himself in a position to attract Julia's attention, this back moved, too, and Noble's nose but pressed black cloth. And the noise everybody made was so baffling that, in order to be heard, Julia herself was shouting. Finally Noble contrived to squirm round the obtrusive back, and protruded his strained face among all the flushed and laughing ones.

"Julia, I got to—" he began.

But this was just at the climax of a story that three people were telling at the same time, Julia being one of them, and he received little attention.

"Julia," he said hoarsely; "I got something I want to *tell* you about—"

He raised his voice: "Julia, come on! Let's go out on the *porch*!"

Nobody even knew that he was there. Nevertheless, the tall and solid Clairdyce was conscious of him, but only, it proved, as one is conscious of something to rest upon. His elbow, a little elevated, was at the height of Noble's shoulder, and this heavy elbow, without its owner's direct or active cognizance, found for itself a comfortable support. Then, as the story reached its conclusion, this old Clairdyce joined the general mirth so heartily as to find himself quite overcome, and he allowed most of his weight to depend upon the supported elbow. Noble sank like feathers.

"Here! What you doin'?" he said hotly. "I'll thank you to keep off o' me!"

Old Baldy recovered his balance without being aware what had threatened it, while his elbow, apparently of its own volition, groped for its former pedestal. Noble evaded it, and pushed forward.

"Julia," he said. "I *got* to say some—"

But the accursed music began again, and horn-rimmed Newland Sanders already had his arm about her waist. They disappeared into the ruck of dancers.

"Well, by George!" said Noble. "By George, I'm goin' to *do* something!"

CHAPTER TWELVE

He went outdoors and smoked Orduma cigarettes, one after the other. Dances and intermissions succeeded each other but Noble had "enough of *that*, for one while!" So he muttered.

And remembering how Julia had told him that he was killing himself with cigarettes, "All right," he said now, as he bitterly lighted his fifth at the spark of the fourth;—"I hope I will!"

"Lot o' difference it'd make!" he said, as he lighted the eighth of a series that must, all told, have contained nearly as much tobacco as a cigar. And, leaning back against the trunk of one of the big old walnut trees in the yard, he gazed toward the house, where the open window nearest him splashed with colour like a bright and crowded aquarium. "To *her*, anyway!" he added, with a slight remorse, remembering that his mother had frequently shown him evidences of affection.

Yes, his mother would care, and his father and sisters would be upset, but Julia—when the friends of the family were asked to walk by for a last look, would she be one? What optimism remained to him presented a sketch of Julia, in black, borne from the room in the arms of girl friends who tried in vain to hush her; but he was unable to give this more hopeful fragment an air of great reality. Much more probably, when word came to her that he had smoked himself to death, she would be a bride, dancing at Niagara Falls with her bald old husband—and she would only laugh and pause to toss a faded rose out of the window, and then go right on dancing. But perhaps, some day, when tears had taught her the real meaning of life with such a man—

"You—*wow*!"

Noble jumped. From the darkness of the yard beside the house there came a grievous howl, distressful to the spinal marrow, a sound of animal pain. It was repeated even more passionately, and another voice was also heard, one both hoarsely bass and falsetto in the articulation of a single syllable. "*Ouch!*" There were sounds of violent scuffing, and the bass-falsetto voice cried: "What's that you *stuck* me with?" and another: "Drag her! Drag her back by her feet!"

These alarms came from the almost impenetrable shadows of the small orchard beside the house; and from the same quarter was heard the repeated contact of a heavy body, seemingly wooden or metallic, with the ground; but high over this there rose a shrieking: "Help! Help! Oh, *hay*-yulp!" This voice was girlish. "Hay-*yulp*!"

Noble dashed into the orchard, and at once fell prostrate upon what seemed a log, but proved to be a large and solidly packed ice-cream freezer lying on its side.

Dark forms scrambled over the fence and vanished, but as Noble got to his feet he was joined by a dim and smallish figure in white—though more light would have disclosed a pink sash girdling its middle. It was the figure of Miss Florence Atwater, seething with furious agitations.

"Vile thieves!" she panted.

"Who?" Noble asked, brushing at his knees, while Florence made some really necessary adjustments of her own attire. "Who were they?"

"It was my own cousin, Herbert, and that nasty little Henry Rooter and their gang. Herbert thinks he hass to act perfectly horrable all the time, now his voice is changing!" said Florence, her emotion not abated. "Tried to steal this whole ice-cream freezer off the back porch and sneak it over the fence and eat it! I stuck a pretty long pin in Herbert and two more of 'em, every bit as far as it would go." And in the extremity of her indignation, she added: "The dirty robbers!"

"Did they hurt you?"

"You bet your life they didn't!" the child responded. "Tried to drag me back to the house! By the feet! I guess I gave 'em enough o' *that*!"

Then, tugging the prostrate freezer into an upright position, she exclaimed darkly: "I expect I gave ole Mister Herbert and some of the others of 'em just a few kicks they won't be in such a hurry to forget!" And in spite of his own gloomy condition, Noble was able, upon thinking over matters, to spare some commiseration for Herbert and his friend, that nasty little Henry Rooter and their gang. They seemed to have been at a disadvantage.

"I suppose I'd better carry the freezer back to the kitchen porch," he said. "Somebody may want it."

"'Somebody'!" Florence exclaimed. "Why, there's only two of these big freezers, and if I hadn't happened to suspeck somep'n and be layin' for those vile thieves, half the party wouldn't get *any*!" And as an afterthought, when Noble had pantingly restored the heavy freezer to its place by the kitchen door, she said: "Or else they'd had to have such little saucers of it nobody would of been any way *like* satisfied, and prob'ly all the fam'ly that's here assisting would of had to go without any at all. That'd 'a' been the worst of it!"

She opened the kitchen door, and to those within explained loudly what dangers had been averted, directing that both freezers be placed indoors under guard; then she rejoined Noble, who was walking slowly back to the front yard.

"I guess it's pretty lucky you happened to be hangin' around out here," she said. "I guess that's about the luckiest thing ever happened to me. The way it looks to me, I guess you saved my life. If you hadn't chased 'em away, I wouldn't been a bit surprised if that gang would killed me!"

"Oh, no!" said Noble. "They wouldn't—"

"You don't know 'em like I do," the romantic child assured him. "I know that gang pretty well, and I wouldn't been a bit surprised. I wouldn't been!"

"But—"

She tossed her head, signifying recklessness.

"Guess 'twouldn't make much difference to anybody particular, whether they did or not," said this strange Florence.

Noble regarded her with astonishment; they had reached the front yard, and paused under the trees where the darkness was mitigated by the light from the shining windows. "Why, you oughtn't to talk that way, Florence," he said. "Think of your mamma and papa and your—and your Aunt Julia."

She tossed her head again. "Pooh! They'd all of 'em just say: 'Good ribbons to bad rubbish,' I guess!" However, she seemed far from despondent about this; in fact, she was naturally pleased with her position as a young girl saved from the power of ruffians by a rescuer who was her Very Ideal. "I bet if I died, they wouldn't even have a funeral," she said cheerfully. "They'd proba'ly just leave me lay."

The curiosities of the human mind are found not in high adventure: they are everywhere in the commonplace. Never for a moment did it strike Noble Dill that Florence's turn to the morbid bore any resemblance to his recent visions of his own funeral. He failed to perceive that the two phenomena were produced out of the same laboratory jar and were probably largely chemical, at that.

"Why, Florence!" he exclaimed. "That's a dreadful way to feel. I'm sure your—your Aunt Julia loves you."

"Oh, well," Florence returned lightly;—"maybe she does. I don't care whether she does or not." And now she made a deduction, the profundity of which his condition made him unable to perceive. "It makes less difference to anybody whether their aunts love 'em or not than whether pretty near anybody else at all does."

"But not your Aunt *Julia*" he urged. "Your Aunt *Julia*—"

"I don't care whether she does than any other aunt I got," said Florence. "All of 'em's just aunts, and that's all there is to it."

"But, Florence, your Aunt *Julia*—"

"She's nothin' in the world but my *aunt*," Florence insisted, and her emphasis showed that she was trying hard to make him understand. "She's just the same as all of 'em. I don't get anything more from her than I do from any the rest of 'em."

Her auditor was dumfounded, but not by Florence's morals. The cold-blooded calculation upon which her family affections seemed to be founded, this aboriginal straightforwardness of hers, passed over him. What shocked him was her appearing to see Julia as all of a piece with a general lot of ordinary aunts. Helplessly, he muttered again:

"But your Aunt *Julia*—"

"There she is now," said Florence, pointing to the window nearest them. "They've stopped dancing for a while so's that ole Mister Clairdyce can get a chance to sing somep'n. Mamma told me he was goin' to."

Dashing chords sounded from a piano invisible to Noble and

his companion; the windows exhibited groups of deferentially expectant young people; and then a powerful barytone began a love song. From the yard the singer could not be seen, but Julia could be: she stood in the demurest attitude; and no one needed to behold the vocalist to know that the scoundrel was looking pointedly and romantically at her.

"Dee-urra-face that holds soswee tasmile for me,
Wairyew nah tmine how darrrk the worrrl dwooed be!"

To Noble, suffering at every pore, this was less a song than a bellowing; and in truth the confident Mr. Clairdyce did "let his voice out," for he was seldom more exhilarated than when he shook the ceiling. The volume of sound he released upon his climaxes was impressive, and the way he slid up to them had a great effect, not indoors alone, but upon Florence, enraptured out under the trees.

"Oh, isn't it be-*you*-tiful!" she murmured.

Her humid eyes were fixed upon Noble, who was unconscious of the honour. Florence was susceptible to anything purporting to be music, and this song moved her. Throughout its delivery from Mr. Clairdyce's unseen chest, her large eyes dwelt upon Noble, and it is not at all impossible that she was applying the tender words to him, just as the vehement Clairdyce was patently addressing them to Julia. On he sang, while Noble, staring glassily at the demure lady, made a picture of himself leaping unexpectedly through the window, striding to the noisy barytone, striking him down, and after stamping on him several times, explaining: "There! That's for your insolence to our hostess!" But he did not actually permit himself these solaces; he only clenched and unclenched his fingers several times, and continued to listen.

"Geev a-mee yewr ra-smile,
The luv va-ligh TIN yew rise,
Life cooed not hold a fairrerr paradise.
Geev a-mee the righ to luv va-yew all the wile,

My worrlda for AIV-vorr,
The sunshigh NUV vyewr-ra-smile!"

The conclusion was thunderous, and as a great noise under such circumstances is an automatic stimulant of enthusiasm, the applause was thunderous too. Several girls were unable to subdue their outcries of "Charming!" and "*Won*-derf'l!"—not even after Mr. Clairdyce had begun to sing the same song as an encore.

When this was concluded, a sigh, long and deep, was heard under the trees. It came from Florence. Her eyes, wanly gleaming, like young oysters in the faint light, were still fixed on Noble; and there can be little doubt that just now there was at least one person in the world, besides his mother, who saw him in a glamour as something rare, obs, exquisite, and elegant. "I think that was the most be-*you*-tiful thing I ever heard!" she said; and then, noting a stir within the house, she became practical. "They're starting refreshments," she said. "We better hurry in, Mr. Dill, so's to get good places. Thanks to me, there's plenty to go round."

She moved toward the house, but, observing that he did not accompany her, paused and looked back. "Aren't you goin' to come in, Mr. Dill?"

"I guess not. Don't tell any one I'm out here."

"I won't. But aren't you goin' to come in for—"

He shook his head. "No, I'm going to wait out here a while longer."

"But," she said, "it's *refreshments!*"

"I don't want any. I—I'm going to smoke some more, instead."

She looked at him wistfully, then even more wistfully toward the house. Evidently she was of a divided mind: her feeling for Noble fought with her feeling for "refreshments." Such a struggle could not endure for long: a whiff of coffee conjured her nose, and a sound of clinking china witched her ear. "Well," she said, "I guess I ought to have some nourishment," and betook herself hurriedly into the house.

Noble lit another Orduma. He would follow the line of conduct he had marked out for himself: he would not take his place by Julia for the supper interval—perhaps that breach of etiquette would "show" her. He could see her no longer—she had moved out of range—but he imagined her, asking everywhere: "Hasn't *any* one seen Mr. Dill?" And he thought of her as biting her lip nervously, perhaps, and replying absently to sallies and quips—perhaps even having to run upstairs to her own room to dash something sparkling from her eyes, and, maybe, to look angrily in her glass for an instant and exclaim, "Fool!" For Julia was proud, and not used to be treated in this way.

He felt the least bit soothed, and, lightly flicking the ash from his Orduma with his little finger, an act indicating some measure of restored composure, he strolled to the other side of the house and brought other fields of vision into view through other windows. Abruptly his stroll came to an end.

There sat Julia, flushed and joyous, finishing her supper in company with old Baldy Clairdyce, Newland Sanders, George Plum, seven or eight other young gentlemen, and some inconsidered adhering girls—the horrible barytone sitting closest of all to Julia. Moreover, upon that very moment the orchestra, in the hall beyond, thought fit to pay the recent vocalist a sickening compliment, and began to play "The Sunshine of Your Smile."

Thereupon, with Julia herself first taking up the air in a dulcet soprano, all of the party, including the people in the other rooms, sang the dreadful song in chorus, the beaming Clairdyce exerting such demoniac power as to be heard tremendously over all other voices. He had risen for this effort, and to Noble, below the window, everything in his mouth was visible.

The lone listener had a bitter thought, though it was a longing, rather than a thought. For the first time in his life he wished that he had adopted the profession of dentistry.

> "Geev a-mee the righ to luv va-yew ALL the wile,
> My worrrlda for AIV-vorr,
> The sunshigh NUV vyewr-ra-smile!"

The musicians swung into dance music; old Baldy closed the exhibition with an operatic gesture (for which alone, if for nothing else, at least one watcher thought the showy gentle-man deserved hanging), and this odious gesture concluded with a seizure of Julia's hand. She sprang up eagerly; he whirled her away, and the whole place fluctuated in the dance once more.

"Well, now," said Noble, between his teeth—"now, I *am* goin' to do something!"

He turned his back upon that painful house, walked out to the front gate, opened it, passed through, and looked southward. Not quite two blocks away there shone the lights of a corner drug store, still open to custom though the hour was nearing midnight. He walked straight to the door of this place, which stood ajar, but paused before entering, and looked long and nervously at the middle-aged proprietor who was unconscious of his regard, and lounged in a chair, drowsily stroking a cat upon his lap. Noble walked in.

"Good evening," said the proprietor, rising and brushing himself languidly. "Cat hairs," he said apologetically. "Sheddin', I reckon." Then, as he went behind the counter, he inquired: "How's the party goin' off?"

"It's—it's—" Noble hesitated. "I stepped in to—to—"

The druggist opened a glass case. "Aw right," he said, blinking, and tossed upon the counter a package of Orduma cigarettes. "Old Atwater'd have convulsions, I reckon," he remarked, "if he had to lay awake and listen to all that noise. Price ain't changed," he added, referring humorously to the purchase he mistakenly supposed Noble wished to make. "F'teen cents, same as yesterday and the day before."

Noble placed the sum upon the counter. "I—I was thinking—" He gulped.

"Huh?" said the druggist placidly, for he was too sleepy to perceive the strangeness of his customer's manner.

Noble lighted an Orduma with an unsteady hand, leaned upon the counter, and inquired in a voice that he strove to make casual: "Is—is the soda fountain still running this late?"

"Sure."

"I didn't know," said Noble. "I suppose you have more calls for soda water than you do for—for—for real liquor?"

The druggist laughed. "Funny thing: I reckon we don't have more'n half the calls for real liquor than what we used to before we went dry."

Noble breathed deeply. "I s'pose you probably sell quite a good deal of it though, at that. By the glass, I mean—such as a glass of something kind of strong—like—like whiskey. That is, I sort of supposed so. I mean I thought I'd ask you about this."

"No," said the druggist, yawning. "It never did pay well—not on this corner, anyhow. Once there used to be a little money in it, but not much." He roused himself somewhat. "Well, it's about twelve. Anything you wanted 'cept them Ordumas before I close up?"

Noble gulped again. He had grown pale. "*I* want—" he said

abruptly, then his heart seemed to fail him. "I want a glass of—" Once more he stopped and swallowed. His shoulders drooped, and he walked across to the soda fountain. "Well," he said, "I'll take a chocolate sundae."

The thought of going back to Julia's party was unendurable, yet a return was necessary on account of his new hat, the abandonment of which he did not for a moment consider. But about half way, as he walked slowly along, he noticed an old horse-block at the curbstone, and sat down there. He could hear the music at Julia's, sometimes loud and close at hand, sometimes seeming to be almost a mile away. "All right!" he said, so bitter had he grown. "Dance! Go on and *dance!*"

... When finally he reentered Julia's gate, he shuffled up the walk, his head drooping, and ascended the steps and crossed the veranda and the threshold of the front door in the same manner.

Julia stood before him.

"Noble *Dill!*" she exclaimed.

As for Noble, his dry throat refused its office; he felt that he might never be able to speak to Julia again, even if he tried.

"Where in the world have you been all evening?" she cried.

"Why, Jew-Julia!" he quavered. "Did you notice that I was gone?"

"Did I 'notice'!" she said. "You never came near me all evening after the first dance! Not even at supper!"

"You wouldn't—you didn't—" he faltered. "You wouldn't do anything all evening except dance with that old Clairdyce and listen to him trying to sing."

But Julia would let no one suffer if she could help it; and she could always help Noble. She made her eyes mysterious and used a voice of honey and roses. "You don't think I'd *rather* have danced with him, do you, Noble?"

Immediately sparks seemed to crackle about his head. He started.

"What?" he said.

The scent of heliotrope enveloped him; she laughed her silver harp-strings laugh, and lifted her arms toward the dazzled young man. "It's the last dance," she said. "Don't you want to dance it with me?"

Then to the spectators it seemed that Noble Dill went hopping upon a waxed floor and upon Julia's little slippers; he was bumped and bumping everywhere; but in reality he floated in Elysian ether, immeasurably distant from earth, his hand just touching the bodice of an angelic doll.

Then, on his way home, a little later, with his new hat on the back of his head, his stick swinging from his hand, and a semi-fragrant Orduma between his lips, his condition was precisely as sweet as the condition in which he had walked to the party.

No echoes of "The Sunshine of Your Smile" cursed his memory—that lover's little memory fresh washed in heliotrope—and when his mother came to his door, after he got home, and asked him if he'd had "a nice time at the party," he said:

"Just glorious!" and believed it.

CHAPTER THIRTEEN

It was a pretty morning, two weeks after Julia's Dance; and blue and lavender shadows, frayed with mid-summer sunshine, waggled gayly across the grass beneath the trees of the tiny orchard, but trembled with timidity as they hurried over the abnormal surfaces of Mrs. Silver as she sat upon the steps of the "back porch." Her right hand held in security one end of a leather leash; the other end of the leash was fastened to a new collar about the neck of an odd and fascinating dog. Seated upon the brick walk at her feet, he was regarding her with a gravity that seemed to discomfort her. She was unable to meet his gaze, and constantly averted her own whenever it furtively descended to his. In fact, her expression and manner were singular, denoting embarrassment, personal hatred, and a subtle bedazzlement. She could not look at him, yet could not keep herself from looking at him. There was something here that arose out of the depths of natural character; it was intrinsic in the two personalities, that is to say; and was in addition to the bitterness consequent upon a public experience, just past, which had been brought upon Mrs. Silver partly by the dog's appearance (in particular the style and colour of his hair) and partly by his unprecedented actions in her company upon the highway.

She addressed him angrily, yet with a profound uneasiness.

"Dog!" she said. "You ain't feelin' as skittish as whut you did, li'l while ago, is you? My glory! I dess would like to lay my han' to you' hide once, Mister! I take an' lam you this livin' minute if I right sho' you wouldn't take an' bite me."

She jerked the leash vindictively, upon which the dog at once "sat up" on his haunches, put his forepaws together above his nose, in an attitude of prayer, and looked at her inscrutably from under the great bang of hair that fell like a black chrysanthemum over his forehead. Beneath this woolly lambrequin his eyes were visible as two garnet sparks of which the coloured woman was only too nervously aware. She gasped.

"Look-a-here, dog, who's went an' ast you to take an' pray fer 'em?"

He remained motionless and devout.

"My goo'niss!" she said to him. "If you goin' keep on thisaway whut you *is* been, I'm goin' to up an' go way from here, ri' now!" Then she said a remarkable thing. "Listen here, Mister! I ain' never los' no gran' child, an' I ain' goin' 'dop' no stranger fer one, neither!"

The explanation rests upon the looks and manners of him whom she addressed. This dog was of a kind at the top of dog kingdoms. His size was neither insignificant nor great; probably his weight would have been between a fourth and a third of a St. Bernard's. He had the finest head for adroit thinking that is known among dogs; and he had an athletic body, the forepart muffled and lost in a mass of corded black fleece, but the rest of him sharply clipped from the chest aft; and his trim, slim legs were clipped, though tufts were left at his ankles, and at the tip of his short tail, with two upon his hips, like fanciful buttons of an imaginary jacket; for thus have such dogs been clipped to a fashion proper and comfortable for them ever since (and no doubt long before) an Imperial Roman sculptor so chiselled one in bas-relief. In brief, this dog, who caused Kitty Silver so much disquietude, as she sat upon the back steps at Mr. Atwater's, belonged to that species of which no Frenchman ever sees a specimen without smiling and murmuring: "*Caniche!*" He was that golden-hearted little clown of all the world, a French Poodle.

To arrive at what underlay Mrs. Silver's declaration that she had never lost a grandchild and had no intention of adopting a stranger in the place of one, it should be first understood that in many respects she was a civilized person. The quality of savagery, barbarism, or civilization in a tribe may be tested by the relations it characteristically maintains with domestic animals; and tribes that eat dogs are often inferior to those inclined to ceremonial cannibalism. Likewise, the civilization, barbarism, or savagery of an individual may be estimated by the same test, which sometimes gives us evidence of sporadic reversions to mud. Such reversions are the stomach priests: whatever does not minister to their own bodily inwards is a "parasite." Dogs are "parasites"; they should not live, because to fat and eat them somehow appears uncongenial. "Kill Dogs and Feed Pigs," they write to the papers, and, with a Velasquez available, would burn it rather than go chilly. "Kill dogs, feed pigs, and let *me* eat the pigs!" they cry, even under no great stress, these stern economists who have not noticed how wasteful the Creator is proved to be if He made themselves. They take the strictly intestinal view of life. It is not intelligent; parasite bacilli will get them in the end.

Mrs. Silver was not of these. True, she sometimes professed herself averse to all "animals," but this meant nothing more than her unwillingness to have her work increased by their introduction into the Atwater household. No; the appearance of the dog had stirred something queer and fundamental within her. All coloured people look startled the first time they see a French Poodle, but there is a difference. Most coloured men do not really worry much about being coloured, but many coloured women do. In the expression of a coloured man, when he looks at a black and woolly French Poodle, there is something fonder and more indulgent than there is in the expression of a coloured woman when she looks at one. In fact, when some coloured women see a French Poodle they have the air of being insulted.

Now, when Kitty Silver had first set eyes on this poodle, an hour earlier, she looked, and plainly was, dumfounded. Never in her life had she seen a creature so black, so incredibly black, or with hair so kinky, so incredibly kinky. Julia had not observed Mrs. Silver closely nor paused to wonder what thoughts were rousing in her mind, but bade her take the poodle forth for exercise outdoors and keep him strictly upon the leash. Without protest, though wearing a unique expression, Kitty obeyed; she walked round the block with this mystifying dog; and during the promenade had taken place the episode that so upset her nerves.

She had given a little jerk to the leash, speaking sharply to the poodle in reproach for some lingering near a wonderful sidewalk smell, imperceptible to any one except himself. Instantly the creature rose and walked beside her on his hind legs. He continued to parade in this manner, rapidly, but nevertheless as if casually, without any apparent inconvenience; and Mrs. Silver, never having seen a dog do such a thing before, for more than a yard or so, and then only under the pressure of many inducements, was unfavourably impressed. In fact, she had definitely a symptom of M. Maeterlinck's awed feeling when he found himself left alone with the talking horses: "With *whom* was she?"

"Look-a-here, dog!" she said breathlessly. "Who you tryin' to skeer? *You* ain't no person!"

And then a blow fell. It came from an elderly but ever undignified woman of her own race, who paused, across the street, and stood teetering from side to side in joyful agitation, as she watched the approach of Mrs. Silver with her woolly little companion beside her. When this smaller silhouette in ink suddenly walked upright, the observer's mouth fell open, and there was reason to hope that it might remain so, in silence, especially as several other pedestrians had stopped to watch the poodle's uncalled-for exhibition. But all at once the elderly rowdy saw fit to become uproarious.

"Hoopsee!" she shouted. "Oooh, *Gran'ma!*"

*   *   *   *   *

And so, when the poodle "sat up," unbid, to pray, while Kitty Silver rested upon the back steps, on her return from the excursion, she fiercely informed him that she had never lost a grandchild and that she would not adopt a stranger in place of one; her implication being that he, a stranger, had been suggested for the position and considered himself eligible for it.

He continued to pray, not relaxing a hair.

"Listen to me, dog," said Kitty Silver. "Is you a dog, or isn't you a dog? Whut *is* you, anyway?"

But immediately she withdrew the question. "I ain't astin' you!" she exclaimed superstitiously. "If you isn't no dog, don't you take an' tell me whut you is: you take an' keep it to you'se'f, 'cause I don' want to listen to it!"

For the garnet eyes beneath the great black chrysanthemum indeed seemed to hint that their owner was about to use human language in a human voice. Instead, however, he appeared to be content with his little exhibition, allowed his forepaws to return to the ground, and looked at her with his head wistfully tilted to one side. This reassured her and even somewhat won her. There stirred within her that curious sense of relationship evoked from the first by his suggestive appearance; fondness was being born, and an admiration that was in a way a form of Narcissism. She addressed him in a mollified voice:

"Whut you want now? Don' tell me you' hungry, 'cause you awready done et two dog biskit an' big saucer milk. Whut you stick you' ole black face crossways at *me* fer, honey?"

But just then the dog rose to look pointedly toward the corner of the house. "Somebody's coming," he meant.

"Who you spectin', li'l dog?" Mrs. Silver inquired.

Florence and Herbert came round the house, Herbert trifling with a tennis ball and carrying a racket under his arm. Florence was peeling an orange.

"For Heavenses' sakes!" Florence cried. "Kitty Silver, where on earth'd this dog come from?"

"B'long you' Aunt Julia."

"When'd she get him?"

"Dess to-day."

"Who gave him to her?"

"She ain't sayin'."

"You mean she won't tell?"

"She ain't sayin'," Kitty Silver repeated. "I ast her. I say, I say: 'Miss Julia, ma'am,' I say, 'Miss Julia, ma'am, who ever sen' you sech a unlandish-lookin' dog?' I say. All she say when I ast her: 'Nemmine!' she say, dess thataway. 'Nemmine!' she say. I reckon she ain't goin' tell nobody who give her this dog."

"He's certainly a mighty queer-lookin' dog," said Herbert. "I've seen a few like that, but I can't remember where. What kind is he, Kitty Silver?"

"Miss Julia tell me he a poogle dog."

"A poodle," Florence corrected her, and then turned to Herbert in supercilious astonishment. "A French Poodle! My goodness! I should think you were old enough to know that much, anyway—goin' on fourteen years old!"

"Well, I did know it," he declared. "I kind of knew it, anyhow; but I sort of forgot it for once. Do you know if he bites, Kitty Silver?"

She was noncommittal. "He ain't bit nobody yit."

"I don't believe he'll bite," said Florence. "I bet he likes me. He looks like he was taking a fancy to me, Kitty Silver. What's his name?"

"Gammire."

"What?"

"Gammire."

"What a funny name! Are you sure, Kitty Silver?"

"Gammire whut you' Aunt Julia tole *me*," Mrs. Silver insisted. "You kin go on in the house an' ast her; she'll tell you the same."

"Well, anyway, I'm not afraid of him," said Florence; and she stepped closer to the poodle, extending her hand to caress him. Then she shouted as the dog, at her gesture, rose to his hind legs, and, as far as the leash permitted, walked forward to meet her. She flung her arms about him rapturously.

"Oh, the lovely thing!" she cried. "He walks on his hind legs! Why, he's crazy about me!"

"Let him go," said Herbert. "I bet he don't like you any more than he does anybody else. Leave go of him, and I bet he shows he likes me better than he does you."

But when Florence released him, Gammire caressed them both impartially. He leaped upon one, then upon the other, and then upon Kitty Silver with a cordiality that almost unseated her.

"Let him off the leash," Florence cried. "He won't run away, 'cause the gates are shut. Let him loose and see what he'll do."

Mrs. Silver snapped the catch of the leash, and Gammire departed in the likeness of a ragged black streak. With his large and eccentric ears flapping back in the wind and his afterpart hunched in, he ran round and round the little orchard like a dog gone wild. Altogether a comedian, when he heard children shrieking with laughter, he circled the more wildly; then all upon an unexpected instant came to a dead halt, facing his audience, his nose on the ground between his two forepaws, his hindquarters high and unstooping. And, seeing they laughed at this, too, he gave them enough of it, then came back to Kitty Silver and sat by her feet, a spiral of pink tongue hanging from a wide-open mouth roofed with black.

Florence resumed the peeling of her orange.

"Who do you *think* gave Gammire to Aunt Julia?" she asked.

"I ain't stedyin' about it."

"Yes, but who do you *guess*?"

"I ain't—"

"Well, but if you had to be burned to death or guess somebody, who would you guess?"

"I haf to git burn' up," said Kitty Silver. "Ev'y las' caller whut comes here *is* give her some doggone animal awready. Mista Sammerses, he give her them two Berjum cats, an' ole Mister Ridgways whut los' his wife, he give you' Aunt Julia them two canaries that tuck an' hopped out the cage an' then out the window, las' week, one day, when you' grampaw was alone in the room with 'em; an' Mista George Plummers, he give her that Airydale dog you' grampaw tuck an' give to the milkman; an' Mista Ushers, he give her them two pups whut you' grampaw tuck an' skeer off the place soon as he laid eyes on 'em, an' thishere Mista Clairidge, he give her that ole live allagatuh from Florida whut I foun' lookin' at me over the aidge o' my kitchen sink—ugly ole thing!—an' you' grampaw tuck an' give it to the greenhouse man. Ain't none nem ge'lmun goin' try an' give her no *mo'* animals, I bet! So how anybody goin' guess who sen' her thishere Gammire? Nobody lef' whut ain't awready sen' her one an' had the gift spile."

"Yes, there is," said Florence.

"Who?"

"Noble Dill."

"That there li'l young Mista Dills?" Kitty Silver cried. "Listen me! Thishere dog 'spensive dog."

"I don't care; I bet Noble Dill gave him to her."

Mrs. Silver hooted. "Go way! That there young li'l Mista Dills, he ain' nev' did show no class, no way nor no time. He be hunderd year ole b'fo' you see him in autamobile whut b'long to him. Look at a way some nem fine big rich men like Mista Clairidge an' Mista Ridgways take an' th'ow they money aroun'! New necktie ev'y time you see 'em; new straw hat right spang the firs' warm day. Ring do' bell. I say, I say: 'Walk right in, Mista Ridgways.' Slip me dollah bill dess like that! Mista Sammerses an' Mista Plummers, an' some nem others, they all show class. Look Mista Sammerses' spectickles made turtle back; fancy turtle, too. I ast Miss Julia; she tell me they fancy turtle. Gol' rim spectickles ain't in it; no ma'am! Mista Sammerses' spectickles—jes' them rims on his spectickles alone—I bet they cos' mo'n all whut thishere young li'l Mista Dills got on him from his toes up an' his skin out. I bet Mista Plummers th'ow mo' money aroun' dess fer gittin' his pants press' than whut Mista Dills afford to spen' to buy his'n in the firs' place! He lose his struggle, 'cause you' Aunt Julia, she out fer the big class. Thishere Gammire, he dog cos' money; he show class same you' Aunt Julia. Ain't neither one of 'em got to waste they time on nobody whut can't show no mo' class than thishere li'l young dish-cumbobbery Mista Dills!"

"I don't care," Florence said stubbornly. "He could of saved up and saved up, and if he saved up long enough he could of got enough money to buy a dog like Gammire, because you can get money enough for anything if you're willing to save up long enough. Anyway, I bet he's the one gave him to her."

Herbert joined Kitty Silver in laughter. "Florence is always talkin' about Noble Dill," he said. "She's sort of crazy, anyway, though."

"It runs in the family," Florence retorted, automatically. "I caught it from my cousins. Anyhow, I don't think there's a single one of any that wants to marry Aunt Julia that's got the slightest co'parison to Noble Dill. I admire him because he's so uncouth."

"He so who?" Kitty Silver inquired.

"Uncouth."

"Yes'm," said Mrs. Silver.

"It's in the ditchanary," Florence explained. "It means rare, elegant, exquisite, obs, unknown, and a whole lot else."

"It does not," Herbert interposed. "It means kind of countrified."

"You go look in the ditchanary," his cousin said severely. "Then, maybe, you'll know what you're talkin' about just for once. Anyhow, I *do* like Noble Dill, and I bet so does Aunt Julia."

Kitty Silver shook her head. "He lose his struggle, honey! Miss Julia, she out fer the big class. She ain't stedyin' about him 'cept maybe dess to let him run her erran's. She treat 'em all mighty nice, 'cause the mo' come shovin' an' pushin' each other aroun', class or no class, why, the mo' harder that big class got to work to git her—an' the mo' she got after her the mo' keeps a-comin'. But thishere young li'l Mista Dills, I kine o' got strong notion he liable not come no mo' 'tall!" Her tone had become one of reminiscent amusement, which culminated in a burst of laughter. "Whee!" she concluded. "After las' night, I reckon thishere Mista Dills better keep away from the place—yes'm!"

Florence looked thoughtful, and for the time said nothing. It was Herbert who asked: "Why'd Noble Dill better stay away from here?"

"You' grampaw," Mrs. Silver said, shaking her head. "You' grampaw!"

"What about grandpa?" said Herbert. "What'd he do last night?"

"'Do'? Oh, me!" Then Mrs. Silver uttered sounds like the lowing of kine, whereby she meant to indicate her inability to describe Mr. Atwater's performance. "Well, ma'am," she said, in the low and husky voice of simulated exhaustion, "all I got to say: you' grampaw beat hisse'f! He beat hisse'f!"

"How d'you mean? How could he—"

"He beat hisse'f! He dess out-talk hisse'f! No, ma'am; I done hear him many an' many an' many's the time, but las' night he beat hisse'f."

"What about?"

"Nothin' in the wide worl' but dess thishere young li'l Noble Dills whut we talkin' about this livin' minute."

"What started him?"

"Whut *start* him?" Mrs. Silver echoed with sudden loudness. "My goo'niss! He *b'en* started ev' since the very firs' time he ev' lay eyes on him prancin' up the front walk to call on Miss Julia. You' grampaw don' like none nem callers, but he everlas'n'ly did up an' take a true spite on thishere li'l Dills!"

"I mean," said Herbert, "what started him last night?"

"Them cigareets," said Kitty Silver. "Them cigareets whut thishere Noble Dills smoke whiles he settin' out on the front po'che callin' on you' Aunt Julia. You' grampaw mighty funny man about smellin'! You know's well's I do he don't even like the smell o' violet. Well, ma'am, if he can't stan' *violet*, how in the name o' misery he goin' stan' the smell nem cigareets thishere Dills smoke? I can't hardly stan' 'em myse'f. When he light one on the front po'che, she sif' all through the house, an' come slidin' right the whole way out to my kitchen, an' *bim*! she take me in the nose! You' grampaw awready tole Miss Julia time an' time again if that li'l Dills light dess one mo' on his front po'che he goin' to walk out there an' do some harm! Co'se she nev' tuck an' pay no 'tention, 'cause Miss Julia, she nev' pay no 'tention to nobody; an' she like caller have nice time—she ain' goin' tell 'em you' grampaw make such a fuss. 'Yes, 'deed, kine frien',' she say, she say, when they ast her: 'Miss Julia, ma'am,' they say, 'I like please strike a match fer to light my cigareet if you please, ma'am.' She say: 'Light as many as you please, kine frien',' she say, she say. She say: 'Smell o' cigareet dess deligh'ful li'l smell,' she say. 'Go 'head an' smoke all you kin stan',' she say, ''cause I want you injoy you'se'f when you pay call on me,' she say. Well, so thishere young li'l Dills settin' there puffin' an' blowin' his ches' out and in, an' feelin' all nice 'cause it about the firs' time this livin' summer he catch you' Aunt Julia alone to hisse'f fer while—an' all time the house dess fillin' up, an' draf' blowin' straight at you' grampaw whur he settin' in his liberry. Ma'am, he sen' me out an' tell her come in, he got message mighty important fer to speak to her. So she tell thishere Dills wait a minute, an' walk in the liberry. Oh, ladies!"

"What'd he say?" Herbert asked eagerly.

"He di'n' say nothin'," Mrs. Silver replied eloquently. "He hollered."

"What did he holler?"

"He want know di'n' he never tell her thishere Dills can't smoke no mo' cigareets on his property, an' di'n' he tell her he was'n' goin' allow him on the place if he did? He say she got to go back on the po'che an' run thishere li'l Dills off home. He say he give her fair choice; she kin run him off, or else he go on out and chase him away hisse'f. He claim li'l Dills ain' got no biznuss roun' callin' nowhere 't all, 'cause he on'y make about eighteen dollars a week an' ain't wuth it. He say—"

She was confirmed in this report by an indignant interruption from Florence. "That's just what he did say, the old thing! I heard him, myself, and if you care to ask *me*, I'll be glad to inform you that I think grandpa's conduck was simply insulting!"

"'Deed it were!" said Mrs. Silver. "An' dess whut he claim hisse'f he mean it fer! But you tell me, please, how you hear whut you' grampaw say? He mighty noisy, but you nev' could a-hear him plumb to whur you live."

"I wasn't home," said Florence. "I was over here."

"Then you mus' 'a' made you'se'f mighty skimpish, 'cause *I* ain't seen you!"

"Nobody saw me. I wasn't in the house," said Florence, "I was out in front."

"Whurbouts 'out in front'?"

"Well, I was sitting on the ground, up against the latticework of the front porch."

"Whut fur?"

"Well, it was dark," said Florence. "I just kind of wanted to see what might be going on."

"An' you hear all whut you' grampaw take on about an' ev'ything?"

"I should say so! You could of heard him *lots* farther than where I was."

"Lan' o' misery!" Kitty Silver cried. "If you done hear him whur you was, thishere li'l Dills mus' a-hear him *mighty* plain?"

"He did. How could he help it? He heard every word, and pretty soon he came down off the porch and stood a minute; then he went on out the gate, and I don't know whether he went home or not, because it was too dark to see. But he didn't come back."

"Yo' right he didn'!" exclaimed Mrs. Silver. "I reckon he got fo'thought 'nough fer that, anyhow! I bet he ain't nev' *goin'* come back neither. You' grampaw say he goin' be fix fer him, if he do."

"Yes, that was while he was standing there," said Florence ruefully. "He heard all that, too."

"Miss Julia, she s'picion' he done hear somep'm 'nother, I guess," Kitty Silver went on. "She shet the liberry do' right almos' on you' grampaw's nose, whiles he still a-rampin', an' she slip out on the po'che, an' take look 'roun'; then go on up to her own room. I 'uz up there, while after that, turn' down her bed; an' she injoyin' herse'f readin' book. She feel kine o' put out, I reckon, but she ain't stedyin' about no young li'l Dills. She want 'em all to have nice time an' like her, but she goin' lose this one, an' she got plenty to spare. She show too much class fer to fret about no Dills."

"I don't care," said Florence. "I think she ought to whether she does or not, because I bet he was feeling just awful. And I think grandpa behaved like an ole hoodlum."

"That'll do," Herbert admonished her sternly. "You show some respect for your relations, if you please."

But his loyalty to the Atwater family had a bad effect on Florence. "Oh, *will* I?" she returned promptly. "Well, then, if you care to inquire *my* opinion, I just politely think grandpa ought to be hanged."

"See here—"

But Florence and Kitty Silver interrupted him simultaneously.

"Look at *that*!" Florence cried.

"My name!" exclaimed Kitty Silver.

It was the strange taste of Gammire that so excited them. Florence had peeled her orange and divided it rather fairly into three parts, but the vehemence she exerted in speaking of her grandfather had caused her to drop one of these upon the ground. Gammire promptly ate it, "sat up" and adjusted his paws in prayer for more.

"Now you listen me!" said Kitty Silver. "I ain't see no dog eat orange in all my days, an' I ain't see nobody else whut see dog eat orange! No, ma'am, an' I ain't nev' hear o' nobody else whut ev' see nobody whut see dog eat orange!"

Herbert decided to be less impressed. "Oh, I've heard of dogs that'd eat apples," he said. "Yes, and watermelon and nuts and things." As he spoke he played with the tennis ball upon his racket, and concluded by striking the ball high into the air. Its course was not true; and it descended far over toward the orchard, where Herbert ran to catch it—but he was not quick enough. At the moment the ball left the racket Gammire abandoned his prayers: his eyes, like a careful fielder's, calculating and estimating, followed the swerve of the ball in the breeze, and when it fell he was on the correct spot. He caught it.

Herbert shouted. "He caught it on the *fly*! It must have been an accident. Here—" And he struck the ball into the air again. It went high—twice as high as the house—and again Gammire "judged" it; continuously shifting his position, his careful eyes never leaving the little white globe, until just before the last instant of its descent he was motionless beneath it. He caught it again, and Herbert whooped.

Gammire brought the ball to him and invited him to proceed with the game. That there might be no mistaking his desire, Gammire "sat up" and prayed; nor did he find Herbert anything loth. Out of nine chances Gammire "muffed" the ball only twice, both times excusably, and Florence once more flung her arms about the willing performer.

"*Who* do you s'pose trained this wonderful, darling doggie?" she cried.

Mrs. Silver shook her marvelling head. "He mus' 'a' *come* thataway," she said. "I bet nobody 't all ain' train him; he do whut he want to hisse'f. That Gammire don' ast nobody to train him."

"Oh, goodness!" Florence said, with sudden despondency. "It's awful!"

"Whut is?"

"To think of as lovely a dog as this having to face grandpa!"

"'Face' him!" Kitty Silver echoed forebodingly. "I reckon you' grampaw do mo'n dess 'face' him."

"That's what I mean," Florence explained. "I expect he's just brute enough to drive him off."

"Yes'm," said Mrs. Silver. "He git madder ev'y time somebody sen' her new pet. You' grampaw mighty nervous man, an' everlas'n'ly do hate animals."

"He hasn't seen Gammire, has he?"

"Don't look like it, do it?" said Kitty Silver. "Dog here yit."

"Well, then I—" Florence paused, glancing at Herbert, for she had just been visited by a pleasant idea and had no wish to share it with him. "Is Aunt Julia in the house?"

"She were, li'l while ago."

"I want to see her about somep'n I ought to see her about," said Florence. "I'll be out in a minute."

CHAPTER FOURTEEN

She ran into the house, and found Julia seated at a slim-legged desk, writing a note.

"Aunt Julia, it's about Gammire."

"Gamin."

"What?"

"His name is Gamin."

"Kitty Silver says his name's Gammire."

"Yes," said Julia. "She would. His name is Gamin, though. He's a little Parisian rascal, and his name is Gamin."

"Well, Aunt Julia, I'd rather call him Gammire. How much did he cost?"

"I don't know; he was brought to me only this morning, and I haven't asked yet."

"But I thought somebody gave him to you."

"Yes; somebody did."

"Well, I mean," said Florence, "how much did the person that gave him to you pay for him?"

Julia sighed. "I just explained, I haven't had a chance to ask."

Florence looked hurt. "I don't mean you *would* ask 'em right out. I just meant: Wouldn't you be liable to kind of hint around an' give 'em a chance to tell you how much it was? You know perfeckly well it's the way most the fam'ly do when they give each other somep'n pretty expensive, Christmas or birthdays, and I thought proba'ly you'd—"

"No. I shouldn't be surprised, Florence, if nobody *ever* got to know how much Gamin cost."

"Well—" Florence said, and decided to approach her purpose on a new tack. "Who was it trained him?"

"I understand that the person who gave him to me has played with him at times during the few days he's been keeping him, but hasn't 'trained' him particularly. French Poodles almost learn their own tricks if you give them a chance. It's natural to them; they love to be little clowns if you let them."

"But who was this person that gave him to you?"

Julia laughed. "It's a secret, Florence—like Gamin's price."

At this Florence looked piqued. "Well, I guess I got *some* manners!" she exclaimed. "I know as well as you do, Aunt Julia, there's no etiquette in coming right square out and asking how much it was when somebody goes and makes you a present. I'm certainly enough of a lady to keep my mouth shut when it's more polite to! But I don't see what harm there is in telling who it is that gives anybody a present."

"No harm at all," Julia murmured as she sealed the note she had written. Then she turned smilingly to face her niece. "Only I'm not going to."

"Well, then, Aunt Julia"—and now Florence came to her point—"what I wanted to know is just simply the plain and simple question: Will you give this dog Gammire to me?"

Julia leaned forward, laughing, and suddenly clapped her hands together, close to Florence's face. "No, I won't!" she cried. "There!"

The niece frowned, lines of anxiety appearing upon her forehead. "Well, why won't you?"

"I won't do it!"

"But, Aunt Julia, I think you ought to!"

"Why ought I to?"

"Because—" said Florence. "Well, it's necessary."

"Why?"

"Because you know as well as I do what's bound to happen to him!"

"What is?"

"Grandpa'll chase him off," said Florence. "He'll take after him the minute he lays eyes on him, and scare him to death—and then he'll get lost, and he won't be *anybody's* dog! I should think you'd just as lief he'd be my dog as have him chased all over town till a street car hits him or somep'n."

But Julia shook her head. "That hasn't happened yet."

"It *did* happen with every other one you ever had," Florence urged plaintively. "He chased 'em every last one off the place, and they never came back. You know perfectly well, Aunt Julia, grandpa's just bound to hate this dog, and you know just exactly how he'll act about him."

"No, I don't," said Julia. "Not just *exactly*."

"Well, anyway, you know he'll behave awful."

"It's probable," the aunt admitted.

"He always does," Florence continued. "He behaves awful about everything I ever heard about. He—"

"I'll go pretty far with you, Florence," Julia interposed, "but we'd better leave him a loophole. You know he's a constant attendant at church and contributes liberally to many good causes."

"Oh, you know what I mean! I mean he always acts horrable about anything pleasant. Of course I know he's a *good* man, and everything; I just mean the way he behaves is perfeckly disgusting. So what's the use your not givin' me this dog? You won't have him yourself as soon as grandpa comes home to lunch in an hour or so."

"Oh, yes, I will!"

"Grandpa hasn't already seen him, has he?"

"No."

"Then what makes you say—"

"He isn't coming home to lunch. He won't be home till five o'clock this afternoon."

"Well, then, about six you won't have any dog, and poor little Gammire'll get run over by an automobile some time this very evening!" Florence's voice became anguished in the stress of her appeal. "Aunt Julia, *won't* you give me this dog?"

Julia shook her head.

"Won't you, *please?*"

"No, dear."

"Aunt Julia, if it was Noble Dill gave you this dog—"

"Florence!" her aunt exclaimed. "What in the world makes you imagine such absurd things? Poor Mr. Dill!"

"Well, if it was, I think you ought to give Gammire to me because I *like* Noble Dill, and I—"

But here her aunt laughed again and looked at her with some curiosity. "You still do?" she asked. "What for?"

"Well," said Florence, swallowing, "he may be rather smallish for a man, but he's very uncouth and distingrished-looking, and I think he doesn't get to enjoy himself much. Grandpa talks about him so torrably and—and—" Here, such was the unexpected depth of her feeling that she choked, whereupon her aunt, overcome with laughter, but nevertheless somewhat touched, sprang up and threw two pretty arms about her charmingly.

"You *funny* Florence!" she cried.

"Then will you give me Gammire?" Florence asked instantly.

"No. We'll bring him in the house now, and you can stay for lunch."

Florence was imperfectly consoled, but she had a thought that brightened her a little.

"Well, there'll be an awful time when grandpa comes home this afternoon—but it certainly will be inter'sting!"

She proved a true prophet, at least to the extent that when Mr. Atwater opened his front gate that afternoon he was already in the presence of a deeply interested audience whose observation was unknown to him. Through the interstices of the lace curtains at an open window, the gaze of Julia and Florence was concentrated upon him in a manner that might have disquieted even so opinionated and peculiar a man as Mr. Atwater, had he been aware of it; and Herbert likewise watched him fixedly from an unseen outpost. Herbert had shown some recklessness, declaring loudly that he intended to lounge in full view; but when the well-known form of the ancestor was actually identified, coming up the street out of the distance, the descendant changed his mind. The good green earth ceased to seem secure; and Herbert climbed a tree. He surrounded himself with the deepest foliage; and beneath him some outlying foothills of Kitty Silver were visible, where she endeavoured to lurk in the concealment of a lilac bush.

Gammire was the only person in view. He sat just in the middle of the top step of the veranda, and his air was that of an endowed and settled institution. What passing traffic there was interested him but vaguely, not affecting the world to which he belonged—that world being this house and yard, of which he felt himself now, beyond all question, the official dog.

It had been a rather hard-working afternoon, for he had done everything suggested to him as well as a great many other things that he thought of himself. He had also made it clear that he had taken a fancy to everybody, but recognized Julia to be the head of the house and of his own universe; and though he was at the disposal of all her family and friends, he was at her disposal first. Whithersoever she went, there would he go also, unless she otherwise commanded. Just now she had withdrawn, closing the door, but he understood that she intended no permanent exclusion. Who was this newcomer at the gate?

The newcomer came to a halt, staring intolerantly. Then he advanced, slamming the gate behind him. "Get out o' here!" he said. "You get off the place!"

Gammire regarded him seriously, not moving, while Mr.

Atwater cast an eye about the lawn, seeming to search for something, and his gaze, thus roving, was arrested by a slight movement of great areas behind a lilac bush. It appeared that the dome of some public building had covered itself with antique textiles and was endeavouring to hide there—a failure.

"Kitty Silver!" he said. "What are you doing?"

"Suh?"

Debouching sidewise she came into fuller view, but retired a few steps. "Whut I doin' whur, Mista Atwater?"

"How'd that dog get on my front steps?"

Her face became noncommittal entirely. "Thishere dog? He just settin' there, suh."

"How'd he get in the yard?"

"Mus' somebody up an' brung him in."

"Who did it?"

"You mean: Who up an' brung him in, suh?"

"I mean: Who does he belong to?"

"Mus' be Miss Julia's. I reckon he is, so fur."

"What! She knows I don't allow dogs on the place."

"Yessuh."

Mr. Atwater's expression became more outraged and determined. "You mean to say that somebody's trying to give her another dog after all I've been through with—"

"It look that way, suh."

"Who did it?"

"Miss Julia ain't sayin'; an' me, I don' know who done it no mo'n the lilies of the valley whut toil not neither do they spins."

In response, Mr. Atwater was guilty of exclamations lacking in courtesy; and turning again toward Gammire, he waved his arm. "Didn't you hear me tell you to get out of here?"

Gammire observed the gesture, and at once "sat up," placing his forepaws over his nose in prayer, but Mr. Atwater was the more incensed.

"Get out of here, you woolly black scoundrel!"

Mrs. Silver uttered a cry of injury before she perceived that she had mistaken her employer's intention. Gammire also appeared to mistake it, for he came down upon the lawn, rose to his full height, on his "hind legs," and in that humanlike posture "walked" in a wide circle. He did this with an affectation of conscientiousness thoroughly hypocritical; for he really meant to be humorous.

"My heavens!" Mr. Atwater cried, lamenting. "Somebody's given her one of those things at last! I don't like *any* kind of dog, but if there's one dam thing on earth I *won't* stand, it's a trick poodle!"

And while the tactless Gammire went on, "walking" a circle round him, Mr. Atwater's eye furiously searched the borders of the path, the lawn, and otherwheres, for anything that might serve as missile. He had never kicked a dog, or struck one with his hand, in his life; he had a theory that it was always better to throw something. "Idiot poodle!" he said.

But Gammire's tricks were not idiocy in the eyes of Mr. Atwater's daughter, as she watched them. They had brought to her mind the tricks of the Jongleur of Notre Dame, who had nothing to offer heaven itself, to mollify heaven's rulers, except his entertainment of juggling and nonsense; so that he sang his thin jocosities and played his poor tricks before the sacred figure of the Madonna; but when the pious would have struck him down for it, she miraculously came to life just long enough to smile on him and show that he was right to offer his absurd best. And thus, as Julia watched the little Jongleur upon the lawn, she saw this was what he was doing: offering all he knew, hoping that someone might laugh at him, and like him. And, not curiously, after all, if everything were known, she found herself thinking of another foolish creature, who had nothing in the world to offer anybody, except what came out of the wistfulness of a foolish, loving heart. Then, though her lips smiled faintly as she thought of Noble Dill, all at once a brightness trembled along the eyelids of the Prettiest Girl in Town, and glimmered over, a moment later, to shine upon her cheek.

"You get out!" Mr. Atwater shouted, "D'ye hear me, you poodle?"

He found the missile, a stone of fair diameter. He hurled it violently.

"*There*, darn you!"

The stone missed, and Gammire fled desperately after it.

"You get over that fence!" Mr. Atwater cried. "You wait till I find another rock and I'll—"

He began to search for another stone, but, before he could find one, Gammire returned with the first. He deposited it upon the ground at Mr. Atwater's feet.

"There's your rock," he said.

Mr. Atwater looked down at him fiercely, and through the black chrysanthemum two garnet sparks glinted waggishly.

"Didn't you hear me tell you what I'd do if you didn't get out o' here, you darn poodle?"

Gammire "sat up," placed his forepaws together over his nose and prayed. "There's your rock," he said. And he added, as clearly as if he used a spoken language, "Let's get on with the game!"

Mr. Atwater turned to Kitty Silver. "Does he—does he know how to speak, or shake hands, or anything like that?" he asked.

*   *   *   *   *

The next morning, as the peculiar old man sat at breakfast, he said to the lady across the table: "Look here. Who did give Gamin to us?"

Julia bit her lip; she even cast down her eyes.

"Well, who was it?"

Her demureness still increased. "It was—Noble Dill."

Mr. Atwater was silent; he looked down and caught a clownish garnet gleam out of a blackness neighbouring his knee. "Well, see here," he said. "Why can't you—why can't you—"

"Why can't I what?"

"Why can't you sit out in the yard the next time he calls here, instead of on the porch where it blows all through the house? It's just as pleasant to sit under the trees, isn't it?"

"Pleasanter," said Julia.

CHAPTER FIFTEEN

By the end of October, with the dispersal of foliage that has served all summer long as a screen for whatever small privacy may exist between American neighbours, we begin to perceive the rise of our autumn high tides of gossip. At this season of the year, in our towns of moderate size and ambition, where apartment houses have not yet condensed and at the same time sequestered the population, one may look over back yard beyond back yard, both up and down the street; especially if one takes the trouble to sit for an hour or so daily, upon the top of a high fence at about the middle of a block.

Of course an adult who followed such a course would be thought peculiar, no doubt he would be subject to inimical comment; but boys are considered so inexplicable that they have gathered for themselves many privileges denied their parents and elders, and a boy can do such a thing as this to his full content, without anybody's thinking about it at all. So it was that Herbert Illingsworth Atwater, Jr., sat for a considerable time upon such a fence, after school hours, every afternoon of the last week in October; and only one person particularly observed him or was stimulated to any mental activity by his procedure. Even at that, this person was affected only because she was Herbert's relative, of an age sympathetic to his and of a sex antipathetic.

In spite of the fact that Herbert, thus seriously disporting himself on his father's back fence, attracted only an audience of one (and she hostile at a rather distant window) his behaviour might well have been thought piquant by anybody. After climbing to the top of the fence he would produce from interior pockets a small memorandum-book and a pencil. His expression was gravely alert, his manner more than business-like; yet nobody could have failed to comprehend that he was enjoying himself, especially when his attitude became tenser, as it frequently did. Then he would rise, balancing himself at adroit ease, his feet one before the other on the inner rail, below the top of the boards, and with eyes dramatically shielded beneath a scoutish palm, he would gaze sternly in the direction of some object or movement that had attracted his attention and then, having satisfied himself of something or other, he would sit and decisively enter a note in his memorandum-book.

He was not always alone; sometimes he was joined by a friend, male, and, though shorter than Herbert, about as old; and this companion was inspired, it seemed, by motives precisely similar to those from which sprang Herbert's own actions. Like Herbert he would sit upon the top of the high fence; like Herbert he would rise at intervals, for the better study of something this side the horizon; then, also like Herbert, he would sit again and write firmly in a little notebook. And seldom in the history of the world have any such sessions been invested by the participants with so intentional an appearance of importance.

That was what most irritated their lone observer at the somewhat distant upstairs back window. The important importance of Herbert and his friend was so extreme as to be all too plainly visible across four intervening broad back yards; in fact, there was sometimes reason to suspect that the two performers were aware of their audience and even of her goaded condition; and that they deliberately increased the outrageousness of their importance on her account. And upon the Saturday of that week, when the notebook writers were upon the fence the greater part of the afternoon, Florence's fascinated indignation became vocal.

"Vile Things!" she said.

Her mother, sewing beside another window of the room, looked up inquiringly.

"What are, Florence?"

"Cousin Herbert and that nasty little Henry Rooter."

"Are you watching them again?" her mother asked.

"Yes, I am," said Florence; and added tartly, "Not because I care to, but merely to amuse myself at their expense."

Mrs. Atwater murmured, "Couldn't you find some other way to amuse yourself, Florence?"

"I don't call this amusement," the inconsistent girl responded, not without chagrin. "Think I'd spend all my days starin' at Herbert Illingsworth Atwater, Junior, and that nasty little Henry Rooter, and call it *amusement*?"

"Then why do you do it?"

"Why do I do *what*, mamma?" Florence inquired, as in despair of Mrs. Atwater's ever learning to put things clearly.

"Why do you 'spend all your days' watching them? You don't seem able to keep away from the window, and it appears to make you irritable. I should think if they wouldn't let you play with them you'd be too proud—"

"Oh, good heavens, mamma!"

"Don't use such expressions, Florence, please."

"Well," said Florence, "I got to use *some* expression when you accuse me of wantin' to 'play' with those two vile things! My goodness mercy, mamma, I don't want to 'play' with 'em! I'm more than four years old, I guess; though you don't ever seem willing to give me credit for it. I don't haf to 'play' all the time, mamma: and anyway, Herbert and that nasty little Henry Rooter aren't playing, either."

"Aren't they?" Mrs. Atwater inquired. "I thought the other day you said you wanted them to let you play with them at being a newspaper reporter or editor or something like that, and they were rude and told you to go away. Wasn't that it?"

Florence sighed. "No, mamma, it cert'nly wasn't."

"They weren't rude to you?"

"Yes, they cert'nly were!"

"Well, then—"

"Mamma, *can't* you understand?" Florence turned from the window to beseech Mrs. Atwater's concentration upon the matter. "It isn't '*playing*'! I didn't want to 'play' being a reporter; *they* ain't 'playing'—"

"*Aren't* playing, Florence."

"Yes'm. They're not. Herbert's got a real printing-press; Uncle Joseph gave it to him. It's a *real* one, mamma, can't you understand?"

"I'll try," said Mrs. Atwater. "You mustn't get so excited about it, Florence."

"I'm not!" Florence returned vehemently. "I guess it'd take more than those two vile things and their old printing-press to get *me* excited! *I* don't care what they do; it's far less than nothing to me! All *I* wish is they'd fall off the fence and break their vile ole necks!"

With this manifestation of impersonal calmness, she turned

again to the window; but her mother protested. "Do quit watching those foolish boys; you mustn't let them upset you so by their playing."

Florence moaned. "They don't 'upset' me, mamma! They have no effects on me by the slightest degree! And I *told* you, mamma, they're not 'playing'."

"Then what are they doing?"

"Well, they're having a newspaper. They got the printing-press and an office in Herbert's stable, and everything. They got somebody to give 'em some ole banisters and a railing from a house that was torn down somewheres, and then they got it stuck up in the stable loft, so it runs across with a kind of a gate in the middle of these banisters, and on one side is the printing-press and a desk from that nasty little Henry Rooter's mother's attic; and a table and some chairs, and a map on the wall; and that's their newspaper office. They go out and look for what's the news, and write it down in lead pencil; and then they go up to their office and write it in ink; and then they print it for their newspaper."

"But what do they do on the fence?"

"That's where they go to watch what the news is," Florence explained morosely. "They think they're so grand, sittin' up there, pokin' around! They go other places, too; and they ask people. That's all they said *I* could be!" Here the lady's bitterness became strongly intensified. "They said maybe I could be one o' the ones they asked if I knew anything, sometimes, if they happened to think of it! I just respectf'ly told 'em I'd decline to wipe my oldest shoes on 'em to save their lives!"

Mrs. Atwater sighed. "You mustn't use such expressions, Florence."

"I don't see why not," the daughter promptly objected.

"They're a lot more refined than the expressions they used on me!"

"Then I'm very glad you didn't play with them."

But at this, Florence once more gave way to filial despair. "Mamma, you just *can't* see through anything! I've said anyhow fifty times they ain't—aren't—playing! They're getting up a *real* newspaper, and have people *buy* it and everything. They been all over this part of town and got every aunt and uncle they have besides their own fathers and mothers, and some people in the neighbourhood, and Kitty Silver and two or three other coloured people besides. They're going to charge twenty-five cents a year, collect-in-advance because they want the money first; and even papa gave 'em a quarter last night; he told me so."

"How often do they intend to publish their paper, Florence?" Mrs. Atwater inquired absently, having resumed her sewing.

"Every week; and they're goin' to have the first one a week from to-day."

"What do they call it?"

"The North End Daily Oriole. It's the silliest name I ever heard for a newspaper; and I told 'em so. I told 'em what *I* thought of it, I guess!"

"Was that the reason?" Mrs. Atwater asked.

"Was it what reason, mamma?"

"Was it the reason they wouldn't let you be a reporter with them?"

"Poot!" Florence exclaimed airily. "*I* didn't want anything to do with their ole paper. But anyway I didn't make fun o' their callin' it 'The North End Daily Oriole' till after they said I couldn't be in it. *Then* I did, you bet!"

"Florence, don't say—"

"Mamma, I got to say somep'n! Well, I told 'em I wouldn't be in their ole paper if they begged me on their bented knees; and I said if they begged me a thousand years I wouldn't be in any paper with such a crazy name and I wouldn't tell 'em any news if I knew the President of the United States had the scarlet fever! I just politely informed 'em they could say what they liked, if they was dying *I* declined so much as wipe the oldest shoes I got on 'em!"

"But why *wouldn't* they let you be on the paper?" her mother insisted.

Upon this Florence became analytical. "Just so's they could act so important." And she added, as a consequence, "They ought to be arrested!"

Mrs. Atwater murmured absently, but forbore to press her inquiry; and Florence was silent, in a brooding mood. The journalists upon the fence had disappeared from view, during her conversation with her mother; and presently she sighed, and quietly left the room. She went to her own apartment, where, at a small and rather battered little white desk, after a period of earnest reverie, she took up a pen, wet the point in purple ink, and without great effort or any critical delayings, produced a poem.

It was in a sense an original poem, though like the greater number of all literary projections, it was so strongly inspirational that the source of its inspiration might easily become manifest to a cold-blooded reader. Nevertheless, to the poetess herself, as she explained later in good faith, the words just seemed to *come to* her;—doubtless with either genius or some form of miracle implied; for sources of inspiration are seldom recognized by inspired writers themselves. She had not long ago been party to a musical Sunday afternoon at her

Great-Uncle Joseph's house, where Mr. Clairdyce sang some of his songs again and again, and her poem may have begun to coagulate within her then.

THE ORGANEST

BY FLORENCE ATWATER

The organest was seated at his organ in a church,
In some beautiful woods of maple and birch,
He was very weary while he played upon the keys,
But he was a great organest and always played with ease,
When the soul is weary,
And the wind is dreary,
I would like to be an organest seated all day at the organ,
Whether my name might be Fairchild or Morgan,
I would play music like a vast amen,
The way it sounds in a church of men.

Florence read her poem seven or eight times, the deepening pleasure of her expression being evidence that repetition failed to denature this work, but on the contrary, enhanced an appreciative surprise at its singular merit. Finally she folded the sheet of paper with a delicate carefulness unusual to her, and placed it in her skirt pocket; then she went downstairs and out into the back yard. Her next action was straightforward and anything but prudish; she climbed the high wooden fences, one after the other, until she came to a pause at the top of that whereon the two journalists had lately made themselves so odiously impressive.

Before her, if she had but taken note of them, were a lesson in history and the markings of a profound transition in human evolution. Beside the old frame stable was a little brick garage, obviously put to the daily use intended by its designer. Quite as obviously the stable was obsolete; anybody would have known from its outside that there was no horse within it. There, visible, was the end of the pastoral age.

All this was lost upon Florence. She sat upon the fence, her gaze unfavourably though wistfully fixed upon a sign of no special aesthetic merit above the stable door.

THE NORTH END DAILY ORIOLE
ATWATER & ROOTER OWNERS &
PROPREITORS SUBSCRIBE NOW 25 CENTS

The inconsistency of the word "daily" did not trouble Florence; moreover, she had found no fault with "Oriole" until the Owners & Propreitors had explained to her in the plainest terms known to their vocabularies that she was excluded from the enterprise. Then, indeed, she had been reciprocally explicit in regard not only to them and certain personal characteristics of theirs, which she pointed out as fundamental, but in regard to any newspaper which should deliberately call itself an "Oriole." The partners remained superior in manner, though unable to conceal a natural resentment; they had adopted "Oriole" not out of a sentiment for the city of Baltimore, nor, indeed, on account of any ornithologic interest of theirs, but as a relic left over from an abandoned club or secret society, which they had previously contemplated forming, its members to be called "The Orioles" for no reason whatever. The two friends had talked of this plan at many meetings throughout the summer, and when Mr. Joseph Atwater made his great-nephew the unexpected present of a printing-press, and a newspaper consequently took the place of the club, Herbert and Henry still entertained an affection for their former scheme and decided to perpetuate the name. They were the more sensitive to attack upon it by an ignorant outsider and girl like Florence, and her chance of ingratiating herself with them, if that could be now her intention, was not a promising one.

She descended from the fence with pronounced inelegance, and, approaching the old double doors of the "carriage-house," which were open, paused to listen. Sounds from above assured her that the editors were editing—or at least that they could be found at their place of business. Therefore, she ascended the cobwebby stairway, emerged from it into the former hay loft, and thus made her appearance in the printing-room of *The North End Daily Oriole*.

Herbert, frowning with the burden of composition, sat at a table beyond the official railing, and his partner was engaged at the press, earnestly setting type. This latter person (whom Florence so seldom named otherwise than as "that nasty little Henry Rooter") was of a pure, smooth, fair-haired appearance, and strangely clean for his age and occupation. His profile was of a symmetry he had not yet himself begun to appreciate; his dress was scrupulous and modish; and though he was short, nothing outward about him confirmed the more sinister of Florence's two adjectives. Nevertheless, her poor opinion of him was plain in her expression as she made her present intrusion upon his working hours. He seemed to reciprocate.

"Listen! Didn't I and Herbert tell you to keep out o' here?" he said. "Look at her, Herbert! She's back again!"

"You get out o' here, Florence," said Herbert, abandoning his task with a look of pain. "How often we got to tell you we don't want you around here when we're in our office like this?"

"For Heaven's sake!" Henry Rooter thought fit to add. "Can't you quit runnin' up and down our office stairs once in a while, long enough for us to get our newspaper work done? Can't you give us a little *peace*?"

The pinkiness of Florence's altering complexion was justified; she had not been within a thousand miles of their old office for four days. With some heat she stated this to be the fact, adding, "And I only came then because I knew somebody ought to see that this stable isn't ruined. It's my own uncle and aunt's stable, I guess, isn't it? Answer me that, if you'll kindly please to do so!"

"It's my father and mother's stable," Herbert asserted. "Haven't I got a right to say who's allowed in my own father and mother's stable?"

"You have not," the prompt Florence replied. "It's my own uncle and aunt's stable, and I got as much right here as anybody."

"You have not!" Henry Rooter protested hotly. "This isn't either your ole aunt and uncle's stable."

"*It isn't?*"

"No, it is not! This isn't anybody's stable. It's my and Herbert's Newspaper Building, and I guess you haven't got the face to stand there and claim you got a right to go in a Newspaper Building and say you got a right there when everybody tells you to stay outside of it, I guess!"

"Oh, haven't I?"

"No, you 'haven't—I'!" Mr. Rooter maintained bitterly. "You just walk down town and go in any Newspaper Buildings down there and tell 'em you got a right to stay there all day long when they tell you to get out o' there! Just try it! That's all I ask!"

Florence uttered a cry of derision. "And pray, whoever told you I was bound to do everything you ask me to, Mister Henry Rooter?" And she concluded by reverting to that hostile impulse, so ancient, which, in despair of touching an antagonist effectively, reflects upon his ancestors. "If you got anything you want to ask, you go ask your grandmother!"

"Here!" Herbert sprang to his feet. "You try and behave like a lady!"

"Who'll make me?" she inquired.

"You got to behave like a lady as long as you're in our Newspaper Building, anyway," Herbert said ominously. "If you expect to come up here after you been told five dozen times to keep out—"

"For Heaven's sakes!" his partner interposed. "When we goin' to get our newspaper *work* done? She's *your* cousin; I should think you could get her out!"

"Well, I'm goin' to, ain't I?" Herbert protested plaintively. "I expect to get her out, don't I?"

"Oh, do you?" Miss Atwater inquired, with severe mockery. "Pray, how would you expect to accomplish it, pray?"

Herbert looked desperate, but was unable to form a reply consistent with a few new rules of etiquette and gallantry that he had begun to observe during the past year or so. "Now, see here, Florence," he said. "You're old enough to know when people tell you to keep out of a place, why, it means they want you to stay away from there."

Florence remained cold to this reasoning. "Oh, Poot!" she said.

"Now, look here!" her cousin remonstrated, and went on with his argument. "We got our newspaper work to do, and you ought to have sense enough to know newspaper work like this newspaper work we got on *our* hands here isn't—well, it ain't any child's play."

His partner appeared to approve of the expression, for he nodded severely and then used it himself. "No, you *bet* it isn't any child's play!" he said.

"No, sir," Herbert continued. "This newspaper work we got on our hands here isn't any child's play."

"No, sir," Henry Rooter again agreed. "Newspaper work like this isn't any child's play at *all*!"

"It isn't any child's play, Florence," said Herbert. "It ain't any child's play at all, Florence. If it was just child's play or something like that, why, it wouldn't matter so much your always pokin' up here, and—"

"Well," his partner interrupted judicially;—"we wouldn't want her around, even if it *was* child's play."

"No, we wouldn't; that's so," Herbert agreed. "We wouldn't want you around, anyhow, Florence." Here his tone became more plaintive. "So, for mercy's sakes can't you go on home and give us a little rest? What you want, anyhow?"

"Well, I guess it's about time you was askin' me that," she said, not unreasonably. "If you'd asked me that in the first place, instead of actin' like you'd never been taught anything, and was only fit to associate with hoodlums, perhaps my time is of *some* value, myself!"

Here the lack of rhetorical cohesion was largely counteracted by the strong expressiveness of her tone and manner, which made clear her position as a person of worth, dealing with the lowest of her inferiors. She went on, not pausing:

"I thought being as I was related to you, and all the family and everybody else is goin' to haf to read your ole newspaper, anyway it'd be a good thing if what was printed in it wasn't *all* a disgrace to the family, because the name of our family's got mixed up with this newspaper;—so here!"

Thus speaking, she took the poem from her pocket and with dignity held it forth to her cousin.

"What's that?" Herbert inquired, not moving a hand. He was but an amateur, yet already enough of an editor to be suspicious.

"It's a poem," Florence said. "I don't know whether I exackly ought to have it in your ole newspaper or not, but on account of the family's sake I guess I better. Here, take it."

Herbert at once withdrew a few steps, placing his hands behind him. "Listen here," he said;—"you think we got time to read a lot o' nothin' in your ole hand-writin' that nobody can read anyhow, and then go and toil and moil to print it on our printin'-press? I guess we got work enough printin' what we write for our newspaper our own selves! My goodness, Florence, I *told* you this isn't any child's play!"

For the moment, Florence appeared to be somewhat baffled. "Well," she said. "Well, you better put this poem in your ole newspaper if you want to have anyhow one thing in it that won't make everybody sick that reads it."

"*I* won't do it!" Herbert said decisively.

"What you take us for?" his partner added.

"All right, then," Florence responded. "I'll go and tell Uncle Joseph and he'll take this printing-press back."

"He will not take it back. I already did tell him how you kept pokin' around, tryin' to *run* everything, and how we just worried our lives out tryin' to keep you away. He said he bet it was a hard job; that's what Uncle Joseph said! So go on, tell him anything you want to. You don't get your ole poem in *our* newspaper!"

"Not if she lived to be two hunderd years old!" Henry Rooter added. Then he had an afterthought. "Not unless she pays for it."

"How do you mean?" Herbert asked, puzzled by this codicil.

Now Henry's brow had become corrugated with no little professional impressiveness. "You know what we were talkin' about this morning?" he said. "How the right way to run our newspaper, we ought to have some advertisements in it and everything? Well, we want money, don't we? We could put this poem in our newspaper like an advertisement;—that is, if

Florence has got any money, we could."

Herbert frowned. "If her ole poem isn't too long I guess we could. Here, let's see it, Florence." And, taking the sheet of paper in his hand, he studied the dimensions of the poem, without paining himself to read it. "Well, I guess, maybe we can do it," he said. "How much ought we to charge her?"

This question sent Henry Rooter into a state of calculation, while Florence observed him with veiled anxiety; but after a time he looked up, his brow showing continued strain. "Do you keep a bank, Florence—for nickels and dimes and maybe quarters, you know?" he inquired.

It was her cousin who impulsively replied for her. "No, she don't," he said.

"Not since I was about seven years old!" And Florence added sharply, though with dignity: "Do you still make mud pies in your back yard, pray?"

"Now, see here!" Henry objected. "Try and be a lady anyway for a few minutes, can't you? I got to figure out how much we got to charge you for your ole poem, don't I?"

"Well, then," Florence returned, "you better ask *me* somep'n about that, hadn't you?"

"Well," said Henry Rooter, "have you got any money at home?"

"No, I haven't."

"Have you got any money with you?"

"Yes, I have."

"How much is it?"

"I won't tell you."

Henry frowned. "I guess we ought to make her pay about two dollars and a half," he said, turning to his partner.

Herbert became deferential; it seemed to him that he had formed a business association with a genius, and for a moment he was dazzled; then he remembered Florence's financial capacities, always well known to him, and he looked depressed. Florence, herself, looked indignant.

"Two dollars and a half!" she cried. "Why, I could buy this whole place for two dollars and a half, printing-press, railing, and all—yes, and you thrown in, Mister Henry Rooter!"

"See here, Florence," Henry said earnestly. "Haven't you got two dollars and a half?"

"Of course she hasn't!" his partner assured him. "She never had two dollars and a half in her life!"

"Well, then," said Henry gloomily, "what we goin' to do about it? How much *you* think we ought to charge her?"

Herbert's expression became noncommittal. "Just let me think a minute," he said, and with his hand to his brow he stepped behind the unsuspicious Florence.

"I got to think," he murmured; then with the straight-forwardness of his age, he suddenly seized his damsel cousin from the rear and held her in a tight but far from affectionate embrace, pinioning her arms. She shrieked, "Murder!" and "Let me go!" and "Help! Hay-yulp!"

"Look in her pocket," Herbert shouted. "She keeps her money in her skirt pocket when she's got any. It's on the left side of her. Don't let her kick you! Look out!"

"I got it!" said the dexterous Henry, retreating and exhibiting coins. "It's one dime and two nickels—twenty cents. Has she got any more pockets?"

"No, I haven't!" Florence fiercely informed him, as Herbert released her. "And I guess you better hand that money back if you don't want to be arrested for stealing!"

But Henry was unmoved. "Twenty cents," he said calculatingly. "Well, all right; it isn't much, but you can have your poem in our newspaper for twenty cents, Florence. If you don't want to pay that much, why, take your ole twenty cents and go on away."

"Yes," said Herbert. "That's as cheap as we'll do it, Florence. Take it or leave it."

"Take it or leave it," Henry Rooter agreed. "That's the way to talk to her; take it or leave it, Florence. If you don't take it you got to leave it."

Florence was indignant, but she decided to take it. "All right," she said coldly. "I wouldn't pay another cent if I died for it."

"Well, you haven't got another cent, so that's all right," Mr. Rooter remarked; and he honourably extended an open palm toward his partner. "Here, Herbert; you can have the dime, or the two nickels, whichever you rather. It makes no difference to me; I'd as soon have one as the other."

Herbert took the two nickels, and turned to Florence. "See here, Florence," he said, in a tone of strong complaint. "This business is all done and paid for now. What you want to hang around here any *more* for?"

"Yes, Florence," his partner faithfully seconded him, at once. "We haven't got any more time to waste around here to-day, and so what you want to stand around in the way and everything for? You ought to know yourself we don't want you."

"I'm not in the way," said Florence hotly. "Whose way am I in?"

"Well, anyhow, if you don't go," Herbert informed her, "we'll carry you downstairs and lock you out."

"I'd just like to see you!" she returned, her eyes flashing. "Just you dare to lay a finger on me again!" And she added, "Anyway, if you did, those ole doors haven't got any lock on 'em: I'll come right back in and walk right straight up the stairs again!"

Herbert advanced toward her. "Now you pay attention, to me," he said. "You've paid for your ole poem, and we got to have some peace around here. I'm goin' straight over to your mother and ask her to come and get you."

Florence gave up. "What difference would *that* make, Mister Taddletale?" she inquired mockingly. "*I* wouldn't be here when she came, would I? I'll thank you to notice there's some value to my time, myself; and I'll just politely ask you to excuse me, pray!"

CHAPTER SIXTEEN

With a proud air she crushingly departed, returning to her own home far from dissatisfied with what she had accomplished. Moreover, she began to expand with the realization of a new importance; and she was gratified with the effect upon her parents, at dinner that evening, when she informed them that she had written a poem, which was to be published in the prospective first number of *The North End Daily Oriole*.

"Written a *poem*?" said her father. "Well, I declare! Why, that's remarkable, Florence!"

"I'm glad the boys were nice about it," said her mother. "I should have feared they couldn't appreciate it, after being so cross to you about letting you have anything to do with the printing-press. They must have thought it was a very good poem."

"Where is the poem, Florence?" Mr. Atwater asked. "Let's read it and see what our little girl can do when she really tries."

Unfortunately Florence had not a copy, and when she informed her father of this fact, he professed himself greatly disappointed as well as eager for the first appearance of *The Oriole*, that he might felicitate himself upon the evidence of his daughter's heretofore unsuspected talent. Florence was herself anxious for the newspaper's debut, and she made her anxiety so clear to Atwater & Rooter, Owners & Propreitors, every afternoon after school, during the following week, that by

Thursday further argument and repartee on their part were felt to be indeed futile; and in order to have a little peace around there, they carried her downstairs. At least, they defined their action as "carrying," and, having deposited her in the yard, they were obliged to stand guard at the doors, which they closed and contrived to hold against her until her strength was worn out for that day.

Florence consoled herself. During the week she dropped in on all the members of "the family"—her grandfather, uncles and aunts and cousins, her great-aunts and great-uncles—and in each instance, after no protracted formal preliminaries, lightly remarked that she wrote poetry now; her first to appear in the forthcoming *Oriole*. And when Great-Aunt Carrie said, "Why, Florence, you're wonderful! I couldn't write a poem to save my life. I never *could* see how they do it," Florence laughed, made a deprecatory little side motion with her head, and responded, "Why, Aunt Carrie, that's nothing! It just kind of comes to you."

This also served as her explanation when some of her school friends expressed their admiration, after being told the news in confidence; though to one of the teachers she said, smiling ruefully, as in remembrance of midnight oil, "It *does* take work, of course!"

*   *   *   *   *

When opportunity offered, upon the street, she joined people she knew (or even rather distant acquaintances) to walk with them a little way and lead the conversation to the subject of poetry, including her own contribution to that art. Altogether, if Florence was not in a fair way to become a poetic celebrity it was not her own fault but entirely that of *The North End Daily Oriole*, which was to make its appearance on Saturday, but failed to do so on account of too much enthusiasm on the part of Atwater & Rooter in manipulating the printing-press. It broke, had to be repaired; and Florence, her nerves upset by the accident, demanded her money back. This was impossible, and the postponement proved to be but an episode; moreover, it gave her time to let more people know of the treat that was coming.

Among these was Noble Dill. Until the Friday following her disappointment she had found no opportunity to acquaint her Very Ideal with the news; and but for an encounter partly due to chance, he might not have heard of it. A sentimental enrichment of colour in her cheeks was the result of her catching sight of him, as she was on the point of opening and entering her own front door, that afternoon, on her return from school. He was passing the house, walking somewhat dreamily.

Florence stepped into the sheltering vestibule, peeping round it with earnest eyes to watch him as he went by; obviously he had taken no note of her. Satisfied of this, she waited until he was at a little distance, then ran lightly down to the gate, hurried after him and joined him.

"Why, Mr. Dill!" she exclaimed, in her mother's most polished manner. "How supprising to see *you*! I presume as we both happen to be walking the same direction we might just's well keep together."

"Surprising to see me?" Noble said vaguely. "I haven't been away anywhere in particular, Florence." Then, at a thought, he brightened. "I'm glad to see you, Florence. Do you know if any of your family or relatives have heard when your Aunt Julia is coming home?"

"Aunt Julia? She's out of town," said Florence. "She's visiting different people she used to know when she was away at school."

"Yes, I know," Mr. Dill returned. "But she's been gone six weeks."

"Oh, I don't believe it's that long," Florence said casually; then with more earnestness: "Mr. Dill, I was goin' to ask you somep'n—it's kind of a funny question for *me* to ask, but—"

"Yes, she has," Noble interrupted, not aware that his remark was an interruption. "Oh, yes, she has!" he said. "It was six weeks day-before-yesterday afternoon. I saw your father downtown this morning, and he said he didn't know that any of the family had heard just when she was coming home. I thought maybe some of your relatives had a letter from her by this afternoon's mail, perhaps."

"I guess not," said Florence. "Mr. Dill, there was a question I thought I'd ask you. It's kind of a funny question for *me*—"

"Are you *sure* nobody's heard from your Aunt Julia to-day?" Noble insisted.

"I guess they haven't. Mr. Dill, I was goin' to ask you—"

"It's strange," he murmured, "I don't see how people can enjoy visits that long. I should think they'd get anxious about what might happen at home."

"Oh, grandpa's all right; he says he kind of likes to have the house nice and quiet to himself; and anyway Aunt Julia enjoys visiting," Florence assured him. "Aunt Fanny saw a newspaper from one the places where Aunt Julia's visiting her school room-mate. It had her picture in it and called her 'the famous Northern Beauty'; it was down South somewhere. Well, Mr. Dill, I was just sayin' I believe I'd ask you—"

But a sectional rancour seemed all at once to affect the young man. "Oh, yes. I heard about that," he said. "Your Aunt Fanny lent my mother the newspaper. Those people in *that* part of the country—well—" He paused, remembering that it was only Florence he addressed; and he withheld from utterance his opinion that the Civil War ought to be fought all over again. "Your father said your grandfather hadn't heard from her for several days, and even then she hadn't said when she was coming home."

"No, I expect she didn't," said Florence. "Mr. Dill, I was goin' to ask you somep'n—it's kind of a queer kind of question for *me* to ask, I guess—" She paused. However, he did not interrupt her, seeming preoccupied with gloom; whereupon Florence permitted herself a deprecatory laugh, and continued, "It might be you'd answer yes, or it might be you'd answer no; but anyway I was goin' to ask you—it's kind of a funny question for *me* to ask, I expect—but do you like poetry?"

"What?"

"Well, as things have turned out lately I guess it's kind of a funny question, Mr. Dill, but do you like poetry?"

Noble's expression took on a coldness; for the word brought to his mind a thought of Newland Sanders. "Do I like poetry?" said Noble. "No, I don't."

Florence was momentarily discouraged; but at her age people usually possess an invaluable faculty, which they lose later in life; and it is a pity that they do lose it. At thirteen—especially the earlier months of thirteen—they are still able to set aside and dismiss from their minds almost any facts, no matter how audibly those facts have asked for recognition. Children superbly allow themselves to become deaf, so to speak, to undesirable circumstances; most frequently, of course, to undesirable circumstances in the way of parental direction; so that fathers, mothers, nurses, or governesses, not comprehending that this mental deafness is for the time being entirely genuine, are liable to hoarseness both of throat and temper. Thirteen is an age when the fading of this gift or talent, one of the most beautiful of childhood, begins to impair its helpfulness under the mistaken stress of discipline; but Florence retained something of it. In a moment or two Noble Dill's disaffection toward poetry was altogether as if it did not exist.

She coughed, inclined her head a little to one side, in her

mother's manner of politeness to callers, and, repeating her deprecatory laugh, remarked: "Well, of course it's kind of a funny question for *me* to ask, of course."

"What is, Florence?" Noble inquired absently.

"Well—what I was saying was that 'course it's sort of queer *me* askin' if you liked poetry, of course, on account of my *writing* poetry the way I do now."

She looked up at him with a bright readiness to respond modestly to whatever exclamation his wonder should dictate; but Noble's attention had straggled again.

"Has she written your mother lately?" he asked.

Florence's expression denoted a mental condition slightly disturbed. "No," she said. "It's goin' to be printed in *The North End Daily Oriole*."

"What?"

"My poem. It's about a vast amen—anyhow, that's proba'ly the best thing in it, I guess—and they're goin' to have it out to-morrow, or else they'll have to settle with *me*; that's one thing certain! I'll bring one over to your house and leave it at the door for you, Mr. Dill."

Noble had but a confused notion of what she thus generously promised. However, he said, "Thank you," and nodded vaguely.

"Of course, I don't know as it's so awful good," Florence admitted insincerely. "The family all seem to think it's something pretty much; but I don't know if it is or not. *Really*, I don't!"

"No," said Noble, still confused. "I suppose not."

"I'm half way through another one I think myself'll be a good deal better. I'm not goin' as fast with it as I did with the other one, and I expect it'll be quite a ways ahead of this one." She again employed the deprecatory little laugh. "I don't know how I do it, myself. The family all think it's sort of funny I don't know how I do it, myself; but that's the way it is. They all say if they could do it they're sure they'd know how they did it; but I guess they're wrong. I presume if you can do it, why, it just *comes* to you. Don't you presume that's the way it is, Mr. Dill?"

"I—guess so." They had reached his gate, and he stopped. "You're sure none of your family have heard anything to-day?" he asked anxiously.

"From Aunt Julia? I don't think they have."

He sighed, and opened the gate. "Well, good evening, Florence."

"Good evening." Her eyes followed him wistfully as he passed within the enclosure; then she turned and walked quickly toward her own home; but at the corner of the next fence she called back over her shoulder, "I'll leave it with your mother for you, if you're not home when I bring it."

"What?" he shouted, from his front door.

"I'll leave it with your *mother*."

"Leave what?"

"The *poem*!"

"Oh!" said Noble. "Thanks!"

But when his mother handed him a copy of the first issue of *The North End Daily Oriole*, the next day, when he came home to lunch, he read it without edification; there was nothing about Julia in it.

THE NORTH END DAILY ORIOLE

Atwater & Rooter Owners & Propreitors

SUBSCRIBE NOW 25 Cents Per Year

Subscriptions shloud be brought to the East etrance of Atwater & Rooter Newspaper Building every afternoon 4.30 to 6. 25 cents.

===

NEWS OF THE CITY

The Candidates for mayor at the election are Mr P. N. Gordon and John T Milo. The contest is very great between these candidates.

Holcombs chickens get in MR. Joseph Atwater's yard a god deal lately. He says chickens are out of place in a city of this size.

Minnie the cook of Mr. F. L. Smith's residisence goes downtown every Thrusday afts about three her regular day for it.

A new ditch is being dug accross the MR. Henry D. Vance backyrad. ;Tis about dug but nobody is working there now. Patty Fairchild received the highest mark in declamation of the 7A at Sumner School last Friday.

Balf's grorcey wagon ran over a cat of the Mr. Rayfort family. Geo. the driver of the wagom stated he had not but was willing to take it away and burg it somewheres Geo. stated regret and claimed nothing but an accident which could not be helped and not his team that did the damage.

MissColfield teacher of the 7A atSumner School was reproted on the sink list. We hope she will soon be well.

There were several deaths in the city this week.

Mr. Fairchild father of Patty Fairchild was on the sick list several days and did not go to his office but is out now.

Been Kriso the cHauffeur of the Mr. R. G. Atwater family washes their car on Monday. In using the hose he turned water over the fence accidently and hit Lonnie the washWOman in back of MRS. Bruffs who called him some low names. Ben told her if he had have been a man he wrould strike her but soon the distrubance was at an end. There is a good deal more of other news which will be printed in our next NO.

        Advertisements & Poems
        20 Cents Each Up.

        JOSEPH K. ATWATER & CO.
        127 South Iowa St,
        Steam Pumps.

THE Organstep
BY Florence Atwater

The Organstep was seated at his organ in a
In some beautifil words of vagle and brir
But he was a gReat organstep and always
When the soil is weary
And the mind is drearq
I would play music like a vast amen
The way it sounds in a church of new
Subscribe NOW 25 cents Adv & Poetry

20 cents up. Atwater & Rooter News
Paper Building 25 cents per YEAR

Such was the first issue, complete, of *The North End Daily Oriole*. What had happened to the poem was due partly to Atwater & Rooter's natural lack of experience in a new and exacting trade; partly to their enviable unconsciousness of any necessity for proof-reading; and somewhat to their haste in getting through the final and least interesting stage of their undertaking; for of course so far as the printers were concerned, the poem was mere hack work anti-climax.

And as they later declared, under fire, anybody that could make out more than three words in five of Florence's ole handwriting was welcome to do it. Besides, what did it matter if a little bit was left out at the end of one or two of the lines? They couldn't be expected to run the lines out over their margin, could they? And they never knew anything crazier than makin' all this fuss, because: Well, what if some of it wasn't printed just exactly right, who in the world was goin' to notice it, and what was the difference of just a few words different in that ole poem, anyhow?

For by the time these explanations (so to call them) took place, Florence was indeed makin' a fuss. Her emotion, at first, had been happily stimulated at sight of "BY Florence Atwater." A singular tenderness had risen in her—a tremulous sense as of something almost sacred coming at last into its own; and she hurried to distribute, gratis, among relatives and friends, several copies of the *Oriole*, paying for them, too (though not without injurious argument), at the rate of two cents a copy. But upon returning to her own home, she became calm enough (for a moment or so) to look over the poem with attention to details. She returned hastily to the Newspaper Building, but would have been wiser to remain away, since all subscribers had received their copies by the time she got there; and under the circumstances little reparation was practicable.

She ended her oration—or professed to end it—by declaring

that she would never have another poem in their ole vile newspaper as long as she lived.

"You're right about that!" Henry Rooter agreed heartily. "We wouldn't *let* another one in it. Not for fifty dollars! Just look at all the trouble we took, moiling and toiling, to get your ole poem printed as nice as we could, so it wouldn't ruin our newspaper, and then you come over here and go on like this, and all this and that, why, I wouldn't go through it again for a *hunderd* dollars! We're makin' good money anyhow, with our newspaper, Florence Atwater. You needn't think we depend on *you* for our living!"

"That's so," his partner declared. "We knew you wouldn't be satisfied, anyway, Florence. Didn't we, Henry?"

"I should say we did!"

"Yes, sir!" said Herbert. "Right when we were havin' the worst time tryin' to print it and make out some o' the words, I said right then we were just throwing away our time. I said, 'What's the use? That ole girl's bound to raise Cain anyhow, so what's the use wastin' a whole lot of our good time and brains like this, just to suit *her*? Whatever we do, she's certain to come over and insult us.' Isn't that what I said, Henry?"

"Yes, it is; and I said then you were right, and you *are* right!"

"Cert'nly I am," said Herbert. "Didn't I tell you she'd be just the way some the family say she is? A good many of 'em say she'd find fault with the undertaker at her own funeral. That's just exactly what I said!"

"Oh, you did?" Florence burlesqued a polite interest. "How *virry* considerate of you! Then, perhaps you'll try to be a gentleman enough for one simple moment to allow me to tell you my last remarks on this subject. I've said enough—"

"Oh, *have* you?" Herbert interrupted with violent sarcasm.

"Oh, no! Say not so! Florence, say not so!"

At this, Henry Rooter loudly shouted with applausive hilarity; whereupon Herbert, rather surprised at his own effectiveness, naturally repeated his waggery.

"Say not so, Florence! Say not so! Say not so!"

"I'll tell you one thing!" his lady cousin cried, thoroughly infuriated. "I wish to make just one last simple remark that I would care to soil myself with in *your* respects, Mister Herbert Illingsworth Atwater and Mister Henry Rooter!"

"Oh, say not so, Florence!" they both entreated. "Say not so! Say not so!"

"I'll just simply state the simple truth," Florence announced. "In the first place, you're goin' to live to see the day when you'll come and beg me on your bented knees to have me put poems or anything I want to in your ole newspaper, but I'll just *laugh* at you! '*Indeed*?' I'll say! 'So you come beggin' around *me*, do you? Ha, ha!' I'll say! 'I guess it's a little too late for that! Why, I wouldn't—'"

"Oh, say not so, Florence! Say not so!"

"'*Me* to allow you to have one of my poems?' I'll say, 'Much less than *that*!' I'll say, 'because even if I was wearing the oldest shoes I got in the world I wouldn't take the trouble to—'"

Her conclusion was drowned out. "Oh, *Florence*, say not so! Say not so, Florence! Say not so!"

CHAPTER SEVENTEEN

The hateful entreaty still murmured in her resentful ears, that night, as she fell asleep; and she passed into the beginnings of a dream with her lips slightly dimpling the surface of her pillow in belated repartee. And upon waking, though it was Sunday, her first words, half slumbrous in the silence of the morning, were, "Vile Things!" Her faculties became more alert during the preparation of a toilet that was to serve not only for breakfast, but with the addition of gloves, a hat, and a blue-velvet coat, for Church and Sunday-school as well; and she planned a hundred vengeances. That is to say, her mind did not occupy itself with plots possible to make real; but rather it dabbled among those fragmentary visions that love to overlap and displace one another upon the changeful retina of the mind's eye.

In all of these pictures, wherein prevailingly she seemed to be some sort of deathly powerful Queen of Poetry, the postures assumed by the figures of Messrs. Atwater and Rooter (both in an extremity of rags) were miserably suppliant. So she soothed herself a little—but not long. Herbert, in the next pew, in church, and Henry in the next beyond that, were perfect compositions in smugness. They were cold, contented, aristo-cratic; and had an imperturbable understanding between themselves (even then perceptible to the sensitive Florence) that she was a nuisance now capably disposed of by their beau-tiful discovery of "Say not so!" Florence's feelings were unbecoming to the place and occasion.

Booth Tarkington

But at four o'clock, that afternoon, she was assuaged into a milder condition by the arrival, according to an agreement made in Sunday-school, of the popular Miss Patty Fairchild.

Patty was thirteen and a half; an exquisite person with gold-dusted hair, eyes of singing blue, and an alluring air of sweet self-consciousness. Henry Rooter and Herbert Illingsworth Atwater, Jr., out gathering news, saw her entering Florence's gate, and immediately forgot that they were reporters. They became silent, gradually moving toward the house of their newspaper's sole poetess.

Florence and Patty occupied themselves indoors for half an hour; then went out in the yard to study a mole's tunnel that had interested Florence recently. They followed it across the lawn at the south side of the house, discussing the habits of moles and other matters of zooelogy; and finally lost the track near the fence, which was here the "side fence" and higher than their heads. Patty looked through a knot-hole to see if the tunnel was visible in the next yard, but, without reporting upon her observations, she turned, as if carelessly, and leaned back against the fence, covering the knot-hole.

"Florence," she said, in a tone softer than she had been using heretofore;—"Florence, do you know what I think?"

"No. Could you see any more tracks over there?"

"Florence," said Patty;—"I was just going to tell you something, only maybe I better not."

"Why not?" Florence inquired. "Go on and tell me."

"No," said Patty gently. "You might think it was silly."

"No, I won't."

"Yes, you *might*."

"I promise I won't."

"Well, then—oh, Florence I'm *sure* you'll think it's silly!"

"I *promised* I wouldn't."

"Well—I don't think I better say it."

"Go on," Florence urged. "Patty, you *got* to."

"Well, then, if I got to," said Patty. "What I was going to say, Florence: Don't you think your cousin Herbert and Henry Rooter have got the nicest eyes of any boy in town?"

"*Who?*" Florence was astounded.

"I do," Patty said in her charming voice. "I think Herbert and Henry've got the nicest eyes of any boy in town."

"You do?" Florence cried incredulously.

"Yes, I really do, Florence. I think Herbert Atwater and Henry Rooter have got the nicest eyes of any boy in town."

"Well, I never heard anything like *this* before!" Florence declared.

"But *don't* you think they've got the nicest eyes of any boy in town?" Patty insisted, appealingly.

"I think," said Florence, "their eyes are just horrable!"

"What?"

"*Herbert's* eyes," continued Florence, ardently, "are the very worst lookin' ole squinty eyes I ever saw, and that nasty little Henry *Rooter's* eyes—"

But Patty had suddenly become fidgety; she hurried away from the fence. "Come over here, Florence," she said. "Let's go over to the other side of the yard and talk."

It was time for her to take some such action. Messrs. Atwater and Rooter, seated quietly together upon a box on the other side of the fence (though with their backs to the knot-hole), were beginning to show signs of inward disturbance. Already flushed with the unexpected ineffabilities overheard, their complexions had grown even pinker upon Florence's open-hearted expressions of opinion. Slowly they turned their heads to look at the fence, upon the other side of which stood the maligner of their eyes. Not that they cared what *that* ole girl thought—but she oughtn't to be allowed to go around talking like this and perhaps prejudicing everybody that had a kind word to say for them.

"Come on over here, Florence," called Patty huskily, from the other side of the yard. "Let's talk over here."

Florence was puzzled, but consented. "What you want to talk over here for?" she asked as she came near her friend.

"Oh, I don't know," said Patty. "Let's go out in the front yard."

She led the way round the house, and a moment later uttered a cry of surprise as the firm of Atwater & Rooter, passing along the pavement, hesitated at the gate. Their celebrated eyes showed doubt for a moment, then a brazenness: Herbert and Henry decided to come in.

"Isn't this the funniest thing?" cried Patty. "After what I just said awhile ago—*you* know, Florence. Don't you dare to tell 'em!"

"I cert'nly won't!" her hostess promised, and, turning inhospitably to the two callers, "What on earth you want around here?" she inquired.

Herbert chivalrously took upon himself the duty of response. "Look here; this is my own aunt and uncle's yard, isn't it? I guess if I want to come in it I got a perfect right to."

"I should say so," his partner said warmly.

"Why, of course!" the cordial Patty agreed. "We can play some nice Sunday games, or something. Let's sit on the porch steps and think what to do."

"*I* just as soon," said Henry Rooter. "*I* got nothin' p'ticular to do."

"I haven't either," said Herbert.

Thereupon, Patty sat between them on the steps.

"This is *per-feckly* grand!" she cried. "Come on, Florence, aren't you going to sit down with all the rest of us?"

"Well, pray kindly excuse *me*!" said Miss Atwater; and she added that she would neither sit on the same steps with Herbert Atwater and Henry Rooter, nor, even if they entreated her with accompanying genuflections, would she have anything else whatever to do with them. She concluded with a reference to the oldest pair of shoes she might ever come to possess; and withdrew to the railing of the veranda at a point farthest from the steps; and, seated there, swinging one foot rhythmically, she sang hymns in a tone at once plaintive and inimical.

It was not lost upon her, however, that her withdrawal had little effect upon her guests. They chattered gaily, and Patty devised, or remembered, harmless little games that could be played by a few people as well as by many; and the three participants were so congenial and noisy and made so merry, that before long Florence was unable to avoid the impression that whether she liked it or not she was giving quite a party.

At times the noted eyes of Atwater & Rooter were gentled o'er with the soft cast of enchantment, especially when Patty felt called upon to reprove the two with little coquetries of slaps and pushes. Noted for her sprightliness, she was never sprightlier; her pretty laughter tooted continuously, and the gentlemen accompanied it with doting sounds so repulsive to Florence that without being actively conscious of what she did, she embodied the phrase, "perfeckly sickening," in the hymn she was crooning, and repeated it over and over to the air of "Rock of Ages."

"Now I tell you what let's play," the versatile Patty proposed, after exhausting the pleasures of "Geography," "Ghosts" and other tests of intellect. "Let's play 'Truth.' We'll each take a piece o' paper and a pencil, and then each of us asks the other one some question, and we haf to write down the answer and sign your name and fold it up so nobody can see it except the one that asked the question, and we haf to keep it a secret and never tell as long as we live."

"All right," said Henry Rooter. "I'll be the one to ask you a question, Patty."

"No," Herbert said promptly. "I ought to be the one to ask Patty."

"Why ought you?" Henry demanded. "Why ought you?"

"Listen!" Patty cried, "*I* know the way we'll do. I'll ask each of you a question—we haf to whisper it—and each one of you'll ask me one, and then we'll write it. That'll be simply grand!" She clapped her hands; then checked herself. "Oh, I guess we can't either. We haven't got any paper and pencils unless—" Here she seemed to recall her hostess. "Oh, Florrie, dear! Run in the house and get us some paper and pencils."

Florence gave no sign other than to increase the volume of her voice as she sang: "Perf'ly sick'ning, clef' for me, let me *perf'*ly sick-kin-*ning*!"

"We got plenty," said Herbert; whereupon he and Henry produced pencils and their professional note-books, and supplied their fair friend and themselves with material for "Truth." "Come on, Patty, whisper me whatever you want to."

"No; I ought to have her whisper *me*, first," Henry Rooter objected. "I'll write the answer to *any* question; I don't care what it's about."

"Well, it's got to be the *truth*, you know," Patty warned them. "We all haf to write down just exackly the truth on our word of honour and sign our name. Promise?"

They promised earnestly.

"All right," said Patty. "Now I'll whisper Henry a question first, and then you can whisper yours to me first, Herbert."

This seemed to fill all needs happily, and the whispering and writing began, and continued with a coziness little to the taste of the piously singing Florence. She altered all previous opinions of her friend Patty, and when the latter finally closed the session on the steps, and announced that she must go home, the hostess declined to accompany her into the house to help her find where she had left her hat and wrap.

"I haven't the *least* idea where I took 'em off!" Patty declared in the airiest manner. "If you won't come with me, Florrie, s'pose you just call in the front door and tell your mother to get 'em for me."

"Oh, they're *somewhere* in there," Florence said coldly, not ceasing to swing her foot, and not turning her head. "You can find 'em by yourself, I presume, or if you can't I'll have our maid throw 'em out in the yard or somep'n to-morrow."

"Well, *thank* you!" Miss Fairchild rejoined, as she entered the house.

The two boys stood waiting, having in mind to go with Patty as far as her own gate. "That's a *pretty* way to speak to company!" Herbert addressed his cousin with heavily marked severity. "Next time you do anything like that I'll march straight in the house and inform your mother of the fact."

Florence still swung her foot and looked dreamily away. She sang, to the air of "Rock of Ages":

"Henry Rooter, Herbert, too—they make me sick, they make me sick, that's what they do."

However, they were only too well prepared with their annihilating response.

"Oh, say not so! Florence, say not so! *Florence!* Say not so!"

They even sent this same odious refrain back to her from the street, as they departed with their lovely companion; and, so tenuous is feminine loyalty sometimes, under these stresses, Miss Fairchild mingled her sweet, tantalizing young soprano with their changing and cackling falsetto.

"Say not so, Florence! Oh, say not so! Say not so!"

CHAPTER EIGHTEEN

They went satirically down the street, their chumminess with one another bountifully increased by their common derision of the outsider on the porch; and even at a distance they still contrived to make themselves intolerable; looking back over their shoulders, at intervals, with say-not-so expressions on their faces. Even when these faces were far enough away to be but yellowish oval planes, their say-not-so expressions were still bitingly eloquent.

Now a northern breeze chilled the air, as the hateful three became indistinguishable in the haze of autumn dusk, whereupon Florence stopped swinging her foot, left the railing, and went morosely into the house. And here it was her fortune to make two discoveries vital to her present career; the first arising out of a conversation between her father and mother in the library, where a gossipy fire of soft coal encouraged this proper Sunday afternoon entertainment for man and wife.

"Sit down and rest, Florence," said her mother. "I'm afraid you play too hard when Patty and the boys are here. Do sit down quietly and rest yourself a little while." And as Florence obeyed, Mrs. Atwater turned to her husband, resuming: "Well, that's what *I* said. I told Aunt Carrie I thought the same way about it that *you* did. Of course nobody *ever* knows what Julia's going to do next, and nobody needs to be surprised at anything she does. Ever since she came home from school, about four-fifths of all the young men in town have been wild about her—and so's every old bachelor, for the matter of that!"

"Yes," Mr. Atwater added. "And every old widower, too."

His wife warmly accepted the amendment. "And every old widower, too," she said, nodding. "Rather! And of course Julia's just done exactly as she pleased about everything, and naturally she's going to do as she pleases about *this*."

"Well, of course it's her own affair, Mollie," Mr. Atwater said mildly. "She couldn't be expected to consult the whole Atwater family connection before she—"

"Oh, no," she agreed. "I don't say she could. Still, it *is* rather upsetting, coming so suddenly like this, when not one of the family has ever seen him—never even heard his very name before."

"Well, that part of it isn't especially strange, Mollie. He was born and brought up in a town three hundred miles from here. I don't see just how we *could* have heard his name unless he visited here or got into the papers in some way."

Mrs. Atwater seemed unwilling to yield a mysterious point. She rocked decorously in her rocking-chair, shook her head, and after setting her lips rigidly, opened them to insist that she could never change her mind: Julia had acted very abruptly. "Why couldn't she have let her poor father know at least a *few* days before she did?"

Mr. Atwater sighed. "Why, she explains in her letter that she only knew it, herself, an hour before she wrote."

"Her poor father!" his wife repeated commiseratingly.

"Why, Mollie, I don't see how father's especially to be pitied."

"Don't you?" said Mrs. Atwater. "That old man, to have to live in that big house all alone, except a few negro servants?"

"Why, no! About half the houses in the neighbourhood, up

and down the street, are fully occupied by close relatives of his: I doubt if he'll be really as lonely as he'd like to be. And he's often said he'd give a great deal if Julia had been a plain, unpopular girl. I'm strongly of the opinion, myself, that he'll be pleased about this. Of course it may upset him a little at first."

"Yes; I think it will!" Mrs. Atwater shook her head forebodingly. "And he isn't the only one it's going to upset."

"No, he isn't," her husband admitted seriously. "That's always been the trouble with Julia; she never could bear to seem disappointing; and so, of course, I suppose every one of 'em has a special idea that he's really about the top of the list with her."

"Every last one of 'em is positive of it," said Mrs. Atwater. "That was Julia's way with 'em!"

"Yes, Julia's always been much too kind-hearted for other people's good." Thus Mr. Atwater summed up Julia; and he was her brother. Additionally, since he was the older, he had known her since her birth.

"If you ask *me*," said his wife, "I'll really be surprised if it all goes through without a suicide."

"Oh, not quite suicide, perhaps," Mr. Atwater protested. "I'm glad it's a fairly dry town though."

She failed to fathom his simple meaning. "Why?"

"Well, some of 'em might feel *that* desperate at least," he explained. "Prohibition's a safeguard for the disappointed in love."

This phrase and a previous one stirred Florence, who had been sitting quietly, according to request, and "resting", but not resting her curiosity. "*Who's* disappointed in love, papa?" she inquired with an explosive eagerness that slightly startled her preoccupied parents. "What *is* all this about Aunt Julia, and grandpa goin' to live alone, and people committing suicide and prohibition and everything? What *is* all this, mamma?"

"Nothing, Florence."

"Nothing! That's what you always say about the very most inter'sting things that happen in the whole family! What *is* all this, papa?"

"It's nothing that would be interesting to little girls, Florence. Merely some family matters."

"My goodness!" Florence exclaimed. "I'm not a 'little girl' any more, papa! You're *always* forgetting my age! And if it's a family matter I belong to the family, I guess, about as much as anybody else, don't I? Grandpa himself isn't any *more* one of the family than I am, I don't care *how* old he is!"

This was undeniable, and her father laughed. "It's really nothing you'd care about one way or the other," he said.

"Well, I'd care about it if it's a secret," Florence insisted. "If it's a secret I'd want to know it, whatever it's about."

"Oh, it isn't a secret, particularly, I suppose. At least, it's not to be made public for a time; it's only to be known in the family."

"Well, didn't I just *prove* I'm as much one o' the family as—"

"Never mind," her father said soothingly. "I don't suppose there's any harm in your knowing it—if you won't go telling everybody. Your Aunt Julia has just written us that she's engaged."

Mrs. Atwater uttered an exclamation, but she was too late to check him.

"I'm afraid you oughtn't to have told Florence. She *isn't* just the most discreet—"

"Pshaw!" he laughed. "She certainly is 'one of the family', however, and Julia wrote that all of the family might be told. You'll not speak of it outside the family, will you, Florence?"

But Florence was not yet able to speak of it, even inside the family; so surprising, sometimes, are parents' theories of what will not interest their children. She sat staring, her mouth open, and in the uncertain illumination of the room these symptoms of her emotional condition went unobserved.

"I say, you won't speak of Julia's engagement outside the family, will you, Florence?"

"Papa!" she gasped. "Did Aunt Julia write she was *engaged*?"

"Yes."

"To get *married*?"

"It would seem so."

"To *who*?"

"'To whom,' Florence," her mother suggested primly.

"Mamma!" the daughter cried. "Who's Aunt Julia engaged to get married to? Noble Dill?"

"Good gracious, *no*!" Mrs. Atwater exclaimed. "What an absurd idea! It's to a young man in the place she's visiting—a stranger to all of us. Julia only met him a few weeks ago." Here she forgot Florence, and turned again to her husband, wearing her former expression of experienced foreboding.

"It's just as I said. It's exactly like Julia to do such a reckless thing!"

"But as we don't know anything at all about the young man," he remonstrated, "how do you know it's reckless?"

"How do you know he's young?" Mrs. Atwater retorted crisply. "All in the world she said about him was that he's a lawyer. He may be a widower, for all we know, or divorced, with seven or eight children."

"Oh, no, Mollie!"

"Why, he *might*!" she insisted. "For all we know, he may be a widower for the third or fourth *time*, or divorced, with any *number* of children! If such a person proposed to Julia, you know yourself she'd hate to be disappointing!"

Her husband laughed. "I don't think she'd go so far as to actually accept 'such a person' and write home to announce her engagement to the family. I suppose most of her swains here have been in the habit of proposing to her just as frequently as she was unable to prevent them from going that far; and while I don't think she's been as discouraging with them as she might have been, she's never really accepted any of 'em. She's never been engaged before."

"No," Mrs. Atwater admitted. "Not to this extent! She's never quite announced it to the family before, that is."

"Yes; I'd hate to have Julia's job when she comes back!" Julia's brother admitted ruefully.

"What job?"

"Breaking it to her admirers."

"Oh, *she* isn't going to do that!"

"She'll have to, now," he said. "She'll either have to write the news to 'em, or else tell 'em, face to face, when she comes home."

"She won't do either."

"Why, how could she get out of it?"

His wife smiled pityingly. "She hasn't set a time for coming home, has she? Don't you know enough of Julia's ways to see she'll never in the world stand up to the music? She writes that all the family can be told, because she knows the news will leak out, here and there, in confidence, little by little, so by the time she gets home they'll all have been through their first spasms, and after that she hopes they'll just send her some forgiving flowers and greet her with manly hand-clasps—and get ready to usher at the wedding!"

"Well," said Mr. Atwater, "I'm afraid you're right. It does seem rather like Julia to stay away till the first of the worst is over. I'm really sorry for some of 'em. I suppose it *will* get whispered about, and they'll hear it; and there are some of the poor things that might take it pretty hard."

"'Take it pretty hard!'" his wife echoed loudly. "There's *one* of 'em, at least, who'll just merely lose his reason!"

"Which one?"

"Noble Dill."

At this, the slender form of Florence underwent a spasmodic seizure in her chair, but as the fit was short and also noiseless, it passed without being noticed.

"Yes," said Mr. Atwater thoughtfully. "I suppose he will."

"He certainly will!" Mrs. Atwater declared. "Noble's mother told me last week that he'd got so he was just as liable to drop a fountain-pen in his coffee as a lump of sugar; and when any one speaks to him he either doesn't know it, or else jumps. When he says anything, himself, she says they can scarcely ever make out what he's talking about. He was trying enough before Julia went away; but since she's been gone Mrs. Dill says he's like nothing in her experience. She says he doesn't inherit it; Mr. Dill wasn't anything like this about her."

Mr. Atwater smiled faintly. "Mrs. Dill wasn't anything like Julia."

"No," said his wife. "She was quite a sensible girl. I'd hate to be in her place now, though, when she tells Noble about *this*."

"How can Mrs. Dill tell him, since she doesn't know it herself?"

"Well—perhaps she ought to know it, so that she *could* tell him. *Somebody* ought to tell him, and it ought to be done with the greatest tact. It ought to be broken to him with the most delicate care and sympathy, or the consequences—"

"Nobody could foretell the consequences," her husband interrupted:—"no matter how tactfully it's broken to Noble."

"No," she said, "I suppose that's true. I think the poor thing's likely to lose his reason unless it *is* done tactfully, though."

"Do you think we really ought to tell Mrs. Dill, Mollie? I mean, seriously: Do you?"

For some moments she considered his question, then replied, "No. It's possible we'd be following a Christian course in doing it; but still we're rather bound not to speak of it outside the family, and when it does get outside the family I think we'd better not be the ones responsible—especially since it might easily be traced to us. I think it's usually better to keep out of things when there's any doubt."

"Yes," he said, meditating. "I never knew any harm to come of people's sticking to their own affairs."

But as he and his wife became silent for a time, musing in the firelight, their daughter's special convictions were far from coinciding with theirs, although she, likewise, was silent—a singularity they should have observed. So far were they from a true comprehension of her, they were unaware that she had more than a casual, young-cousinly interest in Julia Atwater's engagement and in those possible consequences to Noble Dill just sketched with some intentional exaggeration. They did not even notice her expression when Mr. Atwater snapped on the light, in order to read; and she went quietly out of the library and up the stairs to her own room.

* * * * *

On the floor, near her bed, where Patty Fairchild had left her coat and hat, Florence made another discovery. Two small, folded slips of paper lay there, dropped by Miss Fairchild when she put on her coat in the darkening room. They were the replies to Patty's whispered questions in the game on the steps—the pledged Truth, written by Henry Rooter and Herbert Atwater on their sacred words and honours. The infatuated pair had either overestimated Patty's caution, or else each had thought she would so prize his little missive that she would treasure it in a tender safety, perhaps pinned upon her blouse (at the first opportunity) over her heart. It is positively safe to say that neither of the two veracities would ever have been set upon paper had Herbert and Henry any foreshadowing that Patty might be careless; and the partners would have been seized with the utmost horror could they have conceived the possibility of their trustful messages ever falling into the hands of the relentless creature who now, without an instant's honourable hesitation, unfolded and read them.

"*Yes if I got to tell the truth I know I have got pretty eyes,*" Herbert had unfortunately written. "I *am glad you think so too Patty because your eyes are too Herbert Illingsworth Atwater, Jr.*"

And Mr. Henry Rooter had likewise ruined himself in a

coincidental manner:

"Well Patty my eyes are pretty but suppose I would like to trade with yours because you have beautiful eyes also, sure as my name is Henry Rooter."

Florence stood close to the pink-shaded electric drop-light over her small white dressing-table, reading again and again these pathetically honest little confidences. Her eyelids were withdrawn to an unprecedented retirement, so remarkably she stared; while her mouth seemed to prepare itself for the attempted reception of a bulk beyond its capacity. And these plastic tokens, so immoderate as to be ordinarily the consequence of nothing short of horror, were overlaid by others, subtler and more gleaming, which wrought the true significance of the contortion—a joy that was dumfounding.

Her thoughts were first of Fortune's kindness in selecting her for a favour so miraculously dovetailing into the precise need of her life; then she considered Henry and Herbert, each at this hour probably brushing his hair in preparation for the Sunday evening meal, and both touchingly unconscious of the calamity now befalling them; but what eventually engrossed her mind was a thought about Wallie Torbin.

This Master Torbin, fourteen years of age, was in all the town the boy most dreaded by his fellow-boys, and also by girls, including many of both sexes who knew him only by sight—and hearing. He had no physical endowment or attainment worth mention; but boys who could "whip him with one hand" became sycophants in his presence; the terror he inspired was moral. He had a special over-development of a faculty exercised clumsily enough by most human beings, especially in their youth; in other words, he had a genius—not, however, a genius having to do with anything generally recognized as art or science. True, if he had been a violinist prodigy or mathematical prodigy, he would have had some respect from his fellows—about equal to that he might have received if he were gifted with some pleasant deformity, such as six toes on a foot—but he would never have enjoyed such deadly prestige as had actually come to be his. In brief, then, Wallie Torbin had a genius for mockery.

Almost from his babyhood he had been a child of one purpose: to increase by burlesques the sufferings of unfortunate friends. If one of them wept, Wallie incessantly pursued him, yelping in horrid mimicry; if one were chastised he could not appear out-of-doors for days except to encounter Wallie and a complete rehearsal of the recent agony. "Quit, Papa! *Pah*-puh, quee-yet! I'll *never* do it again, Pah-puh! Oh, *lemme* alone, Pah-*puh*!"

As he grew older, his insatiate curiosity enabled him to expose unnumbered weaknesses, indiscretions, and social misfortunes on the part of acquaintances and schoolmates; and to every exposure his noise and energy gave a hideous publicity: the more his victim sought privacy the more persistently he was followed by Wallie, vociferous and attended by hilarious spectators. But above all other things, what most stimulated the demoniac boy to prodigies of satire was a tender episode or any symptom connected with the dawn of love. Florence herself had suffered at intervals throughout her eleventh summer because Wallie discovered that Georgie Beck had sent her a valentine; and the humorist's many, many squealings of that valentine's affectionate quatrain finally left her unable to decide which she hated the more, Wallie or Georgie. That was the worst of Wallie: he never "let up"; and in Florence's circle there was no more sobering threat than, "I'll tell Wallie Torbin!" As for Henry Rooter and Herbert Illingsworth Atwater, Jr., they would as soon have had a Head-hunter on their trail as Wallie Torbin in the possession of anything that could incriminate them in an implication of love—or an acknowledgment (in their own handwriting!) of their own beauty.

The fabric of civilized life is interwoven with blackmail: even some of the noblest people do favours for other people who are depended upon not to tell somebody something that the noblest people have done. Blackmail is born into us all, and our nurses teach us more blackmail by threatening to tell our parents if we won't do this and that—and our parents threaten to tell the doctor—and so we learn! Blackmail is part of the daily life of a child. Displeased, his first resort to get his way with other children is a threat to "tell," but by-and-by his experience discovers the mutual benefit of honour among blackmailers. Therefore, at eight it is no longer the ticket to threaten to tell the teacher; and, a little later, threatening to tell any adult at all is considered something of a breakdown in morals. Notoriously, the code is more liable to infraction by people of the physically weaker sex, for the very reason, of course, that their inferiority of muscle so frequently compels such a sin, if they are to have their way. But for Florence there was now no such temptation. Looking to the demolition of Atwater & Rooter, an exposure before adults of the results of "Truth" would have been an effect of the sickliest pallor compared to what might be accomplished by a careful use of the catastrophic Wallie Torbin.

*   *   *   *   *

On Sunday evening it was her privileged custom to go to the house of fat old Great-Uncle Joseph and remain until nine o'clock, in chatty companionship with Uncle Joseph and Aunt Carrie, his wife, and a few other relatives (including Herbert) who were in the habit of dropping in there, on Sunday evenings. In summer, lemonade and cake were frequently provided; in the autumn, one still found cake, and perhaps a pitcher of clear new cider: apples were a certainty.

This evening was glorious: there were apples and cider and cake, with walnuts, perfectly cracked, and a large open-hearted box of candy; for Uncle Joseph and Aunt Carrie had foreseen the coming of several more Atwaters than usual, to talk over the new affairs of their beautiful relative, Julia. Seldom have any relative's new affairs been more thoroughly talked over than were Julia's that evening; though all the time by means of symbols, since it was thought wiser that Herbert and Florence should not yet be told of Julia's engagement; and Florence's parents were not present to confess their indiscretion. Julia was referred to as "the traveller"; other makeshifts were employed with the most knowing caution, and all the while Florence merely ate inscrutably. The more sincere Herbert was placid; the foods absorbing his attention.

"Well, all I say is, the traveller better enjoy herself on her travels," said Aunt Fanny, finally, as the subject appeared to be wearing toward exhaustion. "She certainly is in for it when the voyaging is over and she arrives in the port she sailed from, and has to show her papers. I agree with the rest of you: she'll have a great deal to answer for, and most of all about the shortest one. My own opinion is that the shortest one is going to burst like a balloon."

"The shortest one," as the demure Florence had understood from the first, was none other than her Very Ideal. Now she looked up from the stool where she sat with her back against a pilaster of the mantelpiece. "Uncle Joseph," she said;—"I was just thinking. What is a person's reason?"

The fat gentleman, rosy with firelight and cider, finished his fifth glass before responding. "Well, there *are* persons I never could find any reason for at all. 'A person's reason'? What do you mean, 'a person's reason,' Florence?"

"I mean: like when somebody says, 'They'll lose their reason,'" she explained. "Has everybody got a reason, and if they have, what is it, and how do they lose it, and what would they do then?"

"Oh! I see!" he said. "You needn't worry. I suppose since you heard it you've been hunting all over yourself for your reason and looking to see if there was one hanging out of anybody else, somewhere. No; it's something you can't see, ordinarily, Florence. Losing your reason is just another way of saying, 'going crazy'!"

"Oh!" she murmured, and appeared to be disturbed.

At this, Herbert thought proper to offer a witticism for the pleasure of the company.

"*You* know, Florence," he said, "it only means acting like *you* most always do." He applauded himself with a burst of changing laughter ranging from a bullfrog croak to a collapsing soprano; then he added: "Espeshually when you come around my and Henry's Newspaper Building! You cert'nly 'lose your reason' every time you come around *that* ole place!"

"Well, course I haf to act like the people that's already there," Florence retorted, not sharply, but in a musing tone that should have warned him. It was not her wont to use a quiet voice for repartee. Thinking her humble, he laughed the more raucously.

"Oh, Florence!" he besought her. "Say not so! Say not so!"

"Children, children!" Uncle Joseph remonstrated.

Herbert changed his tone; he became seriously plaintive. "Well, she does act that way, Uncle Joseph! When she comes around there you'd think we were runnin' a lunatic asylum, the way she takes on. She hollers and bellers and squalls and squawks. The least little teeny thing she don't like about the way we run our paper, she comes flappin' over there and goes to screechin' around you could hear her out at the Poor House Farm!"

"Now, now, Herbert," his Aunt Fanny interposed. "Poor little Florence isn't saying anything impolite to you—not right now, at any rate. Why don't you be a little sweet to her just for once?"

Her unfortunate expression revolted all the manliness in Herbert's bosom. "Be a little *sweet* to her?" he echoed with poignant incredulity, and then in candour made plain how poorly Aunt Fanny inspired him. "I just exackly as soon be a little sweet to an alligator," he said.

"Oh, oh!" said Aunt Carrie.

"I would!" Herbert insisted. "Or a mosquito. I'd rather, to *either* of 'em, 'cause anyway they don't make so much noise. Why, you just ought to *hear* her," he went on, growing more and more severe. "You ought to just come around our Newspaper Building any afternoon you please, after school, when Henry and I are tryin' to do our work in anyway *some* peace. Why, she just squawks and squalls and squ—"

"It must be terrible," Uncle Joseph interrupted. "What do you do all that for, Florence, every afternoon?"

"Just for exercise," she answered dreamily; and her placidity the more exasperated her journalist cousin.

"She does it because she thinks *she* ought to be runnin' our own newspaper, my and Henry's; that's why she does it! She thinks she knows more about how to run newspapers than anybody alive; but there's one thing she's goin' to find out; and that is, she don't get anything *more* to do with my and Henry's newspaper. We wouldn't have another single one of her ole poems in it, no matter how much she offered to pay us! Uncle Joseph, I think you ought to *tell* her she's got no business around my and Henry's Newspaper Building."

"But, Herbert," Aunt Fanny suggested;—"you might let Florence have a little share in it of some sort. Then everything would be all right."

"It would?" he said. "It *woo*-wud? Oh, my goodness, Aunt Fanny, I guess you'd like to see our newspaper just utterly ruined! Why, we wouldn't let that girl have any more to do with it than we would some horse!"

"Oh, oh!" both Aunt Fanny and Aunt Carrie exclaimed, shocked.

"We wouldn't," Herbert insisted. "A horse would know any amount more how to run a newspaper than she does. Soon as we got our printing-press, we said right then that we made up our minds Florence Atwater wasn't ever goin' to have a single thing to do with our newspaper. If you let her have anything to do with anything she wants to run the whole thing. But she might just as well learn to stay away from our Newspaper Building, because after we got her out yesterday we fixed a way so's she'll never get in *there* again!"

Florence looked at him demurely. "Are you sure, Herbert?" she inquired.

"Just you try it!" he advised her, and he laughed tauntingly. "Just come around to-morrow and try it; that's all I ask!"

"I cert'nly intend to," she responded with dignity. "I may have a slight supprise for you."

"Oh, *Florence*, say not so! Say not so, Florence! Say not so!"

At this, she looked full upon him, and already she had something in the nature of a surprise for him; for so powerful was the still balefulness of her glance that he was slightly startled. "I might say not so," she said. "I might, if I was speaking of what pretty eyes you say yourself you know you have, Herbert."

It staggered him. "What—what do you mean?"

"Oh, nothin'," she replied airily.

Herbert began to be mistrustful of the solid earth: somewhere there was a fearful threat to his equipoise. "What you talkin' about?" he said with an effort to speak scornfully; but his sensitive voice almost failed him.

"Oh, nothin'," said Florence. "Just about what pretty eyes you know you have, and Patty's being pretty, too, and so you're glad she thinks yours are pretty, the way *you* do—and everything!"

Herbert visibly gulped. He believed that Patty had betrayed him; had betrayed the sworn confidence of "Truth!"

"That's all I was talkin' about," Florence added. "Just about how you knew you had such pretty eyes. Say not so, Herbert! Say not so!"

"Look here!" he said. "When'd you see Patty again between this afternoon and when you came over here?"

"What makes you think I saw her?"

"Did you telephone her?"

"What makes you think so?"

Once more Herbert gulped. "Well, I guess you're ready to believe anything anybody tells you," he said, with palsied bravado. "You don't believe everything Patty Fairchild says, do you?"

"Why, Herbert! Doesn't she always tell the *truth*?"

"Her? Why, half the time," poor Herbert babbled, "you can't tell whether she's just makin' up what she says or not. If you've gone and believed everything that ole girl told you, you haven't got even what little sense I used to think you had!" So base we are under strain, sometimes—so base when our good name is threatened with the truth of us! "I wouldn't believe anything she said," he added, in a sickish voice, "if she told me fifty times and crossed her heart!"

"Wouldn't you if she said you *wrote down* how pretty you knew your eyes were, Herbert? Wouldn't you if it was on paper in your own handwriting?"

"What's this about Herbert having 'pretty eyes'?" Uncle Joe inquired, again bringing general attention to the young cousins; and Herbert shuddered. This fat uncle had an unpleasant reputation as a joker.

The nephew desperately fell back upon the hopeless device of attempting to drown out his opponent's voice as she began to reply. He became vociferous with scornful laughter, badly cracked. "Florence got mad!" he shouted, mingling the purported information with hoots and cacklings. "She got mad because I and Henry played some games with Patty and wouldn't let her play! She's tryin' to make up stories on us to get even. She made it up! It's all made up! She—"

"No, no," Mr. Atwater interrupted. "Let Florence tell us. Florence, what was it about Herbert's knowing he had 'pretty eyes'?"

Herbert attempted to continue the drowning out. He bawled. "She made it *up*! It's somep'n she made up her*self*! She—"

"Herbert," said Uncle Joseph;—"if you don't keep quiet, I'll take back the printing-press."

Herbert substituted a gulp for the continuation of his noise.

"Now, Florence," said Uncle Joseph, "tell us what you were saying about how Herbert knows he has such 'pretty eyes'."

Then it seemed to Herbert that a miracle befell. Florence looked up, smiling modestly. "Oh, it wasn't anything, Uncle Joseph," she said. "I was Just trying to tease Herbert any way I could think of."

"Oh, was that all?" A hopeful light faded out of Uncle Joseph's large and inexpressive face. "I thought perhaps you'd detected him in some indiscretion."

Florence laughed, "I was just teasin' him. It wasn't anything, Uncle Joseph."

Hereupon, Herbert resumed a confused breathing. Dazed, he remained uneasy, profoundly so: and gratitude was no part of his emotion. He well understood that in conflicts such as these Florence was never susceptible to impulses of compassion; in fact, if there was warfare between them, experience had taught him to be wariest when she seemed kindest. He moved away from her, and went into another room where his condition was one of increasing mental discomfort, though he looked over the pictures in his great-uncle's copy of "Paradise Lost." These illustrations, by M. Gustave Dore, failed to aid in reassuring his troubled mind.

When Florence left the house, he impulsively accompanied her, maintaining a nervous silence as they walked the short distance between Uncle Joseph's front gate and her own. There, however, he spoke.

"Look here! You don't haf to go and believe everything that ole girl told you, do you?"

"No," said Florence heartily. "I don't haf to."

"Well, look here," he urged, helpless but to repeat. "You don't haf to believe whatever it was she went and told you, do you?"

"What was it you think she told me, Herbert?"

"All that guff—you know. Well, whatever it was you *said* she told you."

"I didn't," said Florence. "I didn't say she told me anything at all."

"Well, she did, didn't she?"

"Why, no," Florence replied, lightly. "She didn't say anything to *me.* Only I'm glad to have your *opinion* of her, how she's such a story-teller and all—if I ever want to tell her, and everything!"

But Herbert had greater alarms than this, and the greater obscured the lesser. "Look here," he said, "if she didn't tell you, how'd you know it then?"

"How'd I know what?"

"That—that big story about my ever writin' I knew I had"— he gulped again—"pretty eyes."

"Oh, about *that!*" Florence said, and swung the gate shut between them. "Well, I guess it's too late to tell you to-night, Herbert; but maybe if you and that nasty little Henry Rooter do every single thing I tell you to, and do it just *exackly* like I tell you from this time on, why maybe—I only say 'maybe'— well, maybe I'll tell you some day when I feel like it."

She ran up the path and up the veranda steps, but paused before opening the front door, and called back to the waiting Herbert:

"The only person I'd ever *think* of tellin' about it before I tell you would be a boy I know." She coughed, and added as by an afterthought, "He'd just love to know all about it; I know he would. So, when I tell anybody about it I'll only tell just you and this other boy."

"What other boy?" Herbert demanded.

And her reply, thrilling through the darkness, left him demoralized with horror.

"Wallie Torbin!"

CHAPTER NINETEEN

The next afternoon, about four o'clock, Herbert stood gloomily at the main entrance of Atwater & Rooter's Newspaper Building awaiting his partner. The other entrances were not only nailed fast but massively barricaded; and this one (consisting of the ancient carriage-house doors, opening upon a driveway through the yard) had recently been made effective for exclusion. A long and heavy plank leaned against the wall, near by, ready to be set in hook-shaped iron supports fastened to the inner sides of the doors; and when the doors were closed, with this great plank in place, a person inside the building might seem entitled to count upon the enjoyment of privacy, except in case of earthquake, tornado, or fire. In fact, the size of the plank and the substantial quality of the iron fastenings could be looked upon, from a certain viewpoint, as a real compliment to the energy and persistence of Florence Atwater.

Herbert had been in no complimentary frame of mind, however, when he devised the obstructions, nor was he now in such a frame of mind. He was pessimistic in regard to his future, and also embarrassed in anticipation of some explanations it would be necessary to make to his partner. He strongly hoped that Henry's regular after-school appearance at the Newspaper Building would precede Florence's, because these explanations required both deliberation and tact, and he was convinced that it would be almost impossible to make them at all if Florence got there first.

He understood that he was unfortunately within her power; and he saw that it would be dangerous to place in operation for her exclusion from the Building this new mechanism contrived with such hopeful care, and at a cost of two dollars and twenty-five cents taken from the *Oriole's* treasury. What he wished Henry to believe was that for some good reason, which Herbert had not yet been able to invent, it would be better to show Florence a little politeness. He had a desperate hope that he might find some diplomatic way to prevail on Henry to be as subservient to Florence as she had seemed to demand, and he was determined to touch any extremity of unveracity, rather than permit the details of his answer in "Truth" to come to his partner's knowledge. Henry Rooter was not Wallie Torbin; but in possession of material such as this he could easily make himself intolerable.

Therefore, it was in a flurried state of mind that Herbert waited; and when his friend appeared, over the fence, his perturbation was not decreased. He even failed to notice the unusual gravity of Henry's manner.

"Hello, Henry! I thought I wouldn't start in working till you got here. I didn't want to haf to come all the way downstairs again to open the door and hi'st our good ole plank up again."

"I see," said Henry, glancing nervously at their good ole plank. "Well, I guess Florence'll never get in *this* good ole door—that is, she won't if we don't let her, or something."

This final clause would have astonished Herbert if he had been less preoccupied with his troubles. "You bet she won't!" he said mechanically. "She couldn't ever get in here again—if the *family* didn't go intafering around and give me the dickens and everything, because they think—they *say* they do, anyhow—they say they think—they think—"

He paused, disguising a little choke as a cough of scorn for the family's thinking.

"What did you say your family think?" Henry asked absently.

"Well, they say we ought to let her have a share in our news-paper." Again he paused, afraid to continue lest his hypocrisy appear so bare-faced as to invite suspicion. "Well, maybe we *ought*," he said finally, his eyes guiltily upon his toe, which slowly scuffed the ground. "I don't say we ought, and I don't say we oughtn't."

He expected at the least a sharp protest from his partner, who, on the contrary, surprised him. "Well, that's the way *I* look at it," Henry said. "I don't say we ought and I don't say we oughtn't."

And he, likewise, stared at the toe of a shoe that scuffed the ground. Herbert felt a little better; this particular subdivision of his difficulties seemed to be working out with unexpected ease.

"I don't say we will and I don't say we won't," Henry added. "That's the way I look at it. My father and mother are always talkin' to me: how I got to be polite and everything, and I guess maybe it's time I began to pay some 'tention to what they say. You don't have your father and mother for always, you know, Herbert."

Herbert's mood at once chimed with this unprecedented filial melancholy. "No, you don't, Henry. That's what I often think about, myself. No, sir, a fellow doesn't have his father and mother to advise him our whole life, and you ought to do a good deal what they say while they're still alive."

"That's what I say," Henry agreed gloomily; and then, without any alteration of his tone, or of the dejected thoughtfulness of his attitude, he changed the subject in a way that painfully startled his companion. "Have you seen Wallie Torbin to-day, Herbert?"

"What!"

"Have you seen Wallie Torbin to-day?"

Herbert swallowed. "Why, what makes—what makes you ask me that, Henry?" he said.

"Oh, nothin'." Henry still kept his eyes upon his gloomily scuffing toe. "I just wondered, because I didn't happen to see him in school this afternoon when I happened to look in the door of the Eight-A when it was open. I didn't want to know on account of anything particular. I just happened to say that about him because I didn't have anything else to think about just then, so I just happened to think about him, the way you do when you haven't got anything much on your mind and might get to thinkin' about you can't tell what. That's all the way it was; I just happened to kind of wonder if he was around anywhere maybe."

Henry's tone was obviously, even elaborately, sincere; and Herbert was reassured. "Well, I didn't see him," he responded. "Maybe he's sick."

"No, he isn't," his friend said. "Florence said she saw him chasin' his dog down the street about noon."

At this Herbert's uneasiness was uncomfortably renewed. "*Florence* did? Where'd you see Florence?"

Mr. Rooter swallowed. "A little while ago," he said, and again swallowed. "On the way home from school."

"Look—look here!" Herbert was flurried to the point of panic. "Henry—did Florence—did she go and tell you—did she tell you—?"

"*I* didn't hardly notice what she was talkin' about," Henry said doggedly. "She didn't have anything to say that *I'd* ever care two cents about. She came up behind me and walked along with me a ways, but I got too many things on my mind to hardly pay the least attention to anything *she* ever talks about.

She's a girl what I think about her the less people pay any 'tention to what she says the better off they are."

"That's the way with me, Henry," his partner assured him earnestly. "I never pay any notice to what *she* says. The way I figure it out about *her*, Henry, everybody'd be a good deal better off if nobody ever paid the least notice to anything she says. I never even notice what she says, myself."

"I don't either," said Henry. "All *I* think about is what my father and mother say, because I'm not goin' to have their advice all the rest o' my life, after they're dead. If they want me to be polite, why, I'll do it and that's all there is about it."

"It's the same way with me, Henry. If she comes flappin' around here blattin' and blubbin' how she's goin' to have somep'n to do with our newspaper, why, the only reason *I'd* ever let her would be because my *family* say I ought to show more politeness to her than up to now. I wouldn't do it on any other account, Henry."

"Neither would I. That's just the same way *I* look at it, Herbert. If I ever begin to treat her any better, she's got my father and mother to thank, not me. That's the only reason *I'd* be willing to say we better leave the plank down and let her in, if she comes around here like she's liable to."

"Well," said Herbert. "*I'm* willing. I don't want to get in trouble with the family."

And they mounted the stairs to their editorial, reportorial, and printing rooms; and began to work in a manner not only preoccupied but apprehensive. At intervals they would give each other a furtive glance, and then seem to reflect upon their fathers' and mothers' wishes and the troublous state of the times. Florence did not keep them waiting long, however.

She might have been easier to bear had her manner of arrival been less assured. She romped up the stairs, came skipping across the old floor, swinging her hat by a ribbon, flung open the gate in the sacred railing, and, flouncing into the principal chair, immodestly placed her feet on the table in front of that chair. Additionally, such was her lively humour, she affected to light and smoke the stub of a lead pencil. "Well, men," she said heartily, "I don't want to see any loafin' around here, men. I expect I'll have a pretty good newspaper this week; yes, sir, a pretty good newspaper, and I guess you men got to jump around a good deal to do everything I think of, or else maybe I guess I'll have to turn you off. I don't want to haf to do that, men."

The blackmailed partners made no reply, on account of an inability that was perfect for the moment. They stared at her helplessly, though not kindly; for in their expressions the conflict between desire and policy was almost staringly vivid. And such was their preoccupation, each with the bitterness of his own case, that neither wondered at the other's strange complaisance.

Florence made it clear to them that henceforth she was the editor of *The North End Daily Oriole*. (She said she had decided not to change the name.) She informed them that they were to be her printers; she did not care to get all inky and nasty herself, she said. She would, however, do all the writing for her newspaper, and had with her a new poem. Also, she would furnish all the news and it would be printed just as she wrote it, and printed *nicely*, too, or else—She left the sentence unfinished.

Thus did this cool hand take possession of an established industry, and in much the same fashion did she continue to manage it. There were unsuppressible protests; there was covert anguish; there was even a strike—but it was a short one. When the printers remained away from their late Newspaper Building, on Wednesday afternoon, Florence had an interview with Herbert after dinner at his own door. He explained coldly that Henry and he had grown tired of the printing-press and had decided to put in all their spare time building a theatre in

Henry's attic; but Florence gave him to understand that the theatre could not be; she preferred the *Oriole*.

Henry and Herbert had both stopped "speaking" to Patty Fairchild, for each believed her treacherous to himself; but Florence now informed Herbert that far from depending on mere hearsay, she had in her own possession the confession of his knowledge that he had ocular beauty; that she had discovered the paper where Patty had lost it; and that it was now in a secure place, and in an envelope, upon the outside of which was already written, "For Wallie Torbin. Kindness of Florence A."

Herbert surrendered.

So did Henry Rooter, a little later that evening, after a telephoned conversation with the slave-driver.

Therefore, the two miserable printers were back in their places the next afternoon. They told each other that the theatre they had planned wasn't so much after all; and anyhow your father and mother didn't last all your life, and it was better to do what they wanted, and be polite while they were alive.

And on Saturday the new *Oriole*, now in every jot and item the inspired organ of feminism, made its undeniably sensational appearance.

A copy, neatly folded, was placed in the hand of Noble Dill, as he set forth for his place of business, after lunching at home with his mother. Florence was the person who placed it there; she came hurriedly from somewhere in the neighbourhood, out of what yard or alley he did not notice, and slipped the little oblong sheet into his lax fingers.

"There!" she said breathlessly. "There's a good deal about you in it this week, Mr. Dill, and I guess—I guess—"

"What, Florence?"

"I guess maybe you'll—" She looked up at him shyly; then, with no more to say, turned and ran back in the direction whence she had come. Noble walked on, not at once examining her little gift, but carrying it absently in fingers still lax at the end of a dangling arm. There was no life in him for anything. Julia was away.

Away! And yet the dazzling creature looked at him from sky, from earth, from air; looked at him with the most poignant kindness, yet always shook her head! She had answered his first letter by a kind little note, his second by a kinder and littler one, and his third, fourth, fifth, and sixth by no note at all; but by the kindest message (through one of her aunts) that she was thinking about him a great deal. And even this was three weeks ago. Since then from Julia—nothing at all!

But yesterday something a little stimulating had happened. On the street, downtown, he had come face to face, momentarily, with Julia's father; and for the first time in Noble's life Mr. Atwater nodded to him pleasantly. Noble went on his way, elated. Was there not something almost fatherly in this strange greeting?

An event so singular might be interpreted in the happiest way: What had Julia written her father, to change him so toward Noble? And Noble was still dreamily interpreting as he walked down the street with *The North End Daily Oriole* idle in an idle hand.

He found a use for that hand presently, and, having sighed, lifted it to press it upon his brow, but did not complete the gesture. As his hand came within the scope of his gaze, levelled on the unfathomable distance, he observed that the fingers held a sheet of printed paper; and he remembered Florence. Instead of pressing his brow he unfolded the journal she had thrust upon him. As he began to read, his eye was lustreless, his gait slack and dreary; but soon his whole demeanour changed, it cannot be said for the better.

THE NORTH END DAILY ORIOLE

Atwater & Co., Owners & Propietors Subscribe NOW 25 cents Per. Year. Sub-scriptions should be brought to the East Main Entrance of Atwater & Co., News-paper Building every afternoon 430 to VI 25 Cents

POEMS

My Soul by Florence Atwater

When my heart is dreary
Then my soul is weary
As a bird with a broken wing
Who never again will sing
Like the sound of a vast amen
That comes from a church of men.

When my soul is dreary
It could never be cheery
But I think of myideal
And everything seems real
Like the sound of the bright church bells peal.

Poems by Florence Atwater will be in the paper each and every Sat.

Advertisements 45c. each Up

Joseph K. Atwater Co.
127 South Iowa St.
Steam Pumps

The News of the City

Miss Florence Atwater of tHis City received a mark of 94 in History Examination at the concusion of the school Term last June.

Blue hair ribbons are in style again.

Miss Patty Fairchild of this City has not been doing as well in Declamation lately as formerly.

MR. Noble Dill of this City is seldom seen on the streets of the City without smoking a cigarette.

Miss Julia Atwater of this City is out of the City.

The MR. Rayfort family of this City have been presentde with the present of a new Cat by Geo. the man employeD by Balf & CO. This cat is perfectly baeutiful and still quit young.

Miss Julia Atwater of this City is visiting friends in the Soth. The family have had many letters from her that are read by each and all of the famild.

Mr. Noble Dill of this City is in business with his Father.

There was quite a wind storm Thursday doing damage to shade trees in many parts of our beautiful City.

From Letters to the family Miss Julia Atwater of this City is enjoying her visit in the south a greadeal.

Miss Patty Fairchild of the 7 A of this City, will probably not pass in ARithmetiC—unless great improvement takes place before Examination.

Miss Julia Atwater of this City wrote a letter to the family stating while visiting in the SOuth she has made an engagement to be married to MR. Crum of that City. The family do not know who this MR. Crum is but It is said he is a widower though he has been diVorced with a great many children.

The new ditch of the MR. Henry D. Vance, backyard of

this City is about through now as little remain to be done and it is thought the beighborhood will son look better. Subscribe NOW 25c. Per Year Adv. 45c. up. Atwater & Co. Newspaper Building 25 Cents Per Years.

It may be assumed that the last of the news items was wasted upon Noble Dill and that he never knew of the neighbourhood improvement believed to be imminent as a result of the final touches to the ditch of the Mr. Henry D. Vance backyard.

CHAPTER TWENTY

Throughout that afternoon adult members of the Atwater family connection made futile efforts to secure all the copies of the week's edition of *The North End Daily Oriole*. It could not be done.

It was a trying time for "the family." Great Aunt Carrie said that she had the "worst afternoon of any of 'em," because young Newland Sanders came to her house at two and did not leave until five; all the time counting over, one by one, the hours he'd spent with Julia since she was seventeen and turned out, unfortunately, to be a Beauty. Newland had not restrained himself, Aunt Carrie said, and long before he left she wished Julia had never been born—and as for Herbert Illingsworth Atwater, Junior, the only thing to do with him was to send him to some strict Military School.

Florence's father telephoned to her mother from downtown at three, and said that Mr. George Plum and the ardent vocalist, Clairdyce, had just left his office. They had not called in company, however, but coincidentally; and each had a copy of *The North End Daily Oriole*, already somewhat worn with folding and unfolding. Mr. Clairdyce's condition was one of desperate calm, Florence's father said, but Mr. Plum's agitation left him rather unpresentable for the street, though he had finally gone forth with his hair just as he had rumpled it, and with his hat in his hand. They wished the truth, they said: Was it true or was it not true? Mr. Atwater had told them that he feared Julia was indeed engaged, though he knew nothing of her fiance's previous marriage or marriages, or of the number of his children. They had responded that they cared nothing about that. This man Crum's record was a matter of indifference to them, they said. All they wanted to know was whether Julia was engaged or not—and she was!

"The odd thing to *me*," Mr. Atwater continued to his wife, "is where on earth Herbert could have got his story about this Crum's being a widower, and divorced, and with all those children. Do you know if Julia's written any of the family about these things and they haven't told the rest of us?"

"No," said Mrs. Atwater. "I'm sure she hasn't. Every letter she's written to any of us has passed all through the family, and I know I've seen every one of 'em. She's never said anything about him at all, except that he was a lawyer. I'm sure *I* can't imagine where Herbert got his awful information; I never thought he was the kind of boy to just make up such things out of whole cloth."

Florence, sitting quietly in a chair near by, with a copy of "Sesame and Lilies" in her lap, listened to her mother's side of this conversation with an expression of impersonal interest; and if she could have realized how completely her parents had forgotten (naturally enough) the details of their first rambling discussion of Julia's engagement, she might really have felt as little alarm as she showed.

"Well," said Mr. Atwater, "I'm glad *our* branch of the family isn't responsible. That's a comfort, anyhow, especially as people are reading copies of Herbert's dreadful paper all up and down the town, my clerk says. He tells me that over at the Unity Trust Company, where young Murdock Hawes is cashier, they only got hold of one copy, but typewrote it and multigraphed it, and some of 'em have already learned it by heart to recite to poor young Hawes. He's the one who sent Julia the three fivepound boxes of chocolates from New York all at the same time, you remember."

"Yes," Mrs. Atwater sighed. "Poor thing!"

"Florence is out among the family, I suppose?" he inquired.

"No; she's right here. She's just started to read Ruskin this afternoon. She says she's going to begin and read all of him straight through. That's very nice, don't you think?"

He seemed to muse before replying.

"I think that's very nice, at her age especially," Mrs. Atwater urged. "Don't you?"

"Ye-es! Oh, yes! At least I suppose so. Ah—you don't think— of course she hasn't had anything at all to do with this?"

"Well, I don't *see* how she could. You know Aunt Fanny told us how Herbert declared before them all, only last Sunday night, that Florence should never have one thing to do with his printing-press, and said they wouldn't even let her come near it."

"Yes, that's a fact. I'm glad Herbert made it so clear that she can't be implicated. I suppose the family are all pretty well down on Uncle Joseph?"

"Uncle Joseph is being greatly blamed," said Mrs. Atwater primly. "He really ought to have known better than to put such an instrument as a printing-press into the hands of an irresponsible boy of that age. Of course it simply encouraged him to print all kinds of things. We none of us think Uncle Joseph ever dreamed that Herbert would publish, anything exactly like *this*, and of course Uncle Joseph says himself he never dreamed such a thing; he's said so time and time and time again, all afternoon. But of course he's greatly blamed."

"I suppose there've been quite a good many of 'em over there blaming him?" her husband inquired.

"Yes—until he telephoned to a garage and hired a car and went for a drive. He said he had plenty of money with him and didn't know when he'd be back."

"Serves him right," said Mr. Atwater. "Does anybody know where Herbert is?"

"Not yet!"

"Well—" and he returned to a former theme. "I *am* glad we aren't implicated. Florence is right there with you, you say?"

"Yes," Mrs. Atwater replied. "She's right here, reading. You aren't worried about her, are you?" she added.

"Oh, no; I'm sure it's all right. I only thought—"

"Only thought what?"

"Well, it *did* strike me as curious," said Mr. Atwater; "especially after Aunt Fanny's telling us how Herbert declared Florence could never have a single thing to do with his paper again—"

"Well, what?"

"Well, here's her poem right at the top of it, and a *very* friendly item about her history mark of last June. It doesn't seem like Herbert to be so complimentary to Florence, all of a sudden. Just struck me as rather curious; that's all."

"Why, yes," said Mrs. Atwater, "it does seem a little odd, when you think of it."

"Have you *asked* Florence if she had anything to do with getting out this week's *Oriole?*"

"Why, no; it never occurred to me, especially after what Aunt Fanny told us," said Mrs. Atwater. "I'll ask her now."

But she was obliged to postpone putting the intended question. "Sesame and Lilies" lay sweetly upon the seat of the chair that Florence had occupied; but Florence herself had gone somewhere else.

She had gone for a long, long ramble; and pedestrians who encountered her, and happened to notice her expression, were interested; and as they went on their way several of them interrupted the course of their meditations to say to themselves that she was the most thoughtful looking young girl they had ever seen. There was a touch of wistfulness about her, too; as of one whose benevolence must renounce all hope of comprehension and reward.

Now, among those who observed her unusual expression was a gentleman of great dimensions disposed in a closed automobile that went labouring among mudholes in an unpaved outskirt of the town. He rapped upon the glass before him, to get the driver's attention, and a moment later the car drew up beside Florence, as she stood in a deep reverie at the intersection of two roads.

Uncle Joseph opened the door and took his cigar from his mouth. "Get in, Florence," he said. "I'll take you for a ride." She started violently; whereupon he restored the cigar to his mouth, puffed upon it, breathing heavily the while as was his wont, and added, "I'm not going home. I'm out for a nice long ride. Get in."

"I was takin' a walk," she said dubiously. "I haf to take a whole lot of exercise, and I ought to walk and walk and walk. I guess I ought to keep on walkin'."

"Get in," he said. "I'm out riding. I don't know *when* I'll get home!"

Florence stepped in, Uncle Joseph closed the door, and the car slowly bumped onward.

"You know where Herbert is?" Uncle Joseph inquired.

"No," said Florence, in a gentle voice.

"I do," he said. "Herbert and your friend Henry Rooter came to our house with one of the last copies of the *Oriole* they were distributing to subscribers; and after I read it I kind of foresaw that the feller responsible for their owning a printing-press was going to be in some sort of family trouble or other. I had quite a talk with 'em and they hinted they hadn't had much to do with this number of the paper, except the mechanical end of it; but they wouldn't come out right full with what they meant. They seemed to have some good reason for protecting a third party, and said quite a good deal about their fathers and mothers being but mortal and so on; so Henry and Herbert thought they oughtn't to expose this third party—whoever she may happen to be. Well, I thought they better not stay too long, because I was compromised enough already, without being seen in their company; and I gave 'em something to help 'em out with at the movies. You can stay at movies an awful long time, and if you've got money enough to go to several of 'em, why, you're fixed for pretty near as long as you please. A body ought to be able to live a couple o' months at the movies for nine or ten dollars, I should think."

He was silent for a time, then asked, "I don't suppose your papa and mamma will be worrying about you, will they, Florence?"

"Oh, no!" she said quickly. "Not in the least! There was nothin' at all for me to do at our house this afternoon."

"That's good," he said, "because before we go back I was thinking some of driving around by way of Texas."

Florence looked at him trustfully and said nothing. It seemed to her that he suspected something; she was not sure; but his conversation was a little peculiar, though not in the least sinister. Indeed she was able to make out that he had more the air of an accomplice than of a prosecutor or a detective. Nevertheless, she was convinced that far, far the best course for her to pursue, during the next few days, would be one of steadfast reserve. And such a course was congenial to her mood, which was subdued, not to say apprehensive; though she was sure her recent conduct, if viewed sympathetically, would be found at least Christian. The trouble was that probably it would not be viewed sympathetically. No one would understand how carefully and tactfully she had prepared the items of the *Oriole* to lead suavely up to the news of Aunt Julia's engagement and break it to Noble Dill in a manner that would save his reason.

Therefore, on account of this probable lack of comprehension on the part of the family and public, it seemed to her that the only wise and good course to follow would be to claim nothing for herself, but to allow Herbert and Henry to remain undisturbed in full credit for publishing the *Oriole*. This involved a disappointment, it is true; nevertheless, she decided to bear it.

She had looked forward to surprising "the family" delightfully. As they fluttered in exclamation about her, she had expected to say, "Oh, the *poem* isn't so much, I guess—I wrote it quite a few days ago and I'm writing a couple new ones now—but I did take quite a lot o' time and trouble with the rest of the paper, because I had to write every single word of it, or else let Henry and Herbert try to, and 'course they'd just of ruined it. Oh, it isn't so much to talk about, I guess; it just sort of *comes* to me to do things that way."

Thirteen attempts to exercise a great philanthropy, and every grown person in sight, with the possible exception of Great-Uncle Joseph, goes into wholly unanticipated fits of horror. Cause and effect have no honest relation: Fate operates without justice or even rational sequence; life and the universe appear to be governed, not in order and with system, but by Chance, becoming sinister at any moment without reason.

And while Florence, thus a pessimist, sat beside fat Uncle

Joseph during their long, long drive, relatives of hers were indeed going into fits; at least, so Florence would have described their gestures and incoherences of comment. Moreover, after the movies, straight into such a fitful scene did the luckless Herbert walk when urged homeward by thoughts of food, at about six that evening. Henry Rooter had strongly advised him against entering the house.

"You better not," he said earnestly. "*Honest*, you better not, Herbert!"

"Well, we got apple dumplings for dinner," Herbert said, his tone showing the strain of mental uncertainty. "Eliza told me this morning we were goin' to have 'em. I kind of hate to go in, but I guess I better, Henry."

"*You* won't see any apple dumplings," Henry predicted.

"Well, I believe I better try it, Henry."

"You better come home with me. My father and mother'll be perfectly willing to have you."

"I know that," said Herbert. "But I guess I better go in and try it, anyhow, Henry. I didn't have anything to do with what's in the *Oriole*. It's every last word ole Florence's doing. I haven't got any more right to be picked on for that than a child."

"Yes," Henry admitted. "But if you go and tell 'em so, I bet she'd get even with you some way that would probably get *me* in trouble, too, before we get through with the job. *I* wouldn't tell 'em if I was you, Herbert!"

"Well, I wasn't intending to," Herbert responded gloomily; and the thought of each, unknown to the other, was the same, consisting of a symbolic likeness of Wallie Torbin at his worst. "I *ought* to tell on Florence; by rights I ought," said Herbert; "but I've decided I won't. There's no tellin' what she wouldn't do. Not that she could do anything to *me*, particyourly—"

"Nor me, either," his friend interposed hurriedly. "I don't worry about anything like that! Still, if I was you I wouldn't tell. She's only a girl, we got to remember."

"Yes," said Herbert. "That's the way *I* look at it, Henry; and the way I look at it is just simply this: long as she *is* a girl, why, simply let her go. You can't tell what she'd do, and so what's the use to go and tell on a girl?"

"That's the way *I* look at it," Henry agreed. "What's the use? If I was in your place, I'd act just the same way you do."

"Well," said Herbert, "I guess I better go on in the house, Henry. It's a good while after dark."

"You're makin' a big mistake!" Henry Rooter called after him. *You* won't see any apple dumplings, I bet a hunderd dollars! You better come on home with me."

Herbert no more than half opened his front door before he perceived that his friend's advice had been excellent. So clearly Herbert perceived this, that he impulsively decided not to open the door any farther, but on the contrary to close it and retire; and he would have done so, had his mother not reached forth and detained him. She was, in fact, just inside that door, standing in the hall with one of his great-aunts, one of his aunts, two aunts-by-marriage, and an elderly unmarried cousin, who were all just on the point of leaving. However, they changed their minds and decided to remain, now that Herbert was among them.

The captive's father joined them, a few minutes later, but it had already become clear to Herbert that *The North End Daily Oriole* was in one sense a thing of the past, though in another sense this former owner and proprietor was certain that he would never hear the last of it. However, on account of the life of blackmail and slavery now led by the members of the old regime, the *Oriole's* extinction was far less painful to Herbert than his father supposed; and the latter wasted a great deal of severity, insisting that the printing-press should be returned that very night to Uncle Joseph. Herbert's heartiest retrospective wish was that the ole printing-press had been returned to Uncle Joseph long ago.

"If you can find him to give it to!" Aunt Harriet suggested. "Nobody *knows* where he goes when he gets the way he did this afternoon when we were discussing it with him! I only hope he'll be back to-night!"

"He can't stay away forever," Aunt Fanny remarked. "That garage is charging him five dollars an hour for the automobile he's in, and surely even Joseph will decide there's a limit to wildness *some* time!"

"I don't care when he comes back," Herbert's father declared grimly. "Whenever he does he's got to take that printing-press back—and Herbert will be let out of the house long enough to carry it over. His mother or I will go with him."

Herbert bore much more than this. He had seated himself on the third step of the stairway, and maintained as much dogged silence as he could. Once, however, they got a yelp of anguish out of him. It was when Cousin Virginia said: "Oh, Herbert, Herbert! How could you make up that terrible falsehood about Mr. Crum? And, *think* of it; right on the same page with your cousin Florence's pure little poem!"

Herbert uttered sounds incoherent but loud, and expressive of a supreme physical revulsion. The shocked audience readily understood that he liked neither Cousin Virginia's chiding nor Cousin Florence's pure little poem.

"Shame!" said his father.

Herbert controlled himself. It could be seen that his spirit was broken, when Aunt Fanny mourned, shaking her head at him, smiling ruefully:

"Oh, if boys could only be girls!"

Herbert just looked at her.

"The worst thing," said his father;—"that is, if there's any part of it that's worse than another—the worst thing about it all is this rumour about Noble Dill."

"What about that poor thing?" Aunt Harriet asked. "We haven't heard."

"Why, I walked up from downtown with old man Dill," said Mr. Atwater, "and the Dill family are all very much worried. It seems that Noble started downtown after lunch, as usual, and pretty soon he came back to the house and he had a copy of this awful paper that little Florence had given him, and—"

"*Who* gave it to him?" Aunt Fanny asked. "*Who*?"

"Little Florence."

"Why, that's curious," Cousin Virginia murmured. "I must telephone and ask her mother about that."

The brooding Herbert looked up, and there was a gleam in his dogged eye; but he said nothing.

"Go on," Aunt Harriet urged. "What did Noble do?"

"Why, his mother said he just went up to his room and changed his shoes and necktie—"

"I thought so," Aunt Fanny whispered. "Crazy!"

"And then," Mr. Atwater continued, "he left the house and she supposed he'd gone down to the office; but she was uneasy, and telephoned his father. Noble hadn't come. He didn't come all afternoon, and he didn't go back to the house; and they telephoned around to every place he *could* go that they know of, and they couldn't find him or hear anything about him at all—not anywhere." Mr. Atwater coughed, and paused.

"But what," Aunt Harriet cried;—"*what* do they think's become of him?"

"Old man Dill said they were all pretty anxious," said Mr. Atwater. "They're afraid Noble has—they're afraid he's disappeared."

Aunt Fanny screamed.

Then, in perfect accord, they all turned to look at Herbert, who rose and would have retired upstairs had he been permitted.

As that perturbing evening wore on, word gradually reached the most outlying members of the Atwater family connection that Noble Dill was missing. Ordinarily, this bit of news would have caused them no severe anxiety. Noble's person and intellect were so commonplace—"insignificant" was the term usually preferred in his own circle—that he was considered to be as nearly negligible as it is charitable to consider a fellow-being. True, there was one thing that set him apart; he was found worthy of a superlative when he fell in love with Julia; and of course this distinction caused him to become better known and more talked about than he had been in his earlier youth.

However, the eccentricities of a person in such an extremity of love are seldom valued except as comedy, and even then with no warmth of heart for the comedian, but rather with an incredulous disdain; so it is safe to say that under other circumstances, Noble might have been missing, indeed, and few of the Atwaters would have missed him. But as matters stood they worried a great deal about him, fearing that a rash act on his part might reflect notoriety upon themselves on account of their beautiful relative—and *The North End Daily Oriole*. And when nine o'clock came and Mrs. Dill reported to

Herbert's father, over the telephone, that nothing had yet been heard of her son, the pressure of those who were blaming the *Oriole* more than they blamed Julia became so wearing that Herbert decided he would rather spend the remaining days of his life running away from Wallie Torbin than put in any more of such a dog's evening as he *was* putting in. Thus he defined it.

He made a confession; that is to say, it was a proclamation. He proclaimed his innocence. He began history with a description of events distinctly subsequent to Sunday pastimes with Patty Fairchild, and explained how he and Henry had felt that their parents would not always be with them, and as their parents wished them to be polite, they had resolved to be polite to Florence. Proceeding, he related in detail her whole journalistic exploit.

Of the matter in hand he told the perfect and absolute truth— and was immediately refuted, confuted, and demonstrated to be a false witness by Aunt Fanny, Aunt Carrie, and Cousin Virginia, who had all heard him vehemently declare, no longer ago than the preceding Sunday evening, that he and his partner had taken secure measures to prevent Florence from ever again setting foot within the Newspaper Building. In addition, he was quite showered with definitions; and these, though so various, all sought to phrase but the one subject: his conduct in seeking to drag Florence into the mire, when she was absent and could not defend herself. Poor Florence would answer later in the evening, he was told severely; and though her cause was thus championed against the slander, it is true that some of her defenders felt stirrings of curiosity in regard to Florence. In fact, there was getting to be something almost like a cloud upon her reputation. There were several things for her to explain;—among them, her taking it upon herself to see that Noble received a copy of the *Oriole*, and also her sudden departure from home and rather odd protraction of absence therefrom. It was not thought she was in good company. Uncle Joseph had telephoned from a suburb that they were dining at a farmhouse and would thence descend to the general region of the movies.

"*Nobody* knows what that man'll do, when he decides to!" Aunt Carrie said nervously. "Letting the poor child stay up so late! She ought to be in bed this minute, even if it is Saturday night! Or else she ought to be here to listen to her own bad little cousin trying to put his terrible responsibility on her shoulders."

One item of this description of himself the badgered Herbert could not bear in silence, although he had just declared that since the truth was so ill-respected among his persecutors he would open his mouth no more until the day of his death. He passed over "bad," but furiously stated his height in feet, inches, and fractions of inches.

Aunt Fanny shook her head in mourning. "That may be, Herbert," she said gently. "But you must try to realize it can't bring poor young Mr. Dill back to his family."

Again Herbert just looked at her. He had no indifference more profound than that upon which her strained conception of the relation between cause and effect seemed to touch;—from his point of view, to be missing should be the lightest of calamities. It is true that he was concerned with the restoration of Noble Dill to the rest of the Dills so far as such an event might affect his own incomparable misfortunes, but not otherwise. He regarded Noble and Noble's disappearance merely as unfair damage to himself, and he continued to look at this sorrowing great-aunt of his until his thoughts made his strange gaze appear to her so hardened that she shook her head and looked away.

"Poor young Mr. Dill!" she said. "If someone could only have been with him and kept talking to him until he got used to the idea a little!"

Cousin Virginia nodded comprehendingly. "Yes, it might have tided him over," she said. "He wasn't handsome, nor impressive, of course, nor anything like that, but he always spoke so nicely to people on the street. I'm sure he never harmed even a kitten, poor soul!"

"I'm sure he never did," Herbert's mother agreed gently. "Not even a kitten. I do wonder where he is now."

But Aunt Fanny uttered a little cry of protest. "I'm afraid we may hear!" she said. "Any moment!"

CHAPTER TWENTY-ONE

These sympathetic women had unanimously set their expectation in so romantically pessimistic a groove that the most tragic news of Noble would have surprised them little. But if the truth of his whereabouts could have been made known to them, as they sat thus together at what was developing virtually into his wake, with Herbert as a compulsory participant, they would have turned the session into a riot of amazement. Noble was in the very last place (they would have said, when calmer) where anybody in the world could have even madly dreamed of looking for him! They would have been right about it. No one could have expected to find Noble to-night inside the old, four-square brick house of H. I. Atwater, Senior, chief of the Atwaters and father of too gentle Julia. Moreover, Mr. Atwater himself was not at present in the house; he had closed and locked it the day before, giving the servants a week's vacation and telling them not to return till he sent for them; and he had then gone out of town to look over a hominy-mill he thought of buying. And yet, as the wake went on, there was a light in the house, and under that light sat Noble Dill.

Returning home, after Florence had placed the shattering paper within his hand, Noble had changed his shoes and his tie. He was but a mechanism; he had no motive. The shoes he put on were no better than those he took off; the fresh tie was no lovelier than the one he had worn; nor had it even the lucidity to be a purple one, as the banner of grief. No; his action was, if so viewed, "crazy," as Aunt Fanny had called it. Agitation first took this form; that was all. Love and change of dress are so closely allied; and in happier days, when Noble had come home from work and would see Julia in the evening, he usually changed his clothes. No doubt there is some faint tracery here, probably too indistinct to repay contemplation.

When he left the house he walked rapidly downtown, and toward the end of this one-mile journey he ran; but as he was then approaching the railway station, no one thought him eccentric. He was, however, for when he entered the station he went to a bench and sat looking upward for more than ten minutes before he rose, went to a ticket window and asked for a time-table.

"What road?" the clerk inquired.

"All points South," said Noble.

He placed the time-table, still folded, in his pocket, rested an elbow on the brass apron of the window, and would have given himself up to reflections, though urged to move away. Several people, wishing to buy tickets, had formed a line behind him; they perceived that Noble had nothing more to say to the clerk, and the latter encouraged their protests, even going so far as to inquire: "For heaven's sakes, can't you let these folk buy their tickets?" And since Noble still did not move: "My gosh, haven't you got no *feet?*"

"Feet? Oh, yes," said Noble gently. "I'm going away." And went back to his seat.

Afterwhile, he sought to study his time-table. Ordinarily, his mind was one of those able to decipher and comprehend railway time-tables; he had few gifts, but this was one of them. It failed him now; so he wandered back to the ticket-window, and, after urgent coaching, eventually took his place at the end instead of at the head of the line that waited there. In his turn he came again to the window, and departed from it after a conversation with the clerk that left the latter in accord with Aunt Fanny Atwater's commiserating adjective, though the clerk's own pity was expressed in argot. "The poor nut!" he explained to his next client. "Wants to buy a ticket on a train that don't pull out until ten thirty-five to-night; and me fillin' it all out, stampin' it and everything, what for? Turned out all his pockets and couldn't come within eight dollars o' the price! Where you want to go?"

Noble went back to his bench and sat there for a long time, though there was no time, long or short, for him. He was not yet consciously suffering; nor was he thinking at all. True, he had a dim, persistent impulse to action—or why should he be at the station?—but for the clearest expression of his condition it is necessary to borrow a culinary symbol; he was jelling. But the state of shock was slowly dispersing, while a perception of approaching anguish as slowly increased. He was beginning to swallow nothing at intervals and the intervals were growing shorter.

Dusk was misting down, outdoors, when with dragging steps he came out of the station. He looked hazily up and down the street, where the corner-lamps and shop-windows now were lighted; and, after dreary hesitation, he went in search of a pawn-shop, and found one. The old man who operated it must have been a philanthropist, for Noble was so fortunate as to secure a loan of nine dollars upon his watch. Surprised at this, he returned to the station, and went back to the same old bench.

It was fully occupied, and he stood for some time looking with vague reproach at the large family of coloured people who had taken it. He had a feeling that he lived there and that these coloured people were trespassers; but upon becoming aware that part of an orange was being rubbed over his left shoe by the youngest of the children, he groaned abruptly and found another bench.

A little after six o'clock a clanging and commotion in the train-shed outside, attending the arrival of a "through express," stirred him from his torpor, and he walked heavily across the room to the same ticket-window he had twice blocked; but there was no queue attached to it now. He rested his elbow upon the apron and his chin upon his hand, while the clerk waited until he should state his wishes. This was a new clerk, who had just relieved the other.

"Well! Well!" he said at last.

"I'll take it now," Noble responded.

"What'll you take now?"

"That ticket."

"What ticket?"

"The same one I wanted before," Noble sighed.

The clerk gave him a piercing look, glanced out of the window and saw that there were no other clients, then went to a desk at the farther end of his compartment, and took up some clerical work he had in hand.

Noble leaned upon the apron of the window, waiting; and if he thought anything, he thought the man was serving him.

The high, vaulted room became resonant with voices and the blurred echoes of mingling footsteps on the marble floor, as passengers from the express hurried anxiously to the street, or more gaily straggled through, shouting with friends who came to greet them; and among these moving groups there walked a youthful fine lady noticeably enlivening to the dullest eye. She was preceded by a brisk porter who carried two travelling-bags of a rich sort, as well as a sack of implements for the game of golf; and she was warm in dark furs, against which the vasty clump of violets she wore showed dewy gleamings of blue.

At sight of Noble Dill, more than pensive at the ticket-window, she hesitated, then stopped and observed him. That she should observe anybody was in a way a coincidence, for, as it happened, she was herself the most observed person in all the place. She was veiled in two veils, but she had been seen in the train without these, and some of her fellow-travellers, though strangers to her, were walking near her in a hypocritical way, hoping still not to lose sight of her, even veiled. And although the shroudings permitted the most meagre information of her features, what they did reveal was harmfully piquant; moreover, there was a sweetness of figure, a disturbing grace; while nothing could disguise her air of wearing that many violets casually as a daily perquisite and matter of course.

So this observed lady stopped and observed Noble, who in return observed her not at all, being but semi-conscious. Looked upon thoughtfully, it is a coincidence that we breathe; certainly it is a mighty coincidence that we speak to one another and comprehend; for these are true marvels. But what petty interlacings of human action so pique our sense of the theatrical that we call them coincidences and are astonished! That Julia should arrive during Noble's long process of buying a ticket to go to her was stranger than that she stopped to look at him, though still not comparable in strangeness to the fact that either of them, or any living creature, stood upon the whirling earth;—yet when Noble Dill comprehended what was happening he was amazed.

She spoke to him.

"Noble!" she said.

He stared at her. His elbow sagged away from the window; the whole person of Noble Dill seemed near collapse. He shook; he had no voice.

"I just this minute got off the train," she said. "Are you going away somewhere?"

"No," he whispered; then obtained command of a huskiness somewhat greater in volume. "I'm just standing here."

"I told the porter to get me a taxicab," she said. "If you're going home for dinner I'll drop you at your house."

"I—I'm—I—" His articulation encountered unsurmountable difficulties, but Julia had been with him through many such trials aforetime. She said briskly, "I'm awfully hungry and I want to get home. Come on—if you like?"

He walked waveringly at her side through the station, and followed her into the dim interior of the cab, which became fragrant of violets—an emanation at once ineffable and poisonous.

"I'm so glad I happened to run across you," she said, as they began to vibrate tremulously in unison with the fierce little engine that drew them. "I want to hear all the news. Nobody knows I'm home. I didn't write or telegraph to a soul; and I'll be a complete surprise to father and everybody—I don't know how pleasant a one! *You* didn't seem so frightfully glad to see me, Noble!"

"Am I?" he whispered. "I mean—I mean—I mean: Didn't I?"

"No!" she laughed. "You looked—you looked shocked! It couldn't have been because I'm ill or anything, because I'm not; and if I were you couldn't have told it through these two veils. Possibly I'd better take your expression as a compliment." She paused, then asked hesitatingly, "Shall I?"

This was the style for which the Atwaters held Julia responsible; but they were mistaken: she was never able to control it. Now she went cheerily on: "Perhaps not, as you don't answer. I shouldn't be so bold! Do you suppose anybody at all will be glad to see me?"

"I—I—" He seemed to hope that words would come in their own good time.

"Noble!" she cried. "Don't be so glum!" And she touched his

arm with her muff, a fluffy contact causing within him a short convulsion, naturally invisible. "Noble, aren't you going to tell me what's all the news?"

"There's—some," he managed to inform her. "Some—some news."

"What is it?"

"It's—it's—"

"Never mind," she said soothingly. "Get your breath; I can wait. I hope nothing's wrong in your family, Noble."

"No. Oh, no."

"It isn't just my turning up unexpectedly that's upset you so, of course," she dared to say. "Naturally, I know better than to think such a thing as that."

"Oh, Julia!" he said. "Oh, Julia!"

"What is it, Noble?"

"Noth-ing," he murmured, disjointing the word.

"How odd you happened to be there at the station," she said, "just when my train came in! You're sure you weren't going away anywhere?"

"No; oh, no."

She was thoughtful, then laughed confidentially. "You're the only person in town that knows I'm home, Noble."

"I'm glad," he said humbly.

She laughed again. "I came all of a sudden—on an impulse. It's a little idiotic. I'll tell you all about it, Noble. You see, ten or twelve days ago I wrote the family a more or less indiscreet letter. That is, I told them something I wanted them to be discreet about, and, of course, when I got to thinking it over, I knew they wouldn't. You see, I wrote them something I wanted them to keep a secret, but the more I thought about it, the more I saw I'd better hurry back. Yesterday it got into my head that I'd better jump on the next train for home!"

She paused, then added, "So I did! About ten or twelve days is as long as anybody has a right to expect the Atwater family connection to keep the deadliest kind of a secret, isn't it?" And as he did not respond, she explained, modestly, "Of course, it wasn't a very deadly secret; it was really about something of only the least importance."

The jar of this understatement restored Noble's voice to a sudden and startling loudness. "'Only the least importance'!" he shouted. "With a man named Crum!"

"What!" she cried

"Crum!" Noble insisted. "That's exactly what it said his name was!"

"*What* said his name was?"

"*The North End Daily Oriole!*"

"What in heaven's name is that?"

"It's the children's paper, Herbert's and Florence's: your own niece and nephew, Julia! You don't mean you deny it, do you, Julia?"

She was in great confusion: "Do I deny what?"

"That his name's Crum!" Noble said passionately. "That his name's Crum and that he's a widower and he's been divorced and's got nobody knows how many children!"

Julia sought to collect herself. "I don't know what you're talking about," she said. "If you mean that I happened to meet a very charming man while I was away, and that his name happened to be Crum, I don't know why I should go to the trouble of denying it. But if Mr. Crum has had the experiences you say he has, it is certainly news to me! I think someone told me he was only twenty-six years old. He looked rather younger."

"You 'think someone told' you!" Noble groaned. "Oh, Julia! And here it is, all down in black and white, in my pocket!"

"I haven't the slightest idea what you're talking about." Julia's tone was cold, and she drew herself up haughtily, though the gesture was ineffective in the darkness of that quivering interior. The quivering stopped just then, however, as the taxicab came to a rather abrupt halt before her house.

"Will you come in with me a moment, please?" Julia said as she got out. "There are some things I want to ask you—and I'm sure my father hasn't come home from downtown yet. There's no light in the front part of the house."

CHAPTER TWENTY-TWO

There was no light in any other part of the house, they discovered, after abandoning the front door bell for an excursion to the rear. "That's disheartening to a hungry person," Julia remarked: and then remembered that she had a key to the front door in her purse. She opened the door, and lighted the hall chandelier while Noble brought in her bags from the steps where the taxicab driver had left them.

"There's nobody home at all," Julia said thoughtfully. "Not even Gamin."

"No. Nobody," her sad companion agreed, shaking his head. "Nobody at all, Julia. Nobody at all." Rousing himself, he went back for the golf tools, and with a lingering gentleness set them in a corner. Then, dumbly, he turned to go.

"Wait, please," said Julia. "I want to ask you a few things— especially about what you've got 'all down in black and white' in your pocket. Will you shut the front door, if you please, and go into the library and turn on the lights and wait there while I look over the house and see if I can find why it's all closed up like this?"

Noble went into the library and found the control of the lights. She came hurrying in after him.

"It's chilly. The furnace seems to be off," she said. "I'll—" But instead of declaring her intentions, she enacted them; taking a match from a little white porcelain trough on the mantelpiece and striking it on the heel of her glittering shoe. Then she knelt before the grate and set the flame to paper beneath the kindling-wood and coal. "You mustn't freeze," she said, with a thoughtful kindness that killed him; and as she went out of the room he died again;—for she looked back over her shoulder.

She had pushed up her veils and this was his first sight of that disastrous face in long empty weeks and weeks. Now he realized that all his aching reveries upon its contours had shown but pallid likenesses; for here was the worst thing about Julia's looks;—even her most extravagant suitor, in absence, could not dream an image of her so charming as he found herself when he saw her again. Thus, seeing Julia again was always a discovery. And this glance over her shoulder as she left a room—not a honeyed glance but rather inscrutable, yet implying that she thought of the occupant, and might continue to think of him while gone from him—this was one of those ways of hers that experience could never drill out of her.

"I'm Robinson Crusoe, Noble," she said, when she came back. "I suppose I might as well take off my furs, though." But first she unfastened the great bouquet she wore and tossed it upon a table. Noble was standing close to the table, and he moved away from it hurriedly—a revulsion that she failed to notice. She went on to explain, as she dropped her cloak and stole upon a chair: "Papa's gone away for at least a week. He's taken his ulster. It doesn't make any difference what the weather is, but when he's going away for a week or longer, he always takes it with him, except in summer. If he's only going to be gone two or three days he takes his short overcoat. And unless I'm here when he leaves town he always gives the servants a holiday till he gets back; so they've gone and even taken Gamin with 'em, and I'm all alone in the house. I can't get even Kitty Silver back until to-morrow, and then I'll probably have to hunt from house to house among her relatives. Papa left yesterday, because the numbers on his desk calender are pulled off up to to-day, and that's the first thing he does when he comes down for breakfast. So here I am, Robinson Crusoe for to-night at least."

"I suppose," said Noble huskily, "I suppose you'll go to some of your aunts or brothers or cousins or something."

"No," she said. "My trunk may come up from the station almost any time, and if I close the house they'll take it back."

"You needn't bother about that, Julia. I'll look after it."

"How?"

"I could sit on the porch till it comes," he said. "I'd tell 'em you wanted 'em to leave it." He hesitated, painfully. "I—if you want to lock up the house I—I could wait out on the porch with your trunk, to see that it was safe, until you come back to-morrow morning."

She looked full at him, and he plaintively endured the examination.

"*Noble!*" Undoubtedly she had a moment's shame that any creature should come to such a pass for her sake. "What crazy nonsense!" she said; and sat upon a stool before the crackling fire. "Do sit down, Noble—unless your dinner will be waiting for you at home?"

"No," he murmured. "They never wait for me. Don't you want me to look after your trunk?"

"Not by sitting all night with it on the porch!" she said. "I'm going to stay here myself. I'm not going out; I don't want to see any of the family to-night."

"I thought you said you were hungry?"

"I am; but there's enough in the pantry. I looked."

"Well, if you don't want to see any of 'em," he suggested, "and they know your father's away and think the house is empty, they're liable to notice the lights and come in, and then you'd have to see 'em."

"No, you can't see the lights of this room from the street, and I lit the lamp at the other end of the hall. The light near the front door," Julia added, "I put out."

"You did?"

"I can't see any of 'em to-night," she said resolutely. "Besides, I want to find out what you meant by what you said in the taxicab before I do anything else."

"What I meant in the taxicab?" he echoed. "Oh, Julia! Julia!"

She frowned, first at the fire, then, turning her head, at Noble. "You seem to feel reproachful about something," she observed.

"No, I don't. I don't feel reproachful, Julia. I don't know what I feel, but I don't feel reproachful."

She smiled faintly. "Don't you? Well, there's something perhaps you do feel, and that's hungry. Will you stay to dinner with me—if I go and get it?"

"What?"

"You can have dinner with me—if you want to? You can stay till ten o'clock—if you want to? Wait!" she said, and jumped up and ran out of the room.

Half an hour later she came back and called softly to him from the doorway; and he followed her to the dining-room.

"It isn't much of a dinner, Noble," she said, a little tremulously, being for once (though strictly as a cook) genuinely apologetic;—but the scrambled eggs, cold lamb, salad, and coffee were quite as "much of a dinner" as Noble wanted. To him everything on that table was hallowed, yet excruciating.

"Let's eat first and talk afterward," Julia proposed; but what she meant by "talk" evidently did not exclude interchange of information regarding weather and the health of acquaintances, for she spoke freely upon these subjects, while Noble murmured in response and swallowed a little of the sacred food, but more often swallowed nothing. Bitterest of all was his thought of what this unexampled seclusion with Julia could have meant to him, were those poisonous violets not at her waist—for she had put them on again—and were there no Crum in the South. Without these fatal obstructions, the present moment would have been to him a bit of what he often thought of as "dream life"; but all its sweetness was a hurt.

"*Now* we'll talk!" said Julia, when she had brought him back to the library fire again, and they were seated before it. "Don't you want to smoke?" He shook his head dismally, having no heart for what she proposed. "Well, then," she said briskly, but a little ruefully, "let's get to the bottom of things. Just what did you mean you had 'in black and white' in your pocket?"

Slowly Noble drew forth the historic copy of *The North End Daily Oriole*; and with face averted, placed it in her extended hand.

"What in the world!" she exclaimed, unfolding it; and then as its title and statement of ownership came into view, "Oh, yes! I see. Aunt Carrie wrote me that Uncle Joseph had given Herbert a printing-press. I suppose Herbert's the editor?"

"And that Rooter boy," Noble said sadly. "I think maybe your little niece Florence has something to do with it, too."

"'Something' to do with it? She usually has *all* to do with anything she gets hold of! But what's it got to do with me?"

"You'll see!" he prophesied accurately.

She began to read, laughing at some of the items as she went along; then suddenly she became rigid, holding the small journal before her in a transfixed hand.

"Oh!" she cried. "*Oh!*"

"That's—that's what—I meant," Noble explained.

Julia's eyes grew dangerous. "The little fiends!" she cried. "Oh, really, this is a long-suffering family, but it's time these outrages were stopped!"

She jumped up. "Isn't it frightful?" she demanded of Noble.

"Yes, it is," he said, with a dismal fervour. "Nobody knows that better than I do, Julia!"

"I mean *this*!" she cried, extending the *Oriole* toward him with a vigorous gesture. "I mean this dreadful story about poor Mr. Crum!"

"But it's true," he said.

"Noble Dill!"

"Julia?"

"Do you dare to say you believed it?"

He sprang up. "It isn't true?"

"Not one word of it! I told you Mr. Crum is only twenty-six. He hasn't been out of college more than three or four years, and it's the most terrible slander to say he's ever been married at all!"

Noble dropped back into his chair of misery. "I thought you

meant it wasn't true."

"I've just told you there isn't one *word* of tr—"

"But you're—engaged," Noble gulped. "You're engaged to him, Julia!"

She appeared not to hear this. "I suppose it *can* be lived down," she said. "To think of Uncle Joseph putting such a thing into the hands of those awful children!"

"But, Julia, you're eng—"

"Noble!" she said sharply.

"Well, you *are* eng—"

Julia drew herself up. "Different people mean different things by that word," she said with severity, like an annoyed school-teacher. "There are any number of shades of meaning to words; and if I used the word you mention, in writing home to the family, I may have used a certain shade and they may have thought I intended another."

"But, Julia—"

"Mr. Crum is a charming young man," she continued with the same primness. "I liked him very much indeed. I liked him very, very much. I liked him very, *very*—"

"I understand," he interrupted. "Don't say it any more, Julia."

"No; you don't understand! At *first* I liked him very much—in fact, I still do, of course—I'm sure he's one of the best and most attractive young men in the world. I think he's a man any girl ought to be happy with, if he were only to be considered by himself. I don't deny that. I liked him very much indeed, and I don't deny that for several days after he— after he proposed to me—I don't deny I thought something serious *might* come of it. But at that time, Noble, I hadn't—hadn't really thought of what it meant to give up living here at home, with all the family and everything—and friends—friends like you, Noble. I hadn't thought what it would mean to me to give all this up. And besides, there was something very important. At the time I wrote that letter mentioning poor Mr. Crum to the family, Noble, I hadn't—I hadn't—" She paused, visibly in some distress. "I hadn't—"

"You hadn't what?" he cried.

"I hadn't met his mother!"

Noble leaped to his feet. "Julia! You aren't—you aren't engaged?"

"I am not," she answered decisively. "If I ever was—in the slightest—I certainly am not now."

Poor Noble was transfigured. He struggled; making half-formed gestures, speaking half-made words. A rapture glowed upon him.

"Julia—Julia—" He choked. "Julia, promise me something. Will you promise me something? Julia, promise to promise me something."

"I will," she said quickly. "What do you want me to do?"

Then he saw that it was his time to speak; that this was the moment for him to dare everything and ask for the utmost he could hope from her.

"Give me your word!" he said, still radiantly struggling. "Give me your word—your word—your word and your sacred promise, Julia—that you'll never be engaged to anybody at all!"

CHAPTER TWENTY-THREE

At six minutes after four o'clock on the second afternoon following Julia's return, Noble Dill closed his own gate behind him and set forth upon the four-minute walk that would bring him to Julia's. He wore a bit of scarlet geranium in the buttonhole of his new light overcoat; he flourished a new walking-stick and new grey gloves. As for his expression, he might have been a bridegroom.

Passing the mouth of an alley, as he swung along the street, he was aware of a commotion, of missiles hurled and voices clashed. In this alley there was a discord: passion and mockery were here inimically intermingled.

Casting *a* glance that way, Noble could see but one person; a boy of fourteen who looked through a crack in a board fence, steadfastly keeping an eye to this aperture and as continuously calling through it, holding his head to a level for this purpose, but at the same time dancing—and dancing tauntingly, it was conveyed—with the other parts of his body. His voice was now sweet, now piercing, and again far too dulcet with the overkindness of burlesque; and if, as it seemed, he was unburdening his spleen, his spleen was a powerful one and gorged. He appeared to be in a torment of tormenting; and his success was proved by the pounding of bricks, parts of bricks and rocks of size upon the other side of the fence, as close to the crack as might be.

"Oh, dolling!" he wailed, his tone poisonously amorous. "Oh, dolling Henery! Oo's dot de mos' booful eyes in a dray bid nasty world. Henery! Oh, *has* I dot booful eyes, dolling Pattywatty? Yes, I *has*! I *has* dot pretty eyes!" His voice rose unbearably. "*Oh*, what prettiest eyes I dot! Me and Herbie Atwater! *Oh*, my booful eyes! Oh, my *booful*—"

But even as he reached this apex, the head, shoulders, and arms of Herbert Atwater rose momentarily above the fence across the alley, behind the tormentor. Herbert's expression was implacably resentful, and so was the gesture with which he hurled an object at the comedian preoccupied with the opposite fence. This object, upon reaching its goal, as it did more with a splash than a thud, was revealed as a tomato, presumably in a useless state. The taunter screamed in astonishment, and after looking vainly for an assailant, began necessarily to remove his coat.

Noble, passing on, thought he recognized the boy as one of the Torbin family, but he was not sure, and he had no idea that the episode was in any possible manner to be connected with his own recent history. How blindly we walk our ways! As Noble flourished down the street, there appeared a wan face at a prison window; and the large eyes looked out upon him wistfully. But Noble went on, as unwitting that he had to do with this prison as that he had to do with Master Torbin's tomato.

The face at the window was not like Charlotte Corday's, nor was the window barred, though the prisoner knew a little solace in wondering if she did not suggest that famous picture. For all purposes, except during school hours, the room was certainly a cell; and the term of imprisonment was set at three days. Uncle Joseph had been unable to remain at the movies forever: people do have to go home eventually, especially when accompanied by thirteen-year-old great-nieces. Florence had finally to face the question awaiting her; and it would have been better for her had she used less imagination in her replies.

Yet she was not wholly despondent as her eyes followed the

disappearing figure of Noble Dill. His wholesome sprightliness was visible at any distance; and who would not take a little pride in having been even the mistaken instrument of saving so gay a young man from the loss of his reason? No; Florence was not cast down. Day-after-to-morrow she would taste Freedom again, and her profoundest regret was that after all her Aunt Julia was not to be married. Florence had made definite plans for the wedding, especially for the principal figure at the ceremony. This figure, as Florence saw things, would have been that of the "Flower Girl," naturally a niece of the bride; but she was able to dismiss the bright dream with some philosophy. And to console her for everything, had she not a star in her soul? Had she not discovered that she could write poetry whenever she felt like it?

Noble passed from her sight, but nevertheless continued his radiant progress down Julia's Street. Life stretched before him, serene, ineffably fragrant, unending. He saw it as a flower-strewn sequence of calls upon Julia, walks with Julia, talks with Julia by the library fire. Old Mr. Atwater was to be away four days longer, and Julia, that great-hearted bride-not-to-be, had given him her promise.

Blushing, indeed divinely, she had promised him upon her sacred word, never so long as she lived, to be engaged to anybody at all.

THE END

Choose from Thousands of 1stWorldLibrary Classics By

A. M. Barnard
Ada Leverson
Adolphus William Ward
Aesop
Agatha Christie
Alexander Aaronsohn
Alexander Kielland
Alexandre Dumas
Alfred Gatty
Alfred Ollivant
Alice Duer Miller
Alice Turner Curtis
Alice Dunbar
Allen Chapman
Alleyne Ireland
Ambrose Bierce
Amelia E. Barr
Amory H. Bradford
Andrew Lang
Andrew McFarland Davis
Andy Adams
Angela Brazil
Anna Alice Chapin
Anna Sewell
Annie Besant
Annie Hamilton Donnell
Annie Payson Call
Annie Roe Carr
Annonaymous
Anton Chekhov
Archibald Lee Fletcher
Arnold Bennett
Arthur C. Benson
Arthur Conan Doyle
Arthur M. Winfield
Arthur Ransome
Arthur Schnitzler
Arthur Train
Atticus
B.H. Baden-Powell
B. M. Bower
B. C. Chatterjee
Baroness Emmuska Orczy
Baroness Orczy
Basil King
Bayard Taylor
Ben Macomber
Bertha Muzzy Bower
Bjornstjerne Bjornson

Booth Tarkington
Boyd Cable
Bram Stoker
C. Collodi
C. E. Orr
C. M. Ingleby
Carolyn Wells
Catherine Parr Traill
Charles A. Eastman
Charles Amory Beach
Charles Dickens
Charles Dudley Warner
Charles Farrar Browne
Charles Ives
Charles Kingsley
Charles Klein
Charles Hanson Towne
Charles Lathrop Pack
Charles Romyn Dake
Charles Whibley
Charles Willing Beale
Charlotte M. Braeme
Charlotte M. Yonge
Charlotte Perkins Stetson
Clair W. Hayes
Clarence Day Jr.
Clarence E. Mulford
Clemence Housman
Confucius
Coningsby Dawson
Cornelis DeWitt Wilcox
Cyril Burleigh
D. H. Lawrence
Daniel Defoe
David Garnett
Dinah Craik
Don Carlos Janes
Donald Keyhoe
Dorothy Kilner
Dougan Clark
Douglas Fairbanks
E. Nesbit
E. P. Roe
E. Phillips Oppenheim
E. S. Brooks
Earl Barnes
Edgar Rice Burroughs
Edith Van Dyne
Edith Wharton

Edward Everett Hale
Edward J. O'Biren
Edward S. Ellis
Edwin L. Arnold
Eleanor Atkins
Eleanor Hallowell Abbott
Eliot Gregory
Elizabeth Gaskell
Elizabeth McCracken
Elizabeth Von Arnim
Ellem Key
Emerson Hough
Emilie F. Carlen
Emily Bronte
Emily Dickinson
Enid Bagnold
Enilor Macartney Lane
Erasmus W. Jones
Ernie Howard Pie
Ethel May Dell
Ethel Turner
Ethel Watts Mumford
Eugene Sue
Eugenie Foa
Eugene Wood
Eustace Hale Ball
Evelyn Everett-green
Everard Cotes
F. H. Cheley
F. J. Cross
F. Marion Crawford
Fannie E. Newberry
Federick Austin Ogg
Ferdinand Ossendowski
Fergus Hume
Florence A. Kilpatrick
Fremont B. Deering
Francis Bacon
Francis Darwin
Frances Hodgson Burnett
Frances Parkinson Keyes
Frank Gee Patchin
Frank Harris
Frank Jewett Mather
Frank L. Packard
Frank V. Webster
Frederic Stewart Isham
Frederick Trevor Hill
Frederick Winslow Taylor

Friedrich Kerst
Friedrich Nietzsche
Fyodor Dostoyevsky
G.A. Henty
G.K. Chesterton
Gabrielle E. Jackson
Garrett P. Serviss
Gaston Leroux
George A. Warren
George Ade
Geroge Bernard Shaw
George Cary Eggleston
George Durston
George Ebers
George Eliot
George Gissing
George MacDonald
George Meredith
George Orwell
George Sylvester Viereck
George Tucker
George W. Cable
George Wharton James
Gertrude Atherton
Gordon Casserly
Grace E. King
Grace Gallatin
Grace Greenwood
Grant Allen
Guillermo A. Sherwell
Gulielma Zollinger
Gustav Flaubert
H. A. Cody
H. B. Irving
H.C. Bailey
H. G. Wells
H. H. Munro
H. Irving Hancock
H. R. Naylor
H. Rider Haggard
H. W. C. Davis
Haldeman Julius
Hall Caine
Hamilton Wright Mabie
Hans Christian Andersen
Harold Avery
Harold McGrath
Harriet Beecher Stowe
Harry Castlemon
Harry Coghill
Harry Houidini

Hayden Carruth
Helent Hunt Jackson
Helen Nicolay
Hendrik Conscience
Hendy David Thoreau
Henri Barbusse
Henrik Ibsen
Henry Adams
Henry Ford
Henry Frost
Henry James
Henry Jones Ford
Henry Seton Merriman
Henry W Longfellow
Herbert A. Giles
Herbert Carter
Herbert N. Casson
Herman Hesse
Hildegard G. Frey
Homer
Honore De Balzac
Horace B. Day
Horace Walpole
Horatio Alger Jr.
Howard Pyle
Howard R. Garis
Hugh Lofting
Hugh Walpole
Humphry Ward
Ian Maclaren
Inez Haynes Gillmore
Irving Bacheller
Isabel Cecilia Williams
Isabel Hornibrook
Israel Abrahams
Ivan Turgenev
J.G.Austin
J. Henri Fabre
J. M. Barrie
J. M. Walsh
J. Macdonald Oxley
J. R. Miller
J. S. Fletcher
J. S. Knowles
J. Storer Clouston
J. W. Duffield
Jack London
Jacob Abbott
James Allen
James Andrews
James Baldwin

James Branch Cabell
James DeMille
James Joyce
James Lane Allen
James Lane Allen
James Oliver Curwood
James Oppenheim
James Otis
James R. Driscoll
Jane Abbott
Jane Austen
Jane L. Stewart
Janet Aldridge
Jens Peter Jacobsen
Jerome K. Jerome
Jessie Graham Flower
John Buchan
John Burroughs
John Cournos
John F. Kennedy
John Gay
John Glasworthy
John Habberton
John Joy Bell
John Kendrick Bangs
John Milton
John Philip Sousa
John Taintor Foote
Jonas Lauritz Idemil Lie
Jonathan Swift
Joseph A. Altsheler
Joseph Carey
Joseph Conrad
Joseph E. Badger Jr
Joseph Hergesheimer
Joseph Jacobs
Jules Vernes
Julian Hawthrone
Julie A Lippmann
Justin Huntly McCarthy
Kakuzo Okakura
Karle Wilson Baker
Kate Chopin
Kenneth Grahame
Kenneth McGaffey
Kate Langley Bosher
Kate Langley Bosher
Katherine Cecil Thurston
Katherine Stokes
L. A. Abbot
L. T. Meade

L. Frank Baum
Latta Griswold
Laura Dent Crane
Laura Lee Hope
Laurence Housman
Lawrence Beasley
Leo Tolstoy
Leonid Andreyev
Lewis Carroll
Lewis Sperry Chafer
Lilian Bell
Lloyd Osbourne
Louis Hughes
Louis Joseph Vance
Louis Tracy
Louisa May Alcott
Lucy Fitch Perkins
Lucy Maud Montgomery
Luther Benson
Lydia Miller Middleton
Lyndon Orr
M. Corvus
M. H. Adams
Margaret E. Sangster
Margret Howth
Margaret Vandercook
Margaret W. Hungerford
Margret Penrose
Maria Edgeworth
Maria Thompson Daviess
Mariano Azuela
Marion Polk Angellotti
Mark Overton
Mark Twain
Mary Austin
Mary Catherine Crowley
Mary Cole
Mary Hastings Bradley
Mary Roberts Rinehart
Mary Rowlandson
M. Wollstonecraft Shelley
Maud Lindsay
Max Beerbohm
Myra Kelly
Nathaniel Hawthrone
Nicolo Machiavelli
O. F. Walton
Oscar Wilde
Owen Johnson
P.G. Wodehouse
Paul and Mabel Thorne

Paul G. Tomlinson
Paul Severing
Percy Brebner
Percy Keese Fitzhugh
Peter B. Kyne
Plato
Quincy Allen
R. Derby Holmes
R. L. Stevenson
R. S. Ball
Rabindranath Tagore
Rahul Alvares
Ralph Bonehill
Ralph Henry Barbour
Ralph Victor
Ralph Waldo Emmerson
Rene Descartes
Ray Cummings
Rex Beach
Rex E. Beach
Richard Harding Davis
Richard Jefferies
Richard Le Gallienne
Robert Barr
Robert Frost
Robert Gordon Anderson
Robert L. Drake
Robert Lansing
Robert Lynd
Robert Michael Ballantyne
Robert W. Chambers
Rosa Nouchette Carey
Rudyard Kipling
Saint Augustine
Samuel B. Allison
Samuel Hopkins Adams
Sarah Bernhardt
Sarah C. Hallowell
Selma Lagerlof
Sherwood Anderson
Sigmund Freud
Standish O'Grady
Stanley Weyman
Stella Benson
Stella M. Francis
Stephen Crane
Stewart Edward White
Stijn Streuvels
Swami Abhedananda
Swami Parmananda
T. S. Ackland

T. S. Arthur
The Princess Der Ling
Thomas A. Janvier
Thomas A Kempis
Thomas Anderton
Thomas Bailey Aldrich
Thomas Bulfinch
Thomas De Quincey
Thomas Dixon
Thomas H. Huxley
Thomas Hardy
Thomas More
Thornton W. Burgess
U. S. Grant
Upton Sinclair
Valentine Williams
Various Authors
Vaughan Kester
Victor Appleton
Victor G. Durham
Victoria Cross
Virginia Woolf
Wadsworth Camp
Walter Camp
Walter Scott
Washington Irving
Wilbur Lawton
Wilkie Collins
Willa Cather
Willard F. Baker
William Dean Howells
William le Queux
W. Makepeace Thackeray
William W. Walter
William Shakespeare
Winston Churchill
Yei Theodora Ozaki
Yogi Ramacharaka
Young E. Allison
Zane Grey